Got Coffee

CLARA ASHBY

ISBN: 978-91-531-6800-3

Book Cover by LunaCco Design

• First edition 2025

Contents

CHAPTER *One*

Ruby Ashworth had fifteen minutes to clear out her desk before security escorted her from the BrewCorp building, which meant she had no time for nostalgia when her manager delivered the final blow.

"It's nothing personal, Ruby," Derek Castellano said with the kind of smile that meant he'd fired people before. "Your ideas are creative—maybe too creative for our current market strategy. The lavender honey latte concept tested well, but corporate feels it doesn't align with our brand consistency goals."

Ruby stared at the cardboard box containing three years of her professional life—her favorite coffee mug, a succulent, and the innovation awards that meant nothing when budget cuts came calling. "Too creative? Derek, that lavender latte increased sales by twelve percent in our Hartford locations."

"Ruby, you pitched a 'seasonal poetry series' where customers would get haikus printed on their coffee cups. Corporate thought you were joking until they realized you'd already designed the templates." Derek paused, and Ruby's fingers tightened on the cardboard box until the edges crumpled. "Look, you're talented, but maybe independent coffee culture would be a better fit. You know, somewhere your... energy... would be more appreciated."

Energy. Like her passion for coffee innovation was a character flaw instead of the reason BrewCorp had hired her in the first place.

In the elevator, Ruby clutched her box and fought back tears. The security guard stood politely silent, making sure she didn't steal corporate secrets on her way out.

Through the elevator's glass walls, she could see the Hartford skyline—all those office buildings full of people with stable jobs and predictable paychecks and managers who didn't think creativity was a liability.

She'd moved to Hartford for this job. Signed a lease, bought professional clothes, learned to navigate corporate meetings where innovation was encouraged in theory but discouraged in practice. Now she was unemployed in a city where she knew three people, all of whom worked at BrewCorp and would probably stop returning her calls by tomorrow.

Ruby's phone buzzed as she reached the lobby. A text from her grandmother's lawyer:

> Estate paperwork finalized. Inheritance check should arrive next week. Let me know if you need anything else during this difficult time.

Ruby stopped walking, causing the security guard to nearly bump into her. Grandma Doris's inheritance. She'd completely forgotten about the modest sum her grandmother had left her—enough for a few months of expenses, maybe, or a really expensive vacation she couldn't afford to take while unemployed. Or maybe, enough for something completely different.

She spent that evening scrolling through commercial real estate listings in small Connecticut towns she'd never heard of. Most were either too expensive or too depressing, but then she found it: Miller's Coffee, a foreclosed coffee shop in Millbrook Falls. Two stories, Main Street location, price slashed because the previous owner couldn't make it work. The listing agent's carefully neutral description—"motivated seller, property needs cosmetic updates"—translated to: someone's dream died here, want to try yours?

The math was tight but possible. Grandma Doris's inheritance for the down payment, a small business loan for equipment and inventory, and maybe—just maybe—enough left over to survive the first few lean months.

In a boost of nervous excitement she called the agent before she could talk herself out of it.

RUBY RAN ON NERVES, sugar, and enough gas-station coffee to keep an entire marching band awake. She pulled up to Main Street in Millbrook Falls, early morning on the second week of August, after the fastest real estate closure in the history of Connecticut.

This was either going to be the best decision of her life or the most expensive mistake she'd ever made. Based on the way her hands were shaking—definitely from nerves, not caffeine—she was leaning toward expensive mistake.

Ruby tried to smooth down her long brown hair, but the ponytail had given up. Coffee stains dotted her moving-day t-shirt from stress drinking since 5 AM, but she still had that stubborn optimism that had gotten her this far. Even if she looked like a disaster, she was a determined disaster.

"Okay, okay, this is happening," she muttered, clutching her cardboard carrier of travel cups like a caffeinated security blanket. "This is really happening. New town, new dream, new life. Very doable. Totally normal. People do this all the time, right?"

The moving guys were already hauling her life out of the truck before Ruby could even get her bearings. She fumbled for her phone, trying to pull up the address while juggling coffee cups and her purse.

A gust of wind chose that moment to snatch her carefully organized business plans right out of her hand, her hair whipping around her face as she turned.

"No, no, NO!" Ruby lunged forward, coffee cups swaying dangerously. "Those napkins have my entire life mapped out on them!"

She watched in horror as her color-coded revenue projections —written on Dunkin' napkins during a particularly inspired moment at 2 AM—went cartwheeling across the town square like caffeinated tumbleweeds.

"Ma'am, where do you want the espresso machine?" called one of the movers, hefting what looked like a small silver spaceship.

"Just—one second! I need to check—" Ruby spun around, chasing after her napkins while trying to unlock her phone. "The address is 142—"

"Lady, you gotta make up your mind," the mover said, not unkindly. "This thing weighs like two hundred pounds."

Ruby looked up from her phone—where she'd accidentally opened her camera app instead of her notes—and saw the movers standing expectantly. Main Street stretched out with its charming historic buildings, all weathered brick and big windows and exactly the kind of picturesque New England aesthetic the listing had promised.

"That one!" she announced, pointing at the nearest building with two stories and big windows, trying to sound confident despite having absolutely no idea if she was right. "Definitely that one. I'm very sure. Extremely confident in my decision."

The movers shrugged and started hauling her belongings up the front steps.

Ruby finally got her phone working and pulled up her closing documents. 142 Main Street. She squinted at the buildings, trying to see numbers, but her business plans chose that moment to blow past her face again and—Wait.

Through the front window of the building where the movers were currently unloading her entire life, Ruby could see... a coffee shop. An actual, functioning, clearly-already-operating coffee shop. With equipment. And a counter. And her boxes being maneuvered past it all. And in the middle of the chaos stood a man, very still, staring at the invasion with an expression that suggested he was reconsidering every decision that had led him to this moment.

She looked down at her phone. 142 Main Street.

She looked up at the building the movers had just entered. A small, tasteful sign read: "Sullivan's Coffee."

"Oh no," Ruby whispered. "Oh no, no, no—"

Ruby dropped her coffee cups (which miraculously didn't spill, because the universe owed her at least one small favor today) and rushed through Sullivan's front door, already apologizing before she'd fully crossed the threshold.

That wasn't her building.

That was Sullivan's Coffee.

And the man standing next to Beatrice, her gleaming espresso machine, holding a coffee pot and staring at the chaos with quiet intensity, looked like he was deciding whether to explode or never speak again. Either way, Ruby was fairly certain he was the most intimidating person she'd ever accidentally invaded.

He was tall—Ruby had to tilt her head to meet his eyes, which were light brown and caught the morning sun like embers. Copper hair that looked finger-combed, broad shoulders filling out a simple grey T-shirt, and hands that knew their way around both coffee equipment and actual work. He looked like someone who'd never stress-eaten cereal for dinner or made impulsive life decisions based on inherited money.

Ruby, who had stress-eaten cereal for dinner three times in the past week, felt immediately outclassed.

"Hi!" Ruby burst out, breathless and manic. "I am so, so sorry about this. There's been a huge mix-up with the addresses and apparently my moving guys can't read or maybe I wrote it down wrong, which would be typical because I do that when I'm nervous, and I'm very nervous right now because this is my first day in town and I'm opening a coffee shop too, which makes us competitors, I guess, but I really hope we can be friendly competitors because I hate conflict and—"

The man just stared at her. He didn't say a word. He just stood there holding his coffee pot, his jaw set in a line that suggested he wasn't particularly thrilled, looking like she was speaking an entirely foreign language.

Which made Ruby's rambling worse, her hands moving expressively as she talked.

"I mean, not that I'm trying to compete with you specifically! I'm sure your coffee is amazing and has lots of loyal customers and I would never want to step on your toes or anything like that. I just always dreamed of having my own place and when my grandmother left me some money it seemed like a sign, you know? Although maybe not a good sign because look at this disaster and we haven't even officially met yet and—"

"Ma'am?" The mover appeared behind her, looking confused. "Where do you want this stuff?"

Ruby turned to point across the street, gesticulating so wildly she nearly knocked over a sugar dispenser. "Over there! The building directly across—with the big windows and the—oh god, is that my mattress?"

Sure enough, her queen-size mattress was currently blocking Sullivan's front door, while what appeared to be her entire wardrobe was stacked in boxes on his front step.

The man finally spoke.

"You're the new coffee shop owner."

His voice was low and calm with rough edges that didn't waste words on small talk. Ruby's stomach flipped.

"Yes! I mean, I will be. I'm trying to be. I'm Ruby, Ruby Ashworth, and I'm opening Scattered Beans right across the street, which I realize probably makes this whole thing super awkward because we're basically going to be business neighbors and competitors and I've just accidentally invaded your space with my entire life—"

"Jake Sullivan," he said, his tone making it clear that was all the introduction she was getting.

Ruby's brain unhelpfully noted that Jake Sullivan was unfairly attractive for someone who probably hated her already. Great. Perfect. Exactly what she needed.

He sat down his coffee pot and walked past her. Ruby watched him start lifting her heavy boxes like they weighed nothing. He handled her belongings carefully despite the chaos she'd brought.

"Where?" he asked the movers, hefting what Ruby was pretty sure was her collection of coffee table books about European cafes.

"Across the street, 142," the head mover said, looking relieved that someone was taking charge.

Jake nodded once and started walking. Just like that. No complaints about the inconvenience, no questions about how this had happened, no commentary on Ruby's obvious inability to manage basic logistics. He just... fixed it.

Ruby stood frozen on his front step, watching him carry her stuff across Main Street with the same methodical care he probably brought to everything.

"Are you coming?" he called back without stopping. His voice carried quiet authority.

"Right! Yes! Coming!" Ruby scrambled to follow, nearly tripping over her own feet in the process. "You really don't have to do this! I can handle it! I mean, obviously I've already proven I can't handle it, but I can learn to handle it! I'm very adaptable!"

Jake didn't respond to her rambling. He just kept walking, carrying her chaos with steady hands and zero commentary.

By the time they'd moved everything across the street—Jake doing most of the heavy lifting while Ruby directed and apologized and explained her entire life story to anyone within earshot—the morning sun had climbed higher and Main Street was starting to show signs of life. A few people had emerged from shops to watch the spectacle, including an older woman with steel-gray hair who stood in front of what appeared to be a yarn shop, arms crossed and lips pursed in obvious disapproval. Ruby caught her eye and waved nervously; the woman just turned and went back inside with a decisive door slam.

"Thank you," Ruby said when the last box had been delivered to her actual front door. "Seriously, I cannot thank you enough. You totally saved me from complete disaster on day one, and I know this probably wasn't how you planned to spend your morning, and I promise I'm not usually this chaotic. Well, okay, I am usually this chaotic, but I'm working on it."

Jake stood on her doorstep, hands empty now, looking like he was searching for something to say. His hair was messed from the work, and there was a small coffee stain on his T-shirt that Ruby definitely wasn't noticing.

"Your espresso machine," he said, meeting her eyes. "It's expensive."

"Beatrice is very expensive," Ruby agreed, tucking her hair behind her ear again. "Probably too expensive for someone who just got fired from their last job, but my grandmother always said you have to invest in quality coffee equipment if you want to make quality coffee, and she knew about these things because she made the best coffee in her entire neighborhood, which is where I got the idea for all of this, actually..."

She was rambling again. She could hear herself doing it, but Jake's steady attention made her nervous and nervousness made her talk and talking while nervous meant sharing way too much with virtual strangers.

"She sounds smart," Jake said quietly. Something in his tone made Ruby stop gesturing.

Her rambling stopped. "She... yeah. She was."

For a moment, they just looked at each other. Ruby caught a glimpse of something softer in his expression, something that made her think there was more to Jake Sullivan than quiet competence and impressive arms.

Then he stepped back, his jaw tightening.

"Next time, double-check your address," he said.

And then Jake Sullivan walked back across the street to his

coffee shop, leaving Ruby standing surrounded by all her worldly possessions, pretty sure her new neighbor thought she was a complete disaster.

She was still standing there, watching him disappear into his shop, when she realized three things:

One: She was still missing those business plans.

Two: Her first interaction with her new business rival involved him carrying her mattress across Main Street.

And three: Jake Sullivan had really nice arms.

Ruby groaned and turned to face her actual building. "Okay, Grandma Doris," she muttered. "I really hope you knew what you were doing with that inheritance."

CHAPTER
Two

Ruby had been awake since before dawn, which was either dedication or insanity, but the distinction didn't matter—Scattered Beans was opening in three hours and she still hadn't figured out how to make Beatrice cooperate with her vision for the perfect opening-day latte.

"Come on, beautiful," she coaxed the gleaming espresso machine, adjusting the grind settings. "We talked about this. Today is our big day. Our debut. Our chance to show this town that we belong here."

Beatrice responded by making a sound that was somewhere between a fizzy hiss and a death rattle.

Ruby stared at the machine, coffee grounds scattered across her counter like caffeinated confetti, and felt panic flutter in her chest. Through her front window, she could see Sullivan's Coffee across the street, where a single warm light glowed behind the simple painted sign. Jake had probably been up for hours, methodically preparing for another ordinary day. No fanfare, no anxiety, no temperamental equipment named after deceased British monarchs.

His coffee shop had been in his family for generations. Hers was a foreclosed property she'd bought at a steep discount because the previous owner couldn't compete with that kind of legacy.

Ruby tried not to think about that parallel. She failed.

"Okay, plan B," she announced to her empty shop. "We're going with plan B."

The problem was, she'd never actually made a plan B.

The weeks between moving day and opening had passed in a blur of permits, equipment installation, renovations and three separate anxiety spirals about whether she'd made a catastrophic mistake. Jake had nodded politely the few times she'd seen him on Main Street, but they hadn't actually spoken since the mattress incident. Ruby wasn't sure if that was a good sign or if he was just avoiding the chaotic woman who'd invaded his shop with her entire life.

But today—September 8th, her official grand opening—there was no more time for doubt.

By 7:30, Ruby had finally coaxed Beatrice into cooperation, flipped her hand-painted "OPEN" sign, and arranged her small collection of pastries—delivered fresh from a bakery two towns over because Millbrook Falls apparently didn't believe in croissants—in a display case. She'd curated a playlist of indie folk music—upbeat but not intrusive—and now it filled the shop with warmth. The volume was perhaps a touch higher than necessary, but it made the empty space feel less lonely.

She was just stepping back to admire her work when she spotted her first customer walking down Main Street.

Not just any customer. Gladys Murphy, the steel-haired woman from the moving day disaster, marching toward her shop like a woman on a mission.

Ruby's stomach dropped. She smoothed her apron, checked her reflection in the window, and realized she had coffee grounds in her hair. Her long waves had come loose from their clip again, framing her face in a way that made her look younger than twenty-eight, especially with the nervous flush spreading across her cheeks.

The door chimed as Gladys entered, and Ruby put on her biggest, most welcoming smile.

"Good morning! Welcome to Scattered Beans! I'm Ruby, and I'm so excited to—"

"I know who you are," Gladys said, looking around the space with the same expression she might wear while inspecting a crime scene. "Heard quite a bit about you already."

"Oh! Well, I hope it was all good things," Ruby laughed, though the sound came out slightly strangled. "Can I get you something to drink? I have a wonderful lavender honey latte that's been really popular in—"

"I'll have coffee," Gladys interrupted. "Black. Large."

"Of course! One black coffee coming right up!" Ruby turned to Beatrice, silently pleading with the machine to cooperate. "So, do you live nearby? I'm still getting to know the neighborhood, and—"

"Been here my whole life," Gladys said. "Watched this town change plenty over the years. Some changes are good. Others..." She let the sentence hang in the air like smoke.

Ruby's hands shook slightly as she operated the espresso machine. "Well, I really hope I can be a positive addition to the community. I know there's already a wonderful coffee shop across the street, but I think there's room for both of us. Different approaches, you know? Like, Sullivan's has that classic, traditional feel, and Scattered Beans is more... contemporary?"

She was rambling. She could hear herself rambling, but Gladys's silence was like a vacuum that demanded to be filled with words.

"Here you go!" Ruby said, handing over the coffee cup with a smile that felt increasingly desperate. "That'll be three dollars."

Gladys took a sip, and her expression didn't change. "Three dollars for black coffee?"

Ruby's throat went dry. "Well, it's single-origin Ethiopian beans, ground fresh for each cup, and the price also includes—"

"Jake charges two."

The simple statement hung between them like a challenge. Ruby's cheeks burned. She wanted to explain that hers wasn't just coffee—it was quality beans, a different kind of shop entirely. But the words jammed in her throat.

"Right, well, different shops have different pricing structures, and—"

But Gladys was already putting three crumpled dollar bills on the counter and heading for the door.

"Nice meeting you," she said, though her tone suggested the opposite. "I'm sure Jake will be interested to hear about your... contemporary approach."

As Gladys left, Ruby stood alone in her beautiful, empty coffee shop, wondering if she'd just lost her first potential customer or if she'd never really had a chance to begin with.

Across the street, she could see a steady stream of people entering Sullivan's Coffee. The morning regulars, probably. People who'd been starting their days with Jake's coffee for years, who knew what they wanted and what they'd pay for it.

People who thought three dollars for coffee was highway robbery.

Ruby slumped against her counter and considered the very real possibility that she'd made a terrible mistake. Miller's Coffee hadn't survived. What made her think Scattered Beans would be any different?

That's when a petite woman about her own age bounced in, radiating enthusiasm. She had short raven-black hair and bright grey eyes full of infectious energy.

"Oh my gosh, you're open!" the woman exclaimed, looking around Scattered Beans with delight. "This place is absolutely adorable! I'm Zara, I work part-time at the bookstore down the street, rest of the time trying to become the next Colleen Hoover," she laughed, "and I have been so excited about this opening. Please tell me you have something more interesting than Jake's reliable but predictable coffee."

Ruby smiled for the first time all morning.

"I have a lavender honey latte that I think you might love," she offered.

"Sold," Zara said immediately. "Make it large, and tell me everything about how you ended up in our little town."

As Ruby started working Beatrice—who seemed to approve of Zara's enthusiasm and cooperated beautifully—some of the morning's anxiety faded. Maybe Gladys spoke for one side of town, but Zara's enthusiasm suggested there were others ready to welcome her.

"Well," Ruby said as she steamed the milk, "the short version is Hartford burnout, my grandmother's influence, and what might have been either the best or worst impulse purchase of my life." She poured carefully, creating a delicate leaf pattern in the foam. "Jury's still out on which."

Zara grinned. "I'm voting best. This town needs more impulse decisions."

"So," Zara said, accepting her latte and taking a generous sip. Her eyes widened. "Oh wow, this is incredible. Okay, Jake's officially been dethroned." She took another sip, savoring it. "How is the grand opening? Lots of curious neighbors stopping by?"

"You're actually my second customer," Ruby admitted. "The first was... well, let's just say she seemed more interested in market research than coffee appreciation."

Zara laughed. "Let me guess. Steel hair, permanent disapproval, looked like she was gathering intelligence for the enemy?"

"That's... surprisingly accurate."

"Gladys Murphy. She owns the yarn shop next to Sullivan's and considers herself the unofficial guardian of Main Street tradition. Don't take it personally—she'd probably disapprove of indoor plumbing if it wasn't already established."

Relief washed over her. "So it wasn't just me?"

"Definitely not just you. There's a whole faction of folks who think change is the end of the world." Zara paused, looking thoughtful. "But there are also plenty of us who've been dying for a good latte in this town. Jake's coffee is... solid. Dependable. Yours is actually exciting."

Zara settled onto one of Ruby's carefully chosen vintage stools, pulling a laptop from her oversized bag. "Do you mind if I camp out for a bit? I'm on deadline for a short story, and your vibe is way more inspiring than my apartment."

"Please do!" Ruby said, genuinely delighted. Her casual comfort made the shop feel less like an empty stage and more like a place people might actually want to stay.

"Speaking of coming around, you should know the town's split into factions over your arrival. It's like watching a very polite civil war unfold."

"Factions?"

"Oh yes. Team Tradition: Gladys, obviously. Frank Kowalski, who's been Jake's first customer every single morning for fifteen years. And Mayor Greene, though she's trying to stay neutral for political reasons." Zara counted on her fingers. "Then there's Team Fresh Start: me, obviously. Tommy Sullivan—that's Jake's brother, he does most of the renovation work around town. He's got the same broad shoulders as Jake but he's blond and way more social. Always grinning about something. And Daisy Hartwell from the flower shop—she's basically the town mom for anyone who wants Millbrook Falls to keep up with the times."

Ruby felt her spirits lift. "And Jake?"

Zara's smile turned knowing. "That's the interesting question. He's loyal to his family legacy, obviously. Sullivan's Coffee has been in his family since his great-grandfather opened it. But..." She leaned forward conspiratorially. "Jake's been watching your shop all morning. Every time someone comes in here, he finds an excuse to be visible in his front window."

Ruby's stomach did a little flip. "Maybe he's just... keeping an eye on the competition?"

"Maybe," Zara said, but her tone suggested she thought otherwise. "Or maybe he's curious about the woman who has Beatrice over there and talks to her espresso machine like it's a person."

"You heard that?"

"Honey, half the street heard that. The walls aren't that thick." Zara grinned. "Don't worry, it's endearing. Very you, from what I can tell."

Ruby felt her cheeks warm. "Great. So the whole town thinks I'm crazy."

"Interesting beats ordinary around these parts. That's practically a superpower here."

As if summoned by their conversation. A woman with flame-red hair swept in, bringing with her the faint scent of earth and roses. She had the kind of warm, maternal presence that immediately put Ruby at ease.

"Excuse me, dear," she said, approaching the counter with a genuine smile. "I'm Daisy Hartwell. I run the flower shop two doors down. I wanted to stop by and wish you good luck on your opening day ."

"That's so sweet of you!" Ruby said, feeling genuinely touched. "I'm Ruby. Can I get you something?"

"I'd love to try whatever smells so wonderful in here," Daisy said, glancing appreciatively at Zara's cup. "Something with lavender?" She smiled warmly at Ruby as she approached the counter. "You know, I have to say, when I heard Doris Ashworth's granddaughter had bought this place, I was absolutely delighted. Your grandmother and I were dear friends."

Ruby's hands stilled on the espresso machine. "You... you knew Grandma Doris?"

"Oh yes, dear. Doris was one of my dearest friends. We wrote letters for years after I moved away from Hartford—I grew up there, you see. She talked about you constantly in those letters—her granddaughter who was going to change the world one cup of coffee at a time."

Ruby felt tears prick at the corners of her eyes. "She really said that?"

"Word for word. She'd be so proud of what you're doing here." Daisy's expression softened, then turned thoughtful. "You know, when I heard this building was being foreclosed, I thought what a shame it was—another failed shop on Main Street. But then I heard you had bought it, and I thought, well, maybe that's exactly what this place needs. Someone with Doris's passion and your fresh perspective."

Ruby's throat tightened. "The real estate agent told me the previous owner couldn't make it work. That... that's been worrying me."

"Miller's?" Daisy waved a hand dismissively. "Don't let that discourage you, dear. Poor Mr. Miller was lovely, but he was trying to be a carbon copy of Sullivan's. You can't compete with a legacy by imitating it. But bringing something new?" She smiled warmly. "That's how you succeed."

As Ruby prepared Daisy's latte—Beatrice purring along cooperatively now—she felt something settle in her chest. Maybe Gladys Murphy and her allies thought Ruby didn't belong here, but her grandmother's friend believed in her. That had to count for something.

"Here you go," she said, handing Daisy the latte.

Daisy took a careful sip, and her face lit up. "Oh my dear, this is absolutely wonderful. Doris would be so proud—you've got her gift for making everything taste like a warm hug."

"Thank you," Ruby said, her voice catching slightly. "That... that means everything to me."

"Don't you worry about the naysayers. Every town needs a little shaking up now and then." Daisy gathered her purse and headed toward the door, pausing to add, "I'll be back tomorrow for another one of these. And I suspect I won't be the only one."

After Daisy left, Ruby found herself blinking back tears as she straightened the pastry display. Her grandmother would have loved this—the bustling shop, the nervous energy, even temperamental Beatrice.

By midday, Ruby had served twelve customers—a respectable showing for opening day, even if half of them were ordering drinks just to get a look at the competition. The other half, thankfully, were genuine converts to the cause of decent coffee in Millbrook Falls.

Across the street, Sullivan's Coffee had maintained its steady stream of regulars, though Ruby had noticed a few familiar faces glancing toward her shop with what looked like curiosity. Through Jake's front window, she'd caught glimpses of him serving his usual customers—Frank Kowalski with his predictable black coffee and blueberry muffin, Mayor Greene with her standard order, a handful of other locals whose routines probably hadn't changed in years.

But she'd also noticed Jake's attention drifting toward her window more than once, especially during the brief moments when she'd had a small line of customers waiting. His expression had been unreadable from across the street, but there was something in the set of his shoulders that suggested he was paying closer attention than he wanted to admit.

Ruby found herself wondering what he was thinking. Competition assessment? Mild concern about losing customers? Or simple curiosity about whether the chaotic woman from moving day disaster could actually run a business?

She was wiping down her counter and feeling cautiously optimistic when she noticed Jake Sullivan standing in his doorway across the street, arms crossed, watching her shop with that same unreadable expression.

Their eyes met through the window, and for a moment, Ruby felt that same flutter she'd experienced when he'd helped move her furniture. But then Jake's gaze shifted to something outside her shop, and his jaw tightened.

He was walking across the street with purposeful strides before Ruby could figure out what had caught his attention.

The door chimed, and Jake Sullivan filled her doorway, all broad shoulders and barely contained irritation.

"Your sign," he said without preamble, "is blocking half the sidewalk."

Ruby blinked, trying to process the accusation. "My... what?"

"The sandwich board. Outside." Jake gestured toward her front window. "It's blocking the pedestrian flow. Someone's going to trip over it."

Ruby's cheeks flushed. She'd been so excited about her hand-painted chalkboard sign advertising her opening-day specials that she hadn't thought about placement. "Oh! I'm so sorry. I'll move it right away—"

"And your music," Jake continued, his voice low but carrying an edge, "is loud enough that I can hear it across the street."

Ruby's embarrassment shifted toward defensiveness. "It's just background music. It creates atmosphere—"

"Your atmosphere is bleeding into my shop."

They stood there, staring at each other across her counter, and Ruby realized this wasn't really about the sign or the music. This was about territory. About a Sullivan who'd been running his family's coffee shop for years suddenly having a competitor directly across the street. A competitor who'd bought a foreclosed property and thought she could succeed where someone else had failed.

She hadn't thought about competition when she bought the building—she'd been too desperate for a fresh start to consider whose territory she was invading.

"I'll move the sign," Ruby said quietly, breaking the standoff. "And turn down the music."

Jake's jaw worked, like he was fighting with himself over something. His gaze flickered to the espresso machine, then back to Ruby. Finally, almost reluctantly, he said, "Your coffee smells good. Different."

It wasn't quite a compliment, but it wasn't an insult either.

"Thank you," Ruby managed.

Jake nodded once, turned, and walked back across the street to Sullivan's Coffee, leaving Ruby standing in her shop, heart racing for reasons she couldn't quite name.

Zara, who'd been typing away at her laptop but clearly watching the entire exchange with barely concealed delight, let out a low whistle.

"Oh, this is going to be interesting," she said.

Ruby wasn't entirely sure she disagreed.

CHAPTER *Three*

Ruby had been in Millbrook Falls for two weeks when she discovered that Jake Sullivan subscribed to The Atlantic, Poetry Magazine, and something called Prairie Schooner that looked suspiciously literary.

Ruby stood in her apartment above Scattered Beans, holding Jake's mail. The mail mix-up had started small—a utility bill here, a pizza coupon there—but this morning's delivery had included a thick manila envelope addressed to Jacob Sullivan at 142 Main Street. Ruby's address. Their street numbers matched; his storefront used 142 A, and hers was 142. The post office, less poetic than Prairie Schooner, kept confusing the doors.

There was also a piece of mail addressed to "Miller's Coffee" at her address—a final notice from a supply company about an outstanding balance. Ruby set it aside with a pang of sympathy for whoever Miller had been. The postal service seemed determined to remind her that someone else's dream had failed here first. "Okay, you two," Ruby said, addressing Jake's literary magazines and Miller's final notice. "We're going to figure this out. The mail situation and probably my entire life situation while we're at it."

She set the magazines on her kitchen counter next to her newly reconstructed collection of business-plan napkins that she still hadn't organized into anything resembling a coherent strategy, and stared at them like they might reveal their secrets. Jake Sullivan read poetry. Jake Sullivan, who communicated primarily in grunts and helpful silences, subscribed to not one but three publications dedicated to the written word.

This was also the same Jake Sullivan who'd probably received her loan paperwork by now, her overdue credit card statements, and that particularly mortifying letter from Brew-Corp's HR department about her final paycheck and "creative differences."

Ruby's phone buzzed with a text from Vi, her oldest and best friend:

VI

How's small town life? Met any cute farmers yet?

Ruby photographed Jake's mail and sent it back:

RUBY

Define cute. Also define farmer. Also my neighbor probably thinks I'm financially irresponsible.

Her phone rang immediately.

"Ruby Ashworth, are you telling me you have a mystery man situation?" Vi's voice carried all the enthusiasm of someone living vicariously through her best friend's romantic possibilities. Ruby could picture her friend pacing around her pristine Hartford office in designer heels, probably scaring her assistant with her sudden burst of matchmaking energy.

"I'm telling you my neighbor reads poetry and probably knows I'm broke," Ruby said, slumping against her window frame.

"Okay, first of all, you are not broke. Second of all, mystery man reading poetry is hot. Third of all, maybe he's not judging your finances as harshly as you think."

"Or maybe he's too polite to mention that his business competitor is a disaster at basic adulting."

"Ruby." Vi's voice carried that particular tone that meant she was about to dispense unsolicited wisdom. "When was the last time you were curious about someone?"

Ruby considered this. When was the last time she'd wondered what someone did when they weren't directly in front of her? Derek from BrewCorp certainly hadn't inspired late-night speculation about his reading habits. Most of her dating life had been refreshingly surface-level.

"That's not the point," Ruby said, though she wasn't entirely sure what the point was anymore.

"That's exactly the point. You're curious. Curiosity is good. Curiosity leads to conversation, conversation leads to connection, connection leads to—"

"Vi."

"I'm just saying, maybe grumpy coffee guy has layers. And maybe you should focus less on whether he's judging your Visa bill and more on the fact that he reads poetry."

After Vi hung up, Ruby stood at her window with Jake's mail in her hands, watching Sullivan's Coffee for signs of life. A light came on behind the painted sign, the front door opened and Jake appeared, methodically setting up the sidewalk chalkboard that advertised "Coffee: $2, Good Coffee: $2."

Ruby had to admit his approach to marketing was refreshingly honest, if completely devoid of creativity.

She watched him work, noting the efficient way he moved, how he checked the street in both directions before adjusting his sign. There was something reassuring about his steadiness—a kind of rhythm Ruby hadn't found yet. When his gaze drifted toward Scattered Beans, Ruby stepped back from the window, though she wasn't sure why.

The rational thing would be to walk across the street, hand over his mail, and ask about the forwarding situation. The normal-human-interaction thing. But there was something about discovering Jake's secret literary life that felt intimate, like she'd accidentally seen him in his underwear. Plus, if he'd gotten her credit card statement, this conversation was going to be awkward in entirely new ways.

Instead, Ruby did what she always did when faced with social uncertainty: she procrastinated.

She spent ten minutes arranging Jake's mail on her counter in different configurations, as if the optimal layout might reveal hidden meaning. She made herself a latte with extra foam because nervous energy required caffeine. Beatrice had been making concerning grinding noises that suggested a mechanical crisis was imminent.

Finally, she grabbed a sticky note. She'd considered writing on another napkin, but this seemed like a situation that called for actual stationery.

Wrong address again.
-Ruby

Simple. Direct. No mention of finances or poetry or the growing complexity of her feelings about her grumpy neighbor.

She opened Scattered Beans and made it through the morning rush despite Beatrice's concerning noises and her distracted state. During the brief lull between customers, Ruby crossed Main Street with Jake's mail tucked under her arm.

Sullivan's Coffee smelled like dark roast and years of accumulated conversation. The interior was like Ruby remembered—worn wooden floors, mismatched chairs, and a collection of coffee-stained newspapers that looked like they'd been there since the Clinton administration. It was the opposite of everything she'd tried to create at Scattered Beans, and somehow it worked perfectly.

Jake was wiping down the coffee machine—a sturdy, no-nonsense model that probably had been brewing the same reliable coffee for decades—when the door chimed. He looked up, and Ruby caught a flicker of something across his face. Surprise? Wariness? Recognition?

"Mail mix-up," she said, holding up the magazines and immediately regretting how breathless she sounded. "I think the postal service is confused about which building is which number, which honestly makes sense because the numbers aren't super clear from the street, and I keep thinking I should maybe paint mine bigger or get one of those fancy address plaques, but then I worry about historic district regulations because I have no idea what those are but I'm sure they exist, and the last thing I need is to get in trouble for unauthorized signage modifications when I'm already probably pushing boundaries with my sidewalk chalkboard situation that you mentioned the other day—"

Jake set down his cleaning cloth and walked over to where she stood, and Ruby's rambling died in her throat. Up close, in his own space, he seemed more settled somehow. The coffee shop smelled like him—dark roast and something woodsy. Ruby noticed the small scar above his left eyebrow and how close he was standing, the warmth radiating from him.

When he reached for the mail, his fingers brushed hers briefly, and Ruby's heart skipped.

"Thanks," he said, his voice a low rumble that had made her forget how to speak. "And I got some of yours."

Ruby's chest tightened slightly. Here it came—the awkward conversation about her financial situation. "Oh. Oh no. Was it... a lot?"

Jake's mouth quirked up slightly. "Credit card statement, something from your bank, loan paperwork."

"Right. Well." Ruby felt her cheeks flush. She knew everyone got bills, knew sealed envelopes didn't reveal anything, but the sheer volume of financial mail in her first weeks probably painted a picture. "I'm sure that looked super professional and financially stable. Multiple pieces of loan and credit mail definitely scream 'successful business owner.'—"

"Ruby." Jake's voice was quiet, but it cut through her spiraling anxiety.

He watched her animated gestures with something that might have been fondness. "It's fine."

"It's not fine, it's just—well, I suppose it's normal? I mean, new businesses always have cash flow issues, and I'm sure you understand that better than anyone, given that you've been running Sullivan's and probably went through the same growing pains when you started, or when your family started, and—"

"Ruby." Jake said her name again, and this time there was definitely amusement in his voice.

She stopped rambling and looked at him. Really looked at him—at the way he stood close enough that made her acutely aware of his presence, at how his voice carried that steady authority that made her feel like everything might actually be okay.

"Everyone's broke when they start a business," he said simply.

Ruby stared at him. "Really?"

"Really." Jake set her mail behind his counter next to his magazines. "Sullivan's barely made money the first two years. Great-grandfather almost lost the building three times."

This was more personal information than Jake had shared in all their previous interactions combined. The air between them felt different now, less tense.

"So you don't think I'm completely hopeless?"

Jake shook his head, and Ruby caught the way his mouth almost curved into a smile. "You're doing better than you think."

The admission was so unexpectedly reassuring that Ruby found herself smiling. "Thank you. That... actually helps."

Jake returned to cleaning his coffee machine, but his shoulders seemed more relaxed now. "You're brave," he said quietly.

The word hit Ruby like a small revelation. Not reckless or foolish or financially irresponsible, but brave.

"I..." she started, then stopped. When was the last time someone had looked at her chaos and seen courage instead of disaster?

"Really?" she finally managed.

Jake nodded. "Really."

The silence stretched between them, and Ruby felt that familiar urge to fill it with words, made worse by the fact that she was standing in Jake's domain, breathing his coffee-scented air, trying not to stare at the way his forearms looked when he worked.

"So," she said, her voice slightly higher than usual, "Poetry Magazine. That's... I didn't know people still subscribed to poetry magazines. I mean, I know poets exist, obviously, because someone has to write all those poems, but I always assumed they just published online now or did those coffee shop reading things where everyone snaps instead of claps, which I never really understood the snapping thing, honestly, because what's wrong with clapping? But maybe that's not the point, maybe the point is that you read poetry and that's actually really cool and intellectual and I'm rambling again, aren't I?"

Jake's cleaning motions paused for just a moment, and Ruby caught what looked like a smile trying to break free. "They do."

"Do you write, or just read, or...?" Ruby let the question trail off, realizing she was venturing into personal territory that Jake clearly didn't want to explore. "I mean, not that it matters, because reading is great, reading is wonderful, I just don't meet many people who read poetry for fun, you know? Most people think poetry is all doom and gloom and roses are red, violets are blue, but there's actually some really beautiful stuff out there, not that I'm an expert or anything, I just remember liking it in college before I got distracted by business classes and the practical realities of making a living wage—"

"Just read," he said, not looking up from his machine.

Ruby stood there for another moment, waiting for elaboration that didn't come. The silence felt different now, though—less awkward, more comfortable. Like they'd established some kind of understanding.

Finally, she said, "Well, I'll try to catch any future mail mix-ups before they pile up. And thanks for not making me feel like a complete disaster about the whole bill situation."

Jake looked up then, and Ruby caught something soft in his expression. "Your coffee really does smell good," he said. "From across the street."

Ruby felt her cheeks warm. "Thank you. That's... actually really nice to hear."

"Maybe sometime I could try it," Jake said, and Ruby's heart made an extra beat in her chest.

"Really? You'd want to try my coffee?" Ruby's voice pitched higher with excitement, her hands moving enthusiastically again. "I mean, obviously you would know good coffee, you've been making it way longer than I have, and your customers seem really happy with what you do here, and I would hate for you to compare it to what you're used to and find it lacking, but if you want to try it, I would love to make you something, maybe not a lavender latte because that might be too weird for your palate, but I do a really good vanilla latte, or just a regular latte, or whatever you prefer—"

"Ruby," Jake said, and there was something almost fond in the way he said her name.

She stopped talking.

"I'd like to try your coffee," he said simply.

Ruby stood there, smiling like an idiot, until she realized she should probably leave before she said something embarrassing about how nice his voice sounded when he said her name.

"Okay," she managed. "Great. Good. I should get back. Customers—" she pointed across the street, "—and Beatrice has been making concerning noises that suggest a mechanical crisis is brewing, which is probably not a great metaphor for my life but might be an accurate one—"

She was backing toward the door as she spoke, and nearly tripped over the threshold.

Jake stepped forward, steadying her with one hand on her arm, and Ruby felt that flutter become a full-fledged swarm of butterflies. Up close like this, she could feel the gentle strength of his hand through her sweater.

"There you go," he said quietly.

And there it was—those three words that turned Ruby's brain to mush and made her forget how to function like a normal human being.

"Thanks," she whispered, looking up at him and wondering when she'd started falling for her grumpy neighbor.

Jake's hand lingered on her arm for just a moment longer than necessary before he stepped back.

"See you around, Ruby," he said.

Ruby managed to make it back across Main Street without falling down, though it was a close thing. She unlocked Scattered Beans and flipped her sign to "OPEN," her mind replaying every moment of their conversation.

Jake thought she was brave. Jake wanted to try her coffee. Jake had said her name in that low, rumbly voice that made her stomach do impossible things.

Maybe Vi was right. Maybe curiosity was good.

Twenty minutes later, one of her customers, an apologetic elderly gentleman, knocked over the small chalkboard sign she'd left by the door. As Ruby rushed outside to help the man, she found a manila envelope on her doorstep with her name written in careful block letters.

Inside was a copy of Prairie Schooner with a sticky note attached:

THOUGHT YOU MIGHT BE CURIOUS. GOOD LUCK WITH BEATRICE.

-J

Ruby stood on Main Street, holding Jake Sullivan's poetry magazine. She reread the sticky note—*Thought you might be curious. Good luck with Beatrice.*—and felt a small smile tug at her lips.

He'd been paying attention. Not just to her questions about poetry, but to her rambling about her temperamental espresso machine.

Vi's voice echoed in her head: *Curiosity leads to conversation, conversation leads to connection.* She'd been curious about the magazines. That curiosity had led her across the street. The conversation had led to Jake calling her brave, offering to try her coffee, and now this—a gesture that proved he'd been listening.

Vi had been right. It wasn't just curiosity anymore—it was the beginning of actual connection.

Maybe Jake Sullivan had layers after all. Maybe she was ready to find out what they were.

CHAPTER *Four*

Ruby discovered that Millbrook Falls took its Fall Harvest Festival very seriously when Mayor Greene appeared at Scattered Beans on a crisp Tuesday morning in mid-September, clipboard in hand and the determined expression of someone about to volun-tell half the town into community service.

"Ruby, dear." Mayor Greene settled onto one of the vintage stools with the practiced ease of a politician who'd spent decades perfecting her approachable-but-authoritative demeanor. "I hope you're settling in well. The town council has been so pleased with the... energy you've brought to Main Street."

Ruby paused in her latte-making, immediately suspicious. In her limited experience, compliments from authority figures usually preceded requests for favors she couldn't afford to decline.

"Thank you? That's really nice to hear."

"Wonderful! Because I have the most exciting opportunity for you." Mayor Greene consulted her clipboard with the enthusiasm of someone who genuinely believed mandatory community participation was a gift. "As you know, our Fall Harvest Festival is this Saturday, and it's one of our biggest events of the year.

Hundreds of visitors, local vendors, live music—it showcases the best of small-town Millbrook Falls."

Ruby nodded, though she had no idea what any of this had to do with her. "It sounds lovely."

"It is! And this year, we're doing something special. Instead of having just one coffee vendor—which has traditionally been Jake's domain—we thought it would be wonderful to showcase both of our Main Street coffee establishments. A sort of... friendly coffee competition."

Ruby's stomach dropped. "A competition?"

"Oh, not a real competition! More like a collaboration. You'll be working side by side at the festival booth, showing visitors the wonderful variety of coffee options we have here in town." Mayor Greene's smile was bright enough to power a ferris wheel. "Won't that be fun?"

Ruby glanced through her front window toward Sullivan's Coffee, where Jake was moving around behind the counter with his usual methodical efficiency. The same Jake who'd called her brave and left poetry magazines on her doorstep. The same Jake who probably had no idea he was about to be voluntold into spending an entire day trapped in a ten-by-ten tent with his scattered, rambling neighbor.

"Has Jake agreed to this?"

"I'm heading over there next! But I'm sure he'll be delighted. Jake's always been so community-minded."

Ruby doubted that Jake would be delighted by anything involving forced cooperation and festival crowds, but she also couldn't think of a polite way to refuse without looking like a terrible new citizen.

"That sounds... great. Really great. I love festivals. And collaboration. And friendly coffee... things."

"Excellent!" Mayor Greene made a satisfied check mark on her clipboard. "Setup starts at 6 AM Saturday morning, and the festival runs until 8 PM. You'll be sharing the main beverage booth right in the center of the town square—prime real estate!

The Parks Department will deliver tables, a tent, and arrange a power hookup for your machines."

It hit Ruby then: fourteen hours of crowds, side by side with Jake, in the dead center of town. Free marketing—or a very public meltdown.

After Mayor Greene left—presumably to steamroll Jake into similar compliance—Ruby collapsed against her counter and wondered how she'd managed to get herself into this situation.

Her phone buzzed with a text from Vi:

VI

How's the small town romance developing?

Ruby typed back:

RUBY

I've been voluntold into working a festival booth with Jake for 14 hours. Send help. Or alcohol. Preferably both.

VI

OMG this is perfect! Forced proximity! Festival atmosphere! You're going to fall in love by sunset!

RUBY

Or die of embarrassment by noon.

VI

Same thing really. What are you going to wear?

Ruby looked down at her current outfit—coffee-stained apron, jeans with a suspicious hole near the knee, and a t-shirt that had definitely seen better days. She hadn't given a single thought to what she'd wear to work a festival booth, mostly because she'd been too busy panicking about the prospect of fourteen uninterrupted hours of trying not to ramble at Jake Sullivan.

I have no idea. What does one wear to a coffee collaboration with one's attractive, grumpy neighbor?

Something cute but practical. You'll be on your feet all day. And maybe something that shows you have a personality beyond coffee anxiety.

All my clothes show coffee anxiety. It's my brand.

She was still googling "comfortable shoes festival" when the bell over the door chimed.

Ruby looked up to see Jake Sullivan standing in her doorway, and her heart tripped over itself in a way that had become embarrassingly familiar.

"Let me guess." Jake's tone suggested he found the concept about as appealing as a root canal. "Mayor Greene."

"Mayor Greene." Ruby noted that he looked about as thrilled by this development as she felt. "So you've been voluntold too?"

"Apparently we're sharing a booth."

Ruby felt a stab of disappointment she tried to ignore. Of course Jake wasn't excited. She was his competition, and an admittedly chaotic one at that. The fact that he'd been kind to her a few times didn't mean he actually wanted to spend fourteen hours listening to her nervous rambling while serving coffee to festival crowds.

"Look, I know this probably isn't your idea of fun, but I promise I'll try to stay out of your way. We can divide the booth down the middle or something, and I'll keep my chaos contained to my half."

Jake was quiet for a long moment, studying her with that unreadable expression she was beginning to recognize. "That's not what I'm worried about."

"Then what are you worried about?"

"You've never worked a festival crowd before."

Ruby blinked. "Is that... bad?"

"They're intense. Lots of people, lots of orders, everything moving fast. Some want their usual, some want to try something new, and some don't know until they see it." He paused, choosing his words carefully. "It can be overwhelming."

"So what do you suggest?"

"We work together. Really together, not divided down the middle. You handle the specialty drinks, I handle the basics. I can prep while you customize."

"You'd want to do that? Even though we're supposed to be competitors?"

Jake's mouth quirked up slightly. "One day won't hurt."

Ruby's heart somersaulted. "Okay. Yes. That sounds... that sounds really good, actually. Thank you."

Jake nodded once and turned to leave, then paused at the door. "Ruby?"

"Yeah?"

"Wear comfortable shoes."

SATURDAY MORNING ARRIVED gray and drizzle-threatening, with a September chill that made Ruby grateful for her coffee-shop lifestyle and constant caffeine supply. She'd taken Jake's advice and worn her most comfortable sneakers, along with dark jeans and the soft green sweater Vi had declared "approachable but put-together" during their emergency FaceTime styling session the night before.

The town square was already bustling with setup activity when Ruby arrived at 5:45 AM, arms full of supplies she'd spent the previous evening organizing and reorganizing in fits of nervous energy. The Parks Department had delivered their promised tent and tables, but everything looked bare and institutional compared to the colorful vendor booths springing up around the square.

Ruby was standing in the middle of the empty tent, trying to figure out how to transform it into a professionally looking coffee-related place, when Jake appeared beside her carrying two large boxes and a thermos.

"Coffee." He held out the thermos. "You'll need it."

Ruby accepted it gratefully and took a long sip. Jake's coffee was strong and perfectly balanced, with a richness that made her question every cup she'd had since college.

"This is really good. I mean, of course it's good—you've been making coffee longer than I've been thinking about making coffee, but it's just—"

"Ruby."

She stopped rambling.

"Let's set up."

For the next thirty minutes, they transformed the bare tent into something professional. Jake had brought his methodical efficiency—supplies arranged by frequency of use, brewing equipment positioned for optimal workflow, even the cash box angled perfectly for quick transactions. When Ruby tried to help by organizing the cups, Jake quietly rearranged them in a more logical order without making her feel incompetent.

Ruby was reaching for the napkin dispenser when she knocked over her entire box of stirring sticks, sending them scattering across the tent floor like wooden confetti.

"Oh, come on. Really? Right now?"

Jake crouched beside her without a word, methodically gathering stirring sticks with the same calm efficiency he brought to everything else.

"I'm sorry. I swear I'm not usually this disaster-prone. Well, actually I kind of am, but I was hoping to keep it under control today, and apparently my nervous energy has other plans, and you're probably wondering why you agreed to work with someone who can't even handle basic setup without creating chaos—"

"Ruby." His voice was quiet, but it cut through her rambling.

She stopped.

He handed her the last of the sticks, and Ruby felt her cheeks warm despite the morning chill.

"Where do you want me to put the syrups?"

Jake looked at her supplies—vanilla, caramel, hazelnut, lavender, and several seasonal options she'd been experimenting with

—and Ruby caught what might have been approval in his amber eyes.

"Here." He set up a station at the front of the booth. "Easy access for custom orders."

"And Beatrice?"

"Next to the main coffee station. We can share the prep space."

As they worked, Ruby became increasingly aware of Jake's presence—the way he moved with quiet confidence around the booth, how he seemed to anticipate what they'd need before they needed it. When he handed her supplies or appeared with things she needed before she even realized she needed them, there was something almost protective in his careful attention. When she struggled with unfolding one of the tables, Jake simply appeared at her side and had it set up before she could even ask for help.

"There you go."

Ruby felt that familiar flutter in her stomach.

BY THE TIME the festival officially opened at 10 AM, their booth looked professional and welcoming, with clear signage for both Sullivan's Coffee and Scattered Beans, and an efficient workflow that Jake had somehow designed to accommodate both of their styles.

"Ready?" Jake asked as the first wave of festival-goers approached their tent.

Ruby took a deep breath, smoothed her apron, and nodded. "Ready."

The morning rush hit them immediately. Within minutes of opening, their booth was surrounded by eager festival-goers clutching cash and crowding close to read the menu board Jake had carefully organized. Ruby's hands moved on autopilot, pulling espresso shots and steaming milk while Jake handled a steady stream of black coffee orders with his usual efficiency.

An hour in, Ruby had found her rhythm. She could hear the

lift in her own voice as she explained options to curious customers, her hands moving expressively as she described flavor combinations. The nervous energy from the morning had transformed into something more purposeful—she was in her element, creating connections one conversation at a time.

"Can you make something fall-flavored but not too sweet?" asked a woman in an elegant coat who was clearly not from Millbrook Falls.

"How about a maple cinnamon latte with just a touch of vanilla? It's like autumn in a cup, but balanced."

"That sounds perfect."

As Ruby worked Beatrice through the specialty order, she was dimly aware of Jake handling orders with the kind of steady competence that made the whole operation look effortless. When she turned to grab milk from the shared prep area, Jake was already there with a fresh pitcher, perfectly steamed.

"There you go."

Heat crept up Ruby's neck despite the September chill.

"Excuse me." A teenager called from the front of the booth. "Do you have anything that's like a coffee milkshake but not too caffeinated? My mom said I could have something coffee-flavored but she doesn't want me bouncing off the walls."

Ruby grinned. "I can do a vanilla latte with half-caff coffee and extra foam. It'll taste like a coffee cloud."

"That sounds awesome!"

The lunch crowd descended in full force. The line at their booth stretched halfway across the square, and Ruby found herself moving faster than she'd ever moved behind a coffee counter. Jake had been right about festival crowds—they were intense, demanding, and seemingly endless. But he'd also been right about their division of labor.

"Behind you." Jake's hand briefly touched her lower back as he moved past her to refill the coffee station—brief, practical—and her breath halted as she caught his woodsy scent mixed with coffee and autumn air. She glanced up to find him watching her with an expression that was warmer than his usual reserve, his amber eyes holding hers for a moment longer than necessary.

"Thanks."

Jake nodded once before returning to his coffee routine.

The lunch rush continued relentlessly. When the line finally thinned to a manageable trickle, Ruby realized she was exhausted, exhilarated, and desperately needed water.

"How are you holding up?" Jake appeared beside her with a bottle of water as if reading her mind.

"Better than I expected. Though I think I understand now why you were worried about the crowds. This is like coffee boot camp."

"You're doing well." There was something in his tone that made Ruby look at him more closely.

"Really?"

"Really. Frank's been watching you all day."

Ruby looked over to where Frank Kowalski was sitting at one of the festival tables, slowly working through his third cup of Jake's coffee while observing their booth with the intensity of someone conducting a scientific study.

"Is that good or bad?"

"With Frank, it's hard to tell. But he hasn't complained, which is usually a good sign."

As if summoned, Frank Kowalski approached their booth with his empty cup and the skeptical expression Ruby had learned to associate with Team Tradition. Frank was shorter than Ruby had expected. Steel-gray hair, sharp blue eyes that moved deliberately from her lavender syrup to her vanilla extract and back again. His arms crossed over his chest. Ruby's hand went to her apron, smoothing it unnecessarily. That look—steady, measuring, unmoved—made her want to defend her flavor choices before he'd even spoken.

Jake started preparing Frank's standard black coffee, but Frank's attention had shifted to Ruby.

"You're the one with the fancy drinks."

"I am. Did you want to try something?"

Frank considered this for a long moment, glancing between Ruby's syrup station and Jake's coffee pot as if weighing loyalty against curiosity. His bushy eyebrows drew together in concentration, and Ruby could see him conducting an internal debate.

"What's that one you made for the lady with the fancy coat?"

"Maple cinnamon latte. Sweet but not too sweet. The cinnamon gives it warmth."

Frank hesitated, then said, "Make it a small one."

Ruby's hands moved automatically through the motions of steaming milk and pulling espresso, but her mind was racing. Frank Kowalski—Jake's most loyal customer, Team Tradition's unofficial spokesman—was ordering a specialty drink. From her.

"Here you go."

When Frank finally tried the maple cinnamon latte, Ruby watched his weathered face carefully. His bushy eyebrows drawn together in concentration, and for a moment his eyes lost their skeptical edge. He took another sip, slower this time, and Ruby caught something that might have been approval in the way his shoulders relaxed slightly.

"Huh."

"Good huh or bad huh?"

"Different huh. Not bad different. Just... different."

Coming from Frank, it felt like getting a five-star review from a famously stingy critic.

"Thank you."

Frank nodded once and returned to his table, maple cinnamon latte in hand. Ruby turned to find Jake watching her with an expression that was definitely approval.

"That was big."

"Really?"

"Frank doesn't try new things. Ever. I've been serving him the same order for fifteen years."

Pride rose bright and quick—partly for Frank's grudging

approval, partly for the way Jake was looking at her, like she'd just pulled off something remarkable.

A familiar laugh drew Ruby's attention to the front of the booth. Zara was approaching with Tommy Sullivan at her side, Jake's younger brother looking relaxed in jeans and a flannel shirt, a coffee cup already in hand.

"Well, well, well." Zara's grin was absolutely wicked as she took in the booth setup. "Look at you two, running a whole operation together. Very cozy."

"Zara." Ruby blushed.

"Hey, Ruby." Tommy's easy smile was so different from Jake's reserved demeanor. "Jake's got you working the festival circuit already? That's how you know you're officially part of Millbrook Falls."

"Don't encourage her," Jake said, but there was no heat in it.

"Don't 'Zara' me," Zara continued, clearly enjoying herself. "I've been watching from the bookstore tent. You've got a whole rhythm going. Very synchronized. Very..." She paused dramatically. "Domestic."

Jake, who was refilling the coffee station and had definitely heard that, said nothing, but Ruby caught the slight quirk of his mouth.

"We're just working efficiently," Ruby said, trying to sound professional while simultaneously fumbling with a cup lid. "It's festival service. High volume. We have to coordinate."

"Uh-huh. And does 'coordinating' usually involve that much eye contact? Because from where I was standing—"

"Zara's been watching you guys all day," Tommy interjected with a grin. "I had to physically drag her away from the bookstore tent to actually see the rest of the festival."

Zara shot him a look that was half-irritation, half-something else entirely. "I was not—I was just observing the foot traffic patterns. For business purposes."

"Right. Business purposes." Tommy's smile widened. "That's why you kept saying 'look how cute they are together.'"

"I said they work well together. That's completely different."

"You said cute."

"Tommy Sullivan, you are the worst—"

"The worst what?" His tone was teasing, and Ruby noticed the slight flush on Zara's cheeks.

"Never mind." Zara turned back to Ruby, clearly trying to regain her composure. "Can I get one of those maple cinnamon lattes I've been hearing about? Frank Kowalski tried one. Frank. The man who thinks flavored coffee is a sign of societal collapse."

Ruby started making Zara's drink, hyperaware of the dynamic playing out in front of her.

"So how much longer are you two stuck in this tiny tent together?" Zara asked, recovering her mischievous grin. "You know, working side by side, sharing space..."

"Four more hours," Ruby said.

"Four whole hours. In close proximity. However will you manage?"

Tommy caught Jake's eye and something passed between the brothers—some silent communication that made Jake's expression soften almost imperceptibly.

"We're managing fine," Jake said quietly.

Ruby handed Zara her latte, and Zara took a sip, her eyebrows rising. "Okay, this is actually amazing. No wonder Frank caved." She pulled out cash, but her teasing grin never wavered. "You two make a good team. A really good team. The kind of team that should maybe keep teaming up. Regularly."

"Zara!"

"I'm just saying what everyone's thinking!"

"Come on," Tommy said, gesturing toward the rest of the festival. "Let's go before you embarrass them any more."

"Fine, fine." Zara allowed herself to be steered away, but not before calling over her shoulder: "Carry on with your very professional coordinating!"

Ruby watched them disappear into the crowd, noting the easy way they moved together.

"She's worse than Mayor Greene," Jake said, but there was definite amusement in his voice.

"She means well. She's just... enthusiastic about things."

A group of customers approached the booth, and they were pulled back into the rhythm of festival service.

But she caught Jake watching her as she started the next order, and wondered if maybe Zara was onto something after all.

The afternoon brought a steadier pace. Families with sticky-fingered children, couples on dates, elderly residents taking their time to chat. The frantic lunch energy had mellowed into something more sustainable, and Ruby found herself settling into an easy rhythm with Jake. Between customers, they restocked supplies and cleaned equipment, moving around each other with increasing comfort.

Ruby noticed their teamwork had become almost choreographed. When she needed clean cups, Jake was already reaching for them. When he ran low on coffee, she had a fresh pot brewing. Their movements around each other became more fluid, less careful, as if some invisible boundary had been crossed without either of them acknowledging it.

"We make a good team." The words slipped out before she could stop them.

Jake looked at her, and something warm flickered in his amber eyes that made her stomach flip.

"Yeah. We do."

Ruby found herself genuinely enjoying the interactions, and she caught Jake watching her more than once with approval mixed with something warmer.

Ruby's feet were aching and her back protested every movement, but she felt energized in a way she hadn't expected. She'd been on her feet for eleven hours straight, but the satisfaction of creating drinks that made people smile kept her going.

The evening rush began as people finished their festival activities and wanted one more coffee before heading home. The line built again, not as intense as lunch but steady enough to keep both of them busy.

When an impatient customer snapped his fingers to get their attention, Ruby's response was immediate—her shoulders tensed, her smile went tight, and her hands fumbled with the cup she was holding. She could feel sweat prickle at her hairline despite the September chill, her rambling starting to spiral.

Jake stepped in smoothly, taking over the order with his usual quiet competence. "I'll handle this one," he said, his calm response somehow containing both authority and courtesy. Ruby watched his steady presence defuse the tension.

The festival crowd was thinning. Vendors around the square were beginning to pack up, and the live music from the main stage had shifted to softer, winding-down melodies. Ruby and Jake served their last few customers with the tired satisfaction of a job well done.

When 8 PM finally arrived, Ruby collapsed against the back table while Jake handled the final transaction. The town square was emptying out, leaving behind the pleasant debris of a successful festival—scattered napkins, the lingering smell of kettle corn, fried dough, and pumpkin spice, the distant sound of maintenance crews beginning cleanup.

"Ruby?"

"Yeah?"

"Good job today."

Ruby felt her cheeks warm. "Thanks. You too. I couldn't have done this without you."

Jake nodded, but there was something in his expression that suggested he might have enjoyed working together as much as she had.

As they packed up their supplies in the warm glow from the street lamps, Ruby found herself reluctant for the day to end. Tomorrow they'd go back to being business competitors across the street, back to their separate routines and careful boundaries.

But today had been something different. Today had been a partnership.

"Jake?"

"Yeah?"

"If Mayor Greene ever volunteers us for another festival, I wouldn't... I mean, this was actually really fun."

Jake's mouth curved up in what was definitely almost a smile. "It was."

Ruby stood in the empty town square, watching Jake walk back toward Sullivan's Coffee. Their relationship had shifted into something entirely new. What started as forced cooperation had become something she didn't want to end—a partnership that felt like it could become something more.

CHAPTER *Five*

Ruby's houseplant died on a Friday.

She discovered the botanical tragedy when she came downstairs to open Scattered Beans and found her succulent had given up sometime during the night. The single plant she'd been determined not to kill in this new chapter of her life had officially joined the ranks of her horticultural failures.

"Well, that's just perfect," Ruby muttered, staring at the shriveled leaves. Her long hair had already escaped from this morning's carefully planned bun, and she could see coffee grounds dusting her sleeve from her pre-opening test runs with Beatrice. So much for looking put-together

"I've officially killed the one green thing that had the misfortune to live with me."

She was still holding the deceased succulent when her first customer arrived—Mrs. Patterson, the sweet elderly woman who'd been cautiously warming up to Scattered Beans ever since the Fall Festival, and who now ordered a vanilla latte with near-religious regularity.

"Oh dear, that's a succulent, isn't it? They're usually so resilient. You probably just overwatered it; they don't like to be too wet."

"I thought I was being so careful." Ruby sighed, setting down the sad little pot. "Maybe plants just aren't my thing."

"Don't give up, dear. My late husband killed a lot of tomato plants before he finally figured out how to grow them. Some people just need a little practice."

After Mrs. Patterson left with her usual vanilla latte, Ruby disposed of the plant with appropriate ceremony and tried not to read it as an omen. She caught her reflection in the front window —hair escaping in dark waves around her face, coffee stains despite only being open an hour, but her eyes still bright with determination. She'd been in Millbrook Falls almost two months now, and while some things were going better than expected— Zara and Daisy felt like real friends, and whatever was happening with Jake was... something—other parts of small-town life were tougher than she'd planned.

Case in point: Gladys Murphy walked through the door, for what had become their weekly dance of polite hostility.

"Good morning, Gladys! The usual black coffee?"

"If you insist on calling it that." Gladys lowered herself onto a stool with the air of someone preparing to endure an unpleasant but necessary medical procedure. "Though I notice you're charging three-fifty now instead of three dollars."

Ruby's smile faltered slightly. She had raised her prices slightly —higher-quality beans and inflation had made it necessary—but somehow Gladys always made it sound like highway robbery.

"Well, the cost of beans has gone up, and I'm sourcing from a local roaster now instead of ordering online, which helps support other small businesses, and I think the quality is really noticeable, plus I've added some seasonal options that required new equipment—"

"Jake's still charging two dollars."

There it was. The Jake comparison that lurked beneath every exchange with Team Tradition. No matter how hard Ruby worked or how much her coffee improved, Sullivan's Coffee and its decades of loyalty loomed across the street.

"We're running different operations with different costs." Ruby kept her voice pleasant despite the irritation prickling at the back of her neck.

Gladys took her coffee without another word, left exact change on the counter, and turned to leave. But at the door, she paused. "Miller tried the same thing, you know. Fancy beans, higher prices. Thought the town would pay premium for coffee." She looked back at Ruby. "Lasted three years before the bank took the building."

Ruby's throat tightened. "I'm not Miller."

"We'll see," Gladys said, and walked out.

Ruby sagged against her counter, Gladys's words echoing in the sudden quiet. *Miller tried the same thing.* The reminder that someone else had failed in this exact space, with these exact ideas, felt like a weight settling on her chest.

That's when the door chimed again, and Tommy Sullivan walked in.

Ruby recognized him immediately—the same easy grin he'd worn at the festival, the same blond hair catching the morning light. Where his brother moved with careful precision, Tommy carried himself with loose-limbed confidence. In the month since the festival, he'd stopped by a few times, always cheerful, always managing to brighten her morning.

"Morning, Ruby!" Tommy's smile was bright despite the early hour. "Thought I'd stop by for one of those fancy drinks before I head to Mrs. Martinez's place. Got any new creations to torture Jake with?"

"Morning, Tommy." Ruby found herself smiling despite the morning's frustrations. She smoothed her apron, suddenly conscious of her scattered appearance. "How about a lavender honey latte? I've been perfecting the recipe."

"Perfect. Make it large and extra fancy-looking so I can make Jake question all his life choices."

Ruby laughed, feeling some of the morning's tension ease. "You really enjoy antagonizing your brother, don't you?"

"It's a sacred sibling duty. Plus, someone needs to shake up his routine. He's been making the same five drinks for fifteen years." Tommy leaned against the counter, completely at ease. "Speaking of which, that festival booth was something else. You two really had a system going."

Ruby's hands moved automatically through the familiar motions of preparing his drink. "We did work well together."

"'Work well together' is an understatement. The whole town's still talking about it. Frank Kowalski trying one of your specialty drinks was front-page news in a town this size. Pretty sure Gladys is still recovering from the shock."

"Is that... good or bad?"

Tommy grinned. "Depends. Good if you're trying to win over the old guard. Bad if you're Gladys and you've spent thirty years assuming change is the enemy."

Ruby couldn't stop herself from laughing while handing over his lavender latte, complete with foam art she'd been practicing. "And what's Jake's perspective on all this?"

Something shifted in Tommy's expression, and Ruby caught a glimpse of someone more serious underneath the charm. "Jake's been watching you handle the pushback with a lot more grace than most people would manage. He's impressed, even if he'd never admit it."

Her cheeks warmed as she wiped down the counter. "He said that?"

"Jake doesn't say much of anything, but he doesn't have to. I know my brother." Tommy took a sip of his latte and his eyebrows shot up. "Holy shit, this is actually incredible."

"Language." Ruby immediately winced at herself.

Tommy laughed. "Sorry. But seriously—this is way better than I expected. No wonder Jake's been—" He cut himself off mid-sentence, grinning. "Never mind."

"Jake's been what?"

"Nothing. Just my brother being his usual mysterious self." Tommy straightened from the counter. "Anyway, I should get back to work before Mrs. Martines sends out a search party. I'm supposed to be fixing her front steps, not gossiping about coffee."

On his way out, Tommy made a point of raising his lavender latte toward Sullivan's front windows in an exaggerated salute. Ruby felt lighter despite the morning's challenges. Maybe Gladys would never approve, but there were others in town starting to see her as more than just the chaotic newcomer with overpriced drinks.

The rest of the morning brought a steady stream of customers, including several faces Ruby was starting to recognize as regulars. Zara stopped in for her usual mid-morning caffeine fix, and Ruby noticed the way her friend's entire demeanor changed the moment she spotted Tommy's truck still parked outside Sullivan's.

"Is that Tommy's truck?" Zara's voice was slightly breathless as she perched on her usual stool. Her short raven-black hair was perfectly styled this morning, and she'd clearly taken extra care with her appearance—subtle makeup that made her grey eyes sparkle, a fitted sweater that flattered her petite frame.

"He was just here. Ordered a lavender latte and complimented my coffee-making skills in very colorful language."

"Did he?" Zara's voice pitched slightly higher, and she tucked her hair behind her ear in a gesture that was purely nervous. "What did he say?"

Ruby grinned, recognizing the signs of a serious crush. "That it was incredible and that he wanted to make Jake question his life choices by waving it around dramatically."

"That sounds like Tommy." She kept glancing toward the window where Tommy's truck was visible, her hands unusually still on the counter instead of gesturing expressively as she normally did.

"Zara Patel, you're completely smitten with Tommy Sullivan."

"Was I that obvious?" Zara groaned. "I thought I played it cool at the festival."

"You literally couldn't take your eyes off him. And the way he was teasing you about watching us all day? That wasn't nothing."

"He was just being Tommy. Charming everyone, making jokes." But Zara's voice pitched higher, hopeful. "You really think there was something there?"

"I think he drove you away from your bookstore tent and made you blush at least three times. And he seemed to really enjoy making you flustered."

Zara's hands stilled on the counter. "I've been crushing on him for months, but the festival was different. We actually talked—like really talked, not just my stammering customer service voice. He was funny and sweet and..." She trailed off, looking almost scared by the admission. "What if I'm reading too much into it?"

"Has he come by the bookstore since then?"

"Twice." Zara's cheeks flushed pink. "Once to pick up a book he ordered—he's reading Steinbeck, can you believe that?—and once just to... I don't know, chat? We talked about books for twenty minutes and he seemed genuinely interested, not just being polite. But maybe that's just Tommy being friendly with everyone."

Zara paused, then her expression shifted to something more mischievous. "Speaking of the Sullivan brothers—what about you and Jake? Because that whole festival thing looked pretty cozy to me."

Ruby felt heat creep up her neck. "We were just working together."

"Ruby. I watched you two for hours. That wasn't 'just working together.' That was..." Zara gestured expressively, her usual animation returning. "I don't even know what to call it. Synchronized? In sync? Like you'd been doing it for years instead of one day?"

"We just found a good rhythm."

"A rhythm. Right." Zara's smile was knowing. "Is that what we're calling the way he kept watching you when you weren't looking? Or how you lit up every time he handed you something?"

"I did not—"

"You absolutely did. And he did that thing—you know, where he gets all quiet and intense but somehow softer at the same time? Jake Sullivan does not look at people like that unless he's feeling something."

Ruby busied herself with wiping down the already-clean counter. "Even if he was—and I'm not saying he was—he's so... steady. Put-together. And I'm..." She gestured at herself, at the coffee shop, at the general chaos of her existence.

"You're adorable when you're in denial," Zara said with a grin. "Come on, Ruby. I watched you two at that festival booth. That level of coordination doesn't just happen. You were finishing each other's sentences."

"We were just being efficient."

"Efficient." Zara laughed. "Right. And I'm sure the way Tommy says Jake's been 'impressed' with how you handle things is also just professional admiration."

Ruby's cheeks warmed. "Tommy talks too much."

"Tommy tells the truth. His brother doesn't impress easily." Zara's expression turned knowing. "But hey, take your time figuring it out. Just don't wait so long that you miss what's right in front of you."

Ruby watched through the window as Tommy emerged from Sullivan's, tool belt slung over his shoulder, moving with that same loose-limbed confidence she'd noticed earlier. When he spotted Zara through the window, he raised his hand in a friendly wave, and Ruby watched her normally articulate friend go completely still, her grey eyes wide with something between panic and delight.

"He's waving."

"Wave back."

"I can't. What if I look desperate? What if he's just being polite? What if—"

"Zara. Wave."

Zara raised her hand in a small, careful wave, and Tommy's grin widened before he climbed into his truck. The moment he drove away, Zara collapsed forward onto the counter with a dramatic groan.

"I am completely hopeless."

"You're completely smitten. There's a difference." Ruby slid Zara's finished latte across to her. "And for what it's worth, I think he likes you too."

"You're just saying that to make me feel better."

"I'm saying it because I watched him light up when he saw you through the window. That wasn't polite-neighbor friendly. That was interested."

Zara took her latte, hope and terror warring on her face. "I should get back to the store before I completely lose my nerve and do something embarrassing like texting him." She stood, smoothing her sweater, then paused. "And Ruby? Don't sell yourself short with Jake. Sometimes the best things happen when two different people find a way to fit together."

Ruby watched her friend leave, those words settling somewhere deep in her chest.

AROUND NOON, during what should have been the usual lull, Ruby was wiping down tables when she noticed Jake through the front window. He stood in Sullivan's doorway, arms crossed, watching something. His copper hair was slightly messed from the morning's work, and there was something in the set of his broad shoulders—a thoughtfulness that went beyond coffee service.

Following his gaze, she realized he was looking at her.

Their eyes met across Main Street, and Jake raised one hand in a small wave. Ruby waved back, her heart doing that familiar skip as she took in his steady presence. Even from a distance, there was something about his amber-colored eyes and quiet competence that made her feel a little less scattered. The way he stood in his doorway, framed by the warm light of Sullivan's Coffee, made her think of reliability and strength and all the things she'd been missing without realizing it.

In the month since the festival, their interactions had developed a comfortable rhythm—small waves across the street, occasional brief conversations when they both stepped outside for air, that one time he'd brought over a package that had been missdelivered to Sullivan's. Nothing dramatic, but something was definitely shifting between them.

A movement in Sullivan's window caught her eye—Frank Kowalski had just arrived for his midday coffee. He settled into his usual spot, newspaper in hand, but instead of burying himself in the headlines, his gaze kept drifting toward Scattered Beans. Ruby could swear he looked thoughtful rather than disapproving.

Maybe Tommy was right. Maybe she was making more progress than she realized.

The afternoon brought Ruby's biggest test yet: a tour bus full of weekenders from Boston, all demanding elaborate drinks and complaining about the wait. She found herself juggling twelve different specialty orders while trying to explain why a "simple" caramel macchiato actually required several steps and couldn't be rushed—even if they had schedules to keep and very important sightseeing to do before the light changed.

Ruby's carefully styled hair had completely given up by this point, dark waves escaping to frame her flushed face as she moved frantically between Beatrice and the milk steamer. Coffee grounds dusted her sleeve despite her best efforts to stay clean, and her animated gestures were becoming more frantic as the orders piled up.

"Excuse me, I ordered my drink fifteen minutes ago."

"It's been seven minutes. It's next up. The espresso needs to be pulled fresh for each cup, but I promise it'll be worth the wait. I can offer you a sample of our seasonal cinnamon blend while—"

"This is ridiculous. At Starbucks, they have three people working and everything comes out in two minutes. I don't understand why a simple latte takes forever here."

Ruby's jaw clenched, frustration flashing across her face as she pushed an escaped strand of hair back from her forehead. She was searching for a polite response that wouldn't tank her Yelp reviews when the door chimed. Jake Sullivan walked in, took one look at the chaos—Ruby flushed and frazzled, Beatrice hissing steam like an angry dragon, customers muttering—and moved to stand beside the espresso machine.

His presence immediately changed the energy in the room.

"Hey," he said quietly, his low voice somehow cutting through the noise. "Need help?"

Ruby wanted to cry with relief but settled for nodding frantically. "I'm drowning."

"You take orders. I'll work Beatrice."

It should have been awkward—Jake operating her espresso machine, invading her space, taking over her crisis. Instead, it felt like the most natural thing in the world. He moved around her with easy efficiency, pulling shots and steaming milk with the same quiet competence he brought to everything. When Ruby fumbled with the caramel sauce, Jake caught the bottle before it could hit the ground and handed it back without a word.

"There you go."

Ruby's brain short-circuited despite the chaos around them, a second later she jolted back to reality.

They worked in tandem for the next twenty minutes, Ruby taking orders and handling payment while Jake managed the actual coffee production. The tourists stopped complaining, maybe because Jake's silent intensity suggested he was not someone to be trifled with, or maybe because the coffee was actually coming out faster now.

When the last customer finally left—appeased by their drinks and Ruby's apologetic offer of a free pastry coupon for their next visit—Ruby leaned against the counter, exhausted but grateful.

"Thank you," she managed. "I don't know what I would have done if you hadn't shown up."

Jake was cleaning Beatrice with the same methodical care he probably brought to his own equipment. "You would have figured it out."

"I'm not sure about that. I was about two minutes from a complete meltdown."

"You're tougher than you think." Jake glanced at her, warmth in his amber eyes. "You handled Gladys this morning. Tour bus is nothing compared to that."

Ruby blinked. "You saw that?"

"Frank told me. Said she laid into you pretty hard about the price increase."

Her cheeks warmed, both from embarrassment and from Jake's unexpected defense. "She mentioned Miller. Said he tried the same thing I'm doing and couldn't make it work."

Jake's expression shifted, became more serious. "Miller's problem wasn't his prices. It was that he was trying to be Sullivan's instead of his own thing. You're different."

"How?"

"You're brave enough to actually be different."

Before Ruby could respond, a well-dressed man in his thirties walked through the door, looking around Scattered Beans with obvious curiosity. He was handsome in that polished, corporate way—pressed shirt, expensive watch, confident smile from years of successful client meetings.

"Ruby! There you are!" The man spread his arms wide like he was greeting an old friend at a reunion. "This place is even cuter than I imagined."

Ruby's heart sank. "Derek?"

Jake's expression went carefully neutral, but Ruby caught the way his jaw tightened slightly. He stepped back from Beatrice, putting professional distance between himself and Ruby's workspace.

"I should get back," Jake said quietly.

"Jake, wait—"

But he was already heading for the door, giving Derek a polite nod as he passed. Derek barely seemed to notice, too busy looking around Scattered Beans with that assessing expression Ruby remembered from his business development days.

"So this is where you ended up," Derek said, settling onto a stool. "It's exactly what I pictured."

Ruby wasn't sure if that was a compliment. And as she watched Jake disappear back into Sullivan's Coffee across the street, she wasn't sure she cared what Derek thought anymore.

"Surprise! I was driving back from a client meeting in Springfield and thought I'd detour to see how my favorite barista is settling in."

Ruby became acutely aware of her disheveled appearance and the lingering aftermath of the rush. "That's... really sweet. How did you find the place?"

"Small town, one main street." Derek's gaze took inventory. "This is cute, Ruby. Very... authentic."

The word landed like a paper cut.

"Can I get you something? Coffee?"

"Just a regular coffee. Black. I don't need anything fancy." He made himself comfortable. "So this is where you landed after BrewCorp."

She pulled his shot and topped the cup, acutely aware of how different her hands felt without Jake beside her.

"The drive up here was interesting. Very... rural. I can see the appeal for a weekend getaway, but living here full-time? Ruby, don't you get bored?"

Before she could answer, the door opened and Daisy breezed in with a terracotta pot cradled in her hands, her usual bright energy filling the space.

"Ruby, dear! I heard about your succulent from Mrs. Patterson." Daisy's eyes sparkled with sympathetic amusement as she set the pot on the counter. "So I brought you something that's practically impossible to kill—chocolate mint. It's beautifully fragrant, perfect for drinks, and will forgive you for just about anything."

She paused, noticing Derek for the first time. "Oh! I didn't realize you had company."

"Not company, just an old friend. Daisy, this is Derek Castellano. He's my former boss from my corporate days."

"How lovely you came to visit!" Daisy offered her hand. "Ruby's become such a treasure here. We're so lucky she found us."

"Found you?" Derek's smile tilted. "That's one way to put it."

Daisy gestured to the mint plant with obvious pride. "This will be wonderful for your seasonal drinks, Ruby. And it grows like wildfire, so you'll have plenty. Even someone with your track record can keep this alive."

Ruby laughed despite herself, touched by the gesture. "Thank you, Daisy. This is really kind of you."

"Your grandmother would be so proud," Daisy added, eyes soft. "Planting roots of your own—she always knew you would."

Derek's focus sharpened. "Grandmother?"

"Oh yes—Doris Ashworth was a dear friend," Daisy said. "She always said Ruby had the gift for making people feel at home."

Ruby watched the moment Derek realized her move wasn't random drift but a chosen landing.

After Daisy left—with a promise to stop by tomorrow—the shop felt too quiet again. Derek sipped his coffee, consideration back in place.

"So, your grandmother funded this venture?"

"It's not a venture, Derek. It's my business."

"Right, of course. Your business." His eyes ticked around the room, doing math. "How's it going? Small town coffee shop, limited customer base... it must be interesting."

There it was—the gentle condescension dressed as concern.

"We're doing well."

"I'm sure you are. For now." He leaned forward, closing like a pitch. "But long term? What's your five-year plan? You can't serve lattes to the same handful of people forever. You're talented—you could be running a regional operation, impacting thousands of customers. Instead, you're playing house in a town where the biggest excitement is probably the county fair."

Playing house. Ruby felt the heat in her chest, banked it. "The Fall Festival was actually really successful—"

"I'm sure it was charming. But charm doesn't pay the bills. Charm doesn't build a retirement fund or create advancement." His voice softened, but the edge remained. "I get the appeal, after corporate stress. But hiding from the real world isn't the same as building a future."

Ruby stared at him and, for once, didn't bother arguing the bullet points. She could have pointed to the cork board of customer notes, to Daisy's deliveries, to Zara's laugh, to the way the bell sounded different when locals walked in. She could have said a dozen names that would call her by hers.

"I'm not hiding," she said simply.

"Aren't you, though?" He checked his watch and stood, efficient as ever. "Think about what I said, okay? They admitted it was a mistake to fire you. You've got too much potential to waste it in a place like this." At the door he added, smile perfectly deployed, "I'll be in touch. There might be opportunities coming up that fit your skills. Maybe even a regional manager position."

When he was gone, Ruby stood in the center of Scattered Beans, surrounded by the life she'd built: Daisy's chocolate mint bright on the counter, warm bulbs casting honeyed light. Across the street, Jake moved through Sullivan's with that quiet steadiness she'd started to think of as home.

Derek saw a dead-end town with limited prospects. Ruby saw connection, names she knew, and the possibility of making something that mattered.

She turned to the window. Her reflection met her there—ponytail half-escaped now, coffee stains like badges on her sleeve, eyes bright with a steadier kind of confidence.

"Okay, little guy," she told the mint, smoothing stray hairs back with both hands. "It's you and me now. Try not to die on me."

She brushed soil from her palms, glanced at the messy stack of business-plan napkins, and made herself a promise. Tomorrow she'd water the mint and finally sort those napkins into an actual plan. Derek's warnings about five-year strategies echoed faintly—but so did Jake's quiet, certain: *You're doing fine.*

It was the beginning of October, and she was finding her footing.

CHAPTER *Six*

Ruby was in the middle of explaining to a confused tourist why a macchiato wasn't the same as a latte when Zara burst through the door of Scattered Beans like a small, enthusiastic tornado.

"Ruby! Emergency coffee meeting. Now."

The tourist looked affronted at the interruption, but Zara was already halfway to the counter, practically vibrating with news.

Ruby quickly finished the tourist's order—a regular latte, despite the macchiato confusion—and sent them on their way with an apologetic smile before turning to Zara.

"What's wrong? Did something happen at the bookstore?"

"Nothing's wrong. Everything is amazing and terrifying and you need to prepare yourself." Zara hopped onto a stool, her grey eyes sparkling with mischief. "Mayor Greene just left the bookstore. Guess what she told me?"

Ruby's stomach dropped. Nothing good ever started with "Mayor Greene just told me." "What?"

"The Millbrook Harvest Fair. This weekend. You and Jake are sharing a booth again."

"Wait—what?" Ruby nearly dropped the milk pitcher she was cleaning. "This weekend? As in three days from now?"

"Seventy-two hours of forced proximity with your favorite grumpy coffee man." Zara's grin was absolutely wicked. "And before you panic—yes, you knew about the festival. You agreed to participate like, a month ago. Remember? You signed the vendor form?"

Ruby did have a vague memory of Mayor Greene appearing with paperwork, and Ruby agreeing because she'd wanted to seem like a committed community member. But she'd assumed it would be like September—maybe a day, but this time with her own small booth, manageable.

"I thought I'd have my own setup! A small table, some seasonal drinks, nothing major—"

"Well, Mayor Greene had other ideas. After how well you two worked together in September, she decided the town should 'showcase our collaborative coffee community' or something equally politician-y. Translation: you and Jake are sharing the main beverage booth for the entire weekend."

Ruby sank against the counter. "The whole weekend."

"Friday through Sunday. Same tent, same space, same constant proximity." Zara was clearly enjoying this far too much. "I believe the exact phrase Mayor Greene used was 'building on their successful partnership.'"

"But—I haven't prepared. I don't have enough supplies ordered. I don't even know what drinks to feature. A whole weekend is completely different from one day, and sharing a booth means coordinating everything, and what if our systems don't work together anymore, and—"

"Ruby. Breathe." Zara reached across the counter and squeezed her hand. "You did this in September. You were amazing. You and Jake had a whole rhythm going."

"That was different. That was one day. We were running on adrenaline and desperation. Multiple days means actually planning things, and you know planning isn't my strong suit—"

"Which is why Jake is perfect for you. He plans everything."

Zara's expression softened slightly. "Look, I know this feels overwhelming. But you've got a few days to prepare, and I'm betting Jake already has half of it figured out. Plus, this is good for business. The Millbrook Harvest Fair is huge—easily twice the size of the Fall Festival. Half the state shows up for this thing."

Ruby's mind was already spiraling through logistics. "I need to order more syrups. And cups. Do I have enough cups? I should probably create a limited menu so I'm not trying to make seventeen different drinks under pressure. And what about Beatrice? Can she handle constant use? What if she breaks down in the middle of service and I'm standing there like an idiot with no way to make espresso—"

"Ruby!"

She stopped.

Zara's smile was knowing and kind. "Talk to Jake. You two figured it out before. You'll figure it out again."

After Zara left—with a promise to stop by during the festival to "observe the romantic tension"—Ruby tried to focus on her remaining customers. But her mind kept spinning through worst-case scenarios. An entire weekend with Jake Sullivan. Days of trying not to ramble, not to fumble equipment, not to reveal just how much his quiet "there you go"s made her brain short-circuit.

She was still spiraling when her phone rang.

Ruby glanced at the screen and her stomach dropped. Derek Castellano.

She considered not answering, but Derek was persistent. If she didn't pick up now, he'd just call back. And back. And back.

"Hello?"

"Ruby! I was hoping I'd catch you." Derek's voice was smooth and confident, with that practiced corporate charm. "How's business?"

Ruby moved away from the counter, toward the back of the shop where customers couldn't overhear. "Business is fine, Derek."

"Right, busy. Which is exactly why I'm calling." Papers rustled in the background. "Remember that regional manager position I mentioned? Well, it's moving forward. Hartford office, overseeing operations in New Haven and possibly expanding into Boston. Real growth opportunity, Ruby. Real future."

Her stomach twisted. Regional manager. It was exactly the kind of role she'd once dreamed about—stable salary, career trajectory, the respect of managing multiple locations. Everything she'd lost when BrewCorp had decided her creativity "didn't align with brand standards."

"Derek, I told you—I'm happy here."

"Are you, though?" His tone shifted, became almost gentle. Concerned. "Ruby, I drove through Millbrook Falls. It's charming for a weekend, but long-term? You're relying on what, three thousand locals to keep your doors open? And winter's coming. Tourist season ends. You'll be serving coffee to the same fifty people every day, hoping they don't get bored of your flavors."

The words found their mark because they echoed her own 3 AM anxieties—the ones that woke her up wondering if Grandma Doris's money would be enough, if she'd made a terrible mistake leaving corporate stability for small-town uncertainty.

"The Millbrook Harvest Fair is this weekend," Ruby said, hating how defensive she sounded. "It's one of the biggest events of the year. Hundreds of people."

"One weekend of hundreds isn't the same as consistent customer base, and you know it. Look, I'm not trying to scare you. I'm trying to help. You're talented, Ruby. Really talented. But talent needs the right environment to thrive. Hartford would give you resources, support, a team. What does Millbrook Falls give you?"

Ruby looked around Scattered Beans. The bulletin board covered in handwritten thank-you notes. Daisy's chocolate mint thriving on the windowsill. The light streaming through windows that overlooked Main Street and Sullivan's Coffee, where Jake was probably serving Frank his midday cup with the same competence he brought to everything.

"It gives me community," she said.

"Community." Derek made it sound quaint. Insufficient. "That's great for your mental health, Ruby, but not for your retirement funds. Promise me you think about it, okay? The position hasn't been officially posted yet, but I could get your name in early. Bypass the whole application circus. We'd be lucky to have you back."

"I'll think about it," Ruby said, just to end the conversation.

"That's all I ask. I'll check in next week."

After he hung up, Ruby stood in the quiet of her shop, Derek's words circling like vultures. *Winter's coming. Tourist season ends. Playing house.*

She busied herself wiping down the counter—already clean, but her hands needed something to do. Through the front window, she could see the maple trees lining Main Street, their leaves brilliant crimson and gold against the October sky. In Hartford, she'd never noticed the trees. Here, she knew which ones turned first, which stayed green the longest.

When had that happened? When had Millbrook Falls stopped being temporary and started feeling like hers?

The bell chimed, and Ruby looked up to see Jake standing in her doorway, broad-shouldered and solid, his copper hair slightly mussed from the October wind. His amber eyes found hers immediately, and he paused, reading her like she was an open book.

"Hey," he said.

"Hey." Ruby tried for a smile, but it felt wobbly. "Let me guess—Mayor Greene?"

"Mayor Greene." Jake's mouth quirked slightly. "Shared booth for the weekend. Sound familiar?"

"Zara already gave me the news. I'm still processing." Ruby pushed her hair back from her face, aware that she probably looked as scattered as she felt. "I'm sorry you got voluntold into this again. I know working with me for one day was probably exhausting enough—"

"Ruby."

She stopped.

Jake moved further into the shop, his presence somehow making the space feel smaller and more settled at the same time. "I talked to Mayor Greene this morning. Told her we should collaborate."

Ruby blinked. "You... what?"

"September worked. The town saw it. Customers saw it." He paused, choosing his words with his usual care. "Made sense to do it again."

Relief flooded through her so suddenly it made her dizzy. Jake had *suggested* this. He'd actively chosen to work with her for an entire weekend, despite how chaotic she was, despite her rambling and her tendency to knock things over.

"You actually want to work together?"

"Yeah." His gaze held hers. "But a weekend is different from one day. We should practice. Make sure we don't kill each other under pressure."

"Practice?"

"Tomorrow night. After we close. We'll set up equipment, test the workflow, figure out what works." There was fondness in his expression now, unmistakable. "If you want to."

Ruby felt her scattered anxiety settling into something more manageable. Jake had a plan. Jake always had a plan. And apparently, his plan included her.

"That's brilliant. Yes. Absolutely yes." The words tumbled out before she could stop them. "I've been panicking about supplies and menu planning and whether Beatrice can handle multiple days of constant use, but a practice run is perfect. We can identify problems before we're in front of hundreds of people, and I can figure out which syrups actually matter instead of bringing my entire collection like last time—"

"Ruby." The corner of his mouth lifted. "Six o'clock. Bring Beatrice."

"Six o'clock. Beatrice. Got it." Ruby paused, then added with a small smile, "Should I bring all seventeen syrups or try to narrow it down?"

"Bring them all," Jake said, deadpan. "We both know you will anyway."

Her laugh was surprised and genuine. "You know me too well already."

"Getting there," he said, and the way he looked at her—like she was worth knowing, worth understanding—made her forget all about Derek's phone call.

After he left, Ruby stood in the autumn sunlight streaming through her windows, feeling like the ground had shifted under her feet. Derek offered safety and salary and a clear path forward. But Jake offered something else entirely—partnership, trust, the certainty that she didn't have to figure everything out alone.

She thought about what Zara had said: *You'll figure it out again.*

Maybe she would.

THE NEXT EVENING, Ruby wheeled Beatrice across Main Street with more supplies than any reasonable person needed for a practice run. Seventeen syrup bottles (she'd promised herself she'd narrow it down but hadn't), backup cups, extra napkins, and enough nervous energy to power the entire festival.

The town square was empty in the October dusk, shop lights glowing warm against the cooling air. Fallen leaves crunched beneath Beatrice's wheels, and Ruby could smell wood smoke and someone's dinner cooking—beef stew, maybe, or pot roast. The kind of small-town October evening that would've been impossible to imagine during her Hartford corporate days.

Jake was already there, setting up their booth space with military precision. He'd marked out their work areas, taped down cords to prevent tripping, arranged coffee urns in a logical sequence. Everything had a place, and every place was labeled with blue painter's tape in his neat handwriting.

"You've been busy," Ruby said, slightly breathless from wheeling Beatrice across uneven cobblestones.

Jake looked up, and his expression softened when he saw her struggling with her supplies. He was there immediately, taking the heavier boxes from her arms before she could protest.

"Wanted to make sure we had enough space." He set her boxes down in the designated prep area. "Where do you want Beatrice?"

"Next to your station? If that works?" Ruby gestured vaguely, already second-guessing herself. "Or maybe on the other side if that's better for workflow, or—"

"Here's good." Jake positioned Beatrice with the same careful precision he brought to everything. "Close enough to share space, far enough to not trip over each other."

"The story of our professional relationship," Ruby said without thinking, then immediately felt her cheeks warm. "I mean—the booth setup. Not our actual relationship. Not that we have a relationship relationship, just a working—I'm going to stop talking now."

Jake's mouth twitched. "Probably wise."

They spent the next twenty minutes arranging equipment, and Ruby noticed how much had shifted since September. Where she'd been nervous and uncertain then, now she found herself anticipating what Jake needed. When he reached for tape, she had the dispenser ready. When she started organizing syrups, he simply adjusted the less-stable bottles without comment.

"So," Ruby said as she arranged her flavor arsenal, "you told Mayor Greene we should do this. Was that before or after you remembered I brought seventeen syrups last time?"

"After." Jake didn't look up from the coffee urn he was positioning. "Figured if you survived one festival with that many bottles, a weekend wouldn't kill you."

"Such faith in my organizational skills."

"Didn't say anything about organizational skills. Just survival instincts."

Ruby laughed, caught off guard by his dry humor. "Are you making fun of me, Jake Sullivan?"

"Observing." But there was definite amusement in his voice. "There's a difference."

"Uh-huh. And what else have you been observing?"

Jake straightened, met her eyes. "That you're better at this than you think you are."

The words settled warm in her chest, chasing away the last echoes of Derek's doubts.

"Okay," Jake said, pulling out his small notebook. "Ready to run through some orders?"

For the next hour, they worked through scenarios—pumpkin spice lattes, maple cappuccinos, elaborate custom orders that required multiple syrups and specific temperatures. Ruby found herself falling into rhythm with Jake's methodical pace, their movements becoming more intuitive with each practice round.

"Two cappuccinos, one vanilla latte, extra hot," Jake called out.

Ruby's hands moved automatically, but she frowned at the espresso machine. "Wait, is Beatrice pulling slower than usual? That shot took an extra three seconds."

"Could be the grind." Jake came over to look. "When did you last adjust it?"

"This morning, but maybe the humidity..." Ruby trailed off, already reaching for the grinder settings.

"Check it now, not during the rush." His tone was matter-of-fact. "Better to fix problems in practice."

They spent ten minutes fine-tuning Beatrice's temperamental espresso extraction, Jake offering suggestions while Ruby made adjustments. It was practical, unglamorous problem-solving—but somehow it felt more intimate than any romantic gesture. This was partnership. This was trust.

"Better?" Jake asked after she pulled a test shot.

Ruby timed it carefully. "Perfect. Thank you."

"Can't have Beatrice failing mid-festival. You'd panic."

"I would not panic. I'd just... have a very intense moment of crisis management."

"That's panicking."

"That's controlled concern."

Jake's lips twitched. "Sure it is."

They kept practicing, the autumn evening settling cool and comfortable around them. The town square's street lamps flickered on, casting everything in warm gold light. Somewhere nearby, the high school band was practicing for the festival, their distant music drifting across the square in cheerful, slightly off-key bursts.

"Behind you," Jake murmured at one point, brushing past to refill supplies. His hand steadied her waist briefly—practical, grounding—and Ruby felt the warmth of his palm even after he'd moved away.

She glanced up and found him watching her, amber eyes unreadable in the lamplight.

"What was the next order?" she managed.

"Two regulars, one decaf."

They were packing up the equipment, moving in comfortable silence, when a car pulled up to the curb near Sullivan's Coffee. An elderly woman emerged—carefully, using the door for support—and Jake immediately set down the box he was holding.

"That's Mrs. Henderson," he said. "She's dropping something off."

Ruby watched as Mrs. Henderson retrieved a large envelope from her passenger seat and made her way slowly toward Sullivan's front door. Jake met her halfway, taking the envelope gently and exchanging a few words Ruby couldn't hear. Mrs. Henderson patted his arm with obvious affection before returning to her car.

When Jake came back, he was studying the envelope with an expression Ruby couldn't quite read.

"Everything okay?" she asked.

"Yeah." He turned the envelope over, and Ruby caught a

glimpse of careful cursive handwriting. "It's from Rose. My grandmother."

"Rose," Ruby repeated. "She's the one who writes you letters, right? Tommy mentioned her once."

"Every week." Jake's thumb traced the edge of the envelope absently. "She lives in Northfield. I visit on Sundays."

Ruby pictured it—Jake driving thirty minutes every week to visit his grandmother, probably bringing her groceries and updates about the coffee shop. It fit perfectly with everything she'd learned about him: loyal, devoted to the people he cared about, showing love through action rather than words.

"That's really sweet. She must love your visits."

"She says they're the highlight of her week." Jake's expression softened in a way Ruby had rarely seen. "She's seventy-eight, still sharp as anything. Loves hearing about the shop."

"Does she know about me? About Scattered Beans?"

Jake was silent for a moment, then said, "Yeah. She knows."

Ruby's breath caught at the way he said it—like Rose knowing about her mattered. "What does she think?"

"She thinks..." Jake paused, choosing his words with care. "She thinks my great-grandfather would be proud to see Sullivan's working with someone bringing new life to Main Street. Said it reminded her of how he used to experiment with new drinks."

Ruby felt her chest tighten. The idea that Rose—someone she'd never met—was writing about her, believing in what she was building, seeing it as honoring rather than threatening the Sullivan legacy.

"That means a lot," she managed.

Jake studied the envelope, turning it over in his hands. "This one's thicker than usual. She mentioned in last week's letter that she's been cleaning out her attic. Said she found some old family things—documents, photographs from when Great-Grandfather ran the shop."

"Really?" Ruby felt curiosity spark bright. "Like what kind of documents?"

"Not sure yet. She wants me to come look through them." Jake glanced at Ruby, uncertainty flickering across his face. "She sounded excited. Said the old days weren't quite what I might think."

"What does that mean?"

"That's what I need to find out." He turned the envelope over again. "I've been meaning to visit, but the festival prep has been taking up all my time. I told her I'd come by after this weekend."

Ruby's mind was already racing with possibilities. Historical documents. Photographs from Sullivan's early days. Stories about Jake's great-grandfather that even Jake didn't know. "That could be really special. Family history you didn't know about."

She stopped herself, realizing she was getting carried away. "Sorry, I'm getting ahead of myself. I just think it's cool that she found all this history."

"You're already imagining what's in there," Jake said, but fondness colored his words.

"It's a gift," Ruby said, grinning. "Or a problem. Probably both."

"Probably both," Jake agreed.

They finished packing in comfortable silence, the envelope from Rose tucked carefully under Jake's arm. Ruby found herself wondering what secrets those old documents held, what stories Rose had discovered that had made her sound so intrigued.

"Same time tomorrow?" she asked, even though tomorrow meant separate shops again, back to their usual routines.

"Same time tomorrow." Jake's gaze lingered on hers for a moment. "And Ruby?"

"Yeah?"

"Stop worrying. The festival's going to be good."

After he left, Ruby stood in the October night, surrounded by their packed equipment and the golden glow of street lamps. Derek's words from earlier echoed faintly—*winter's coming, tourist season ends, playing house*—but they felt distant now, less important.

What mattered was this: Jake had chosen to work with her. Rose believed in what she was building. And somewhere in Northfield, in an elderly woman's attic, there were documents waiting to tell stories about Sullivan's Coffee that no one had heard in decades.

Ruby wheeled Beatrice back across Main Street, her mind already jumping ahead to the festival, to working alongside Jake for an entire weekend, to whatever Rose had found in her attic.

October stretched ahead, full of possibility and pumpkin-spiced promise.

CHAPTER Seven

FRIDAY MORNING DAWNED CRISP AND BRIGHT, THE KIND OF OCTOBER day that made Ruby understand why people wrote poetry about New England autumns. The maples lining Main Street had shifted fully into their fall colors—crimson and gold and burnt orange that caught the early light and made the whole town look like it was glowing.

Ruby arrived at the town square at dawn, arms full of supplies and nerves jangling like wind chimes in a storm. Vendors were already setting up around the square—pumpkin displays appearing like orange constellations, the high school marching band warming up with discordant practice runs, the scent of cider donuts already perfuming the air.

Jake was already at their booth, methodically arranging equipment with the same precision he'd brought to their practice run. But before Ruby could wheel Beatrice over, Daisy appeared at the booth, her arms full of autumn decorations.

"Good morning, dears!" Daisy's smile was warm despite the early hour. She set down a basket overflowing with small pumpkins, gourds, and bundles of dried corn stalks. "I couldn't let you two run the main beverage booth without proper autumn atmosphere."

"Daisy, you didn't have to do this," Ruby said, but she was already eyeing the decorations with delight.

"Nonsense. You're representing Main Street coffee culture. It should look festive." Daisy pulled out a small arrangement of burgundy mums. "Where do you want these?"

For the next half hour, Daisy orchestrated the booth's transformation while Ruby and Jake worked around her. She tucked miniature pumpkins along the front counter, arranged corn stalks at the corners, and positioned the mum arrangement where it would catch the morning light without interfering with workflow.

"There." Daisy stepped back, surveying her work with satisfaction. "Now it looks properly autumn. Welcoming."

"It's perfect," Ruby said, meaning it. The decorations transformed their utilitarian booth into something warm and inviting, the kind of space that made people want to linger.

Jake handed Daisy a thermos. "Coffee. On the house."

"You're a good boy, Jacob Sullivan." Daisy accepted the thermos with obvious pleasure. "I'll stop by tomorrow to make sure the flowers are still fresh. Can't have wilted mums representing our coffee shops."

After Daisy left, Ruby caught Jake studying the decorated booth with approval in his eyes.

"She's right," he said. "It looks good."

"It really does," Ruby agreed.

Jake met her eyes, and an understanding passed between them—this booth, this festival, this partnership was about more than just coffee service. It was about building something that mattered, something that made Main Street feel alive.

"Ready?" Jake asked, holding out their now-traditional thermos.

Ruby accepted the coffee gratefully, taking a long sip. Perfect, as always—strong and balanced, exactly what she needed.

"Ready," she said.

The festival officially opened at ten, but people started arriving early—eager for first dibs on vendor booths and the best parking spots. By 10:15, their coffee booth had a line stretching halfway across the square.

The morning blurred into a symphony of faces and orders. "Can I get extra hot?" "Do you have anything sugar-free?" "What's your most popular drink?" Ruby found herself in her element, explaining flavor combinations to skeptical customers and watching their faces light up after the first sip.

Their September rhythm returned, but this time it felt deeper, more intuitive. Ruby would start calling out a drink order and Jake would already be reaching for the right cup. When she needed clean pitchers, they appeared at her elbow without her asking. Their movements around each other had become fluid, instinctive—less like choreography and more like conversation.

"Maple latte, extra hot," Ruby called out.

"Got the milk," Jake said, already at the steamer.

It worked beautifully until the lunch rush, when Ruby reached for the cinnamon powder at the wrong angle.

The container tipped, and suddenly cinnamon erupted like a fragrant volcano, coating her hair, her apron, and at least two customers in a cloud of sweet spice.

"Oh no, oh no, I'm so sorry—" Ruby was already grabbing napkins, her cheeks flaming. "This is exactly what I feared, and now everyone's sneezing and I've turned the booth into a spice explosion and—"

Jake appeared beside her, calm as ever, wiping down the counter with methodical strokes. His presence immediately cut through her panic spiral.

"There you go."

Ruby coughed, trying to brush cinnamon out of her hair. "I smell like a Yankee Candle exploded."

His lips twitched—an actual, visible reaction. "Could be worse."

"How?"

"You could smell like burnt beans."

Her laugh slipped out before she could stop it, and Jake's hint of a smile widened by a fraction. The affected customers were laughing too, one of them saying something about "festive aromatherapy," and suddenly the disaster didn't feel so disastrous anymore.

"Cinnamon special," Jake said dryly to the next customer in line. "Comes with atmosphere."

"Free aromatherapy with every order," Ruby added, still brushing spice out of her hair. "Very exclusive."

Jake's eyes met hers, warm with amusement. "Should we add it to the menu?"

"'The Cinnamon Explosion—guaranteed to make you smell festive or your money back.'"

"Catchy."

Ruby felt the tension dissolve. He'd turned her catastrophe into a shared joke, made her feel less alone in her chaos.

The cinnamon incident became their running joke for the rest of the day—customers mentioning the "seasonal ambiance," Jake making dry comments about Ruby's "aromatherapy techniques," and Ruby feeling lighter every time their eyes met over the steaming equipment.

By mid-afternoon, during a lull, Mrs. Patterson approached their booth with her usual careful dignity. She was dressed in a pressed cardigan despite the October warmth, her white hair perfectly styled.

"Good afternoon, Ruby dear," she said warmly. "I'll have my usual, please."

"One vanilla latte coming right up." Ruby's hands moved automatically through the familiar order, pleased that Mrs. Patterson now considered her regular enough to have a "usual."

While Ruby steamed the milk, Jake appeared at the counter with his coffee pot. "Mrs. Patterson. How are those MIT applications coming along?"

Mrs. Patterson's entire face lit up. "Oh, Jacob, you remembered! Timothy submitted his last application yesterday. Early action to MIT, just like we discussed. His essay about sustainable engineering was particularly strong, if I do say so myself."

"He's a smart kid. They'd be lucky to have him."

"His mother thinks I'm getting ahead of myself, but I told her —Timothy has the grades, he has the passion, and MIT needs students who care about making a difference." Mrs. Patterson leaned in conspiratorially. "Between you and me, I think he'll get in. Call it grandmother's intuition."

Ruby handed over the finished latte, watching the easy warmth between them. This was what Derek would never understand—that knowing about Timothy's MIT applications, remembering to ask, caring about the outcome, these small connections were what made coffee service feel like community instead of transaction.

"I'm sure he'll do wonderfully," Ruby said. "And if you need someone to proofread future essays, I'm happy to help."

Mrs. Patterson patted Ruby's hand. "That's very kind, dear. I'll tell Timothy he has a whole cheering section here on Main Street." She took her latte and turned to leave, then paused. "You two make quite the team, you know. The booth looks lovely."

After she left, Ruby met Jake's gaze across the counter.

"You offered to help with college essays," he said.

"Was that wrong? I just thought—"

"No." Jake's voice was firm. "It was exactly right."

The afternoon rush built steadily, and Ruby was pulling shots for a trio of pumpkin lattes when Frank Kowalski appeared at their booth. He stood there for a long moment, weathered hands in his jacket pockets, surveying their setup with his usual skeptical expression.

"Frank." Jake had his standard black coffee poured before Frank even opened his mouth. "The usual?"

Frank accepted the cup but didn't move away. His sharp blue eyes tracked Ruby's hands as she worked, watching her add pumpkin syrup and cinnamon to the lattes with the focus of someone conducting a scientific study.

"You're the one who made that maple thing at the September festival," Frank said finally.

Ruby paused mid-pour. "I am. Did you want to try something today?"

"Already got my coffee." But Frank didn't leave. He took a sip of his black coffee, then nodded toward the decorated booth. "Place looks nice. Daisy's work?"

"She came by this morning," Jake confirmed.

"Hmph." Frank's gaze returned to Ruby. "Town's talking about you two. Say you work well together."

Ruby couldn't tell if this was approval or criticism. With Frank, it was hard to distinguish. "We're managing."

"Better than managing, from what I hear." Frank took another sip of his coffee, studying her over the rim of his cup. "Patterson says her grandson's got a whole cheering section now. That your doing?"

"Just offered to help if he needs it."

Frank's bushy eyebrows drew together, and for a moment his expression lost some of its skepticism. "Sullivan's has been part of this town for a decade. Good to see it staying that way." He nodded once —at Ruby, then at Jake—before walking away with his black coffee.

Ruby stared after him. "Did Frank just... approve of me?"

"Looks like it." Jake handed her a clean milk pitcher, and there was definite amusement in his eyes. "Don't let it go to your head."

"Too late. I'm calling Vi immediately to report this historic moment."

By mid-afternoon Saturday, during another lull, Zara appeared at their booth with her usual mischievous energy.

"So," Zara said, leaning against the counter and taking in the cinnamon-dusted surfaces with obvious amusement, "I heard about the aromatherapy incident. The whole town's talking about it."

"Of course they are," Ruby muttered, still finding cinnamon in unexpected places.

"In a good way! People love it. Very festive." Zara's grin widened. "Plus, the way you two handled it was apparently hilarious. Frank said it was the most entertainment he's had at a festival in years."

"Frank said that?" Ruby blinked.

"Frank said that." Zara's eyes sparkled with mischief. "You're winning over Team Tradition one cinnamon explosion at a time."

"I'll add it to my business plan. 'Strategic spice disasters for community integration.'"

Jake, who was refilling the coffee urns, made a sound that might have been a laugh.

"Can I get a maple cinnamon latte?" Zara asked. "Hold the explosive aromatherapy."

Ruby laughed and started making Zara's drink. "One boring, non-exploding latte coming up."

"I didn't say boring. Just controlled chaos instead of uncontrolled chaos." Zara watched Ruby work with obvious fondness. "You look happy. Covered in cinnamon and exhausted, but happy."

"I am happy," Ruby realized, surprised by how true it felt. "This is actually really fun."

"Even the disasters?"

"Especially the disasters." Ruby glanced at Jake, who was methodically organizing cups with his usual precision. "Having backup helps."

"I bet it does," Zara said knowingly, accepting her finished latte. She took a sip and sighed. "Okay, this is perfect. You're a genius."

As Zara walked away from the booth, she nearly collided with Tommy Sullivan, who was heading toward the main stage with his tool belt slung over his shoulder.

"Whoa, sorry!" Tommy caught Zara's elbow to steady her, and Ruby watched her normally articulate friend freeze completely.

"No, that was—I wasn't watching—" Zara's voice went higher. "Hi, Tommy."

"Hey, Zara. Caffeinating for the afternoon?" Tommy nodded at her latte with an easy grin.

"Just visiting Ruby and Jake. Moral support." She held up her cup like evidence.

"Of course. Can't go more than a few hours without checking on them, right?" Tommy's expression turned teasing. "Or maybe you just needed an excuse to walk by the stage?"

Ruby couldn't hear Zara's response, but she saw her friend's cheeks flush before they both continued in opposite directions—Zara toward the bookstore tent, Tommy toward the stage setup. Both glanced back once before disappearing into the festival crowd.

"Those two," Ruby murmured.

Jake appeared beside her with fresh cups. "They'll figure it out eventually."

"You think so?"

"Tommy's not subtle. Neither is Zara." His mouth quirked. "Just taking them a while to realize everyone else already knows."

Later that afternoon, Daisy reappeared at their booth with fresh flowers and a critical eye.

"Let me see how everything's holding up," she said, immediately fussing with the mum arrangement. "Oh, these are wilting already. The sun's stronger than I thought."

She produced fresh burgundy mums from her bag and began swapping out the tired blooms. "Can't have droopy flowers. What would people think?"

"That we've been too busy serving coffee to worry about horticulture?" Ruby suggested.

Daisy gave her a look. "Presentation matters, dear. Even when you're busy." She adjusted a small pumpkin that had been knocked askew. "Besides, I wanted to see how you two were managing. A whole weekend is a long time to work together."

"We're managing fine," Jake said.

"Better than fine, from what I've heard." Daisy's eyes sparkled as she stepped back from the refreshed flowers. "Mrs. Patterson said you two move like you've been running this booth together for years. And Frank hasn't complained once, which is practically a miracle."

Ruby felt her cheeks warm. "We just found a good system."

"Mmm." Daisy's smile was knowing. "Well, keep up the good work. And Jacob, make sure Ruby actually drinks water occasionally. She gets so focused she forgets."

After Daisy left, Ruby met Jake's amused gaze.

"What?"

"You do forget to drink water."

"I do not—" Ruby stopped, realizing her water bottle was still full from hours ago. "Okay, maybe sometimes."

"Drink," Jake said, pushing the bottle toward her. "Can't have you passing out on day two."

By Saturday night, Ruby had served more drinks than her entire first month in business. Her body ached in muscles she'd forgotten she had, but she was buzzing with energy that had nothing to do with caffeine. Customers were coming back, asking about Scattered Beans' location, treating her like she belonged here instead of like a curious outsider.

"Not bad," Jake said as they packed up, "for someone who brought seventeen syrups."

Ruby laughed. "Better too many than not enough."

He shook his head, but she saw genuine amusement cross his face. "Heard all your rambling today."

Her cheeks warmed. "And?"

"And it's not as bad as you think." Jake's voice was firm. "You connect with people. That matters more than being polished."

Ruby felt the words land somewhere deep. Not irritation or patience, but genuine appreciation. Like her scattered, animated way of talking to customers wasn't a flaw to tolerate but a strength he'd come to value.

"Thanks," she managed. "For saying that."

"Just the truth."

Sunday dawned gray and misty, drizzle softening the air and blurring the festival lights into watercolor smudges. Ruby pulled on an extra sweater and wrapped her hands around her morning coffee, breathing in the scent of wood smoke and damp leaves.

By now their rhythm felt effortless—Jake started steaming milk as soon as she called an order, she slid cups into his hand without looking, and they moved around each other with an ease that felt second nature.

"I'm going to miss this," Ruby blurted during a mid-afternoon lull, watching Jake methodically clean the espresso machine.

"Miss what?"

"This." She gestured at the booth, at their shared workspace, at the easy partnership they'd discovered. "Working together. Having backup. Tomorrow we're back to separate shops, but... I really liked this."

Jake met her gaze, considering. "Doesn't have to end."

Ruby's breath caught, her heart doing that stupid hammering thing it always did around Jake. His words just hung there, and suddenly all the festival chaos—the music, people yelling about kettle corn, some kid having a meltdown near the face-painting booth—went weirdly quiet in her head.

She looked at him, trying to figure out if he meant what she thought he meant, as the final rush of festival-goers surged toward their booth.

By dusk, the square was nearly empty. Lanterns glowed like fireflies in the cool October dark, and vendors were packing up around them with the satisfied exhaustion of a successful weekend. Ruby and Jake worked side by side, the air between them changed—not uncomfortable, but weighted with things neither had quite said yet.

They were almost finished when Jake spoke, his voice low enough that Ruby had to lean in to hear. "I'm going to visit Rose next week."

Ruby looked up from the box she was packing. "To see what she found?"

"Yeah." Jake's expression was thoughtful, almost hesitant. "She's been calling all week. Says she wants me to see the documents before she donates them to the historical society. Seems to think there's information I should know."

"That sounds like it could be really special. Family history and all that."

"Maybe." Jake was silent for a moment, then added: "She mentioned you again in last week's letter."

Ruby's breath caught. "She did?"

"Said she'd like to meet you someday. The young woman who's making Main Street feel alive again." His amber eyes found hers in the lantern light.

"What do you think?" Ruby asked softly.

Jake's mouth curved—not quite a smile, but close. "I think she might be right."

They finished packing without speaking, but the silence felt full rather than empty. When everything was loaded and ready to transport back to their respective shops, Jake paused.

"Ruby?"

"Yeah?"

"Same time Monday?"

She knew he meant their usual coffee shop hours, their normal routines. But the way he said it made her wonder if normal would ever feel quite the same again.

"Same time Monday," she agreed.

Ruby wheeled Beatrice home through the October night, past the packed-up vendor booths and darkened festival lights. Derek's job offer felt like distant static now, easy to ignore. What lingered instead was Rose—an elderly woman in Northfield writing weekly letters, believing in family and coffee and the possibility that tradition and innovation could work together.

And soon Jake would visit her, would see what she'd discovered in her attic, would learn stories about Sullivan's Coffee that he'd never heard before.

As Ruby locked up Scattered Beans and went up the stairs to her apartment, she found herself wondering what those old documents would reveal. Whatever secrets Rose had found, Ruby had a feeling everything was about to change.

CHAPTER
Eight

Ruby's morning began with a crisis that had nothing to do with coffee and everything to do with her apartment's ancient radiator, which had died sometime during the night. She woke to a temperature best described as arctic, layered all her sweaters—including one that had been intended for Halloween, not survival—and shuffled downstairs in fuzzy slippers to coax Beatrice into cooperation.

"Don't give me attitude," she muttered, patting the side of the machine like it was a stubborn mule. "You get hot water. I get heat. That's teamwork."

Beatrice hissed in reply, which Ruby decided to interpret as agreement.

The door swung open, letting in Daisy with a scarf the size of a small continent. She headed straight for the counter, checking on the mum arrangement she'd placed there days ago. "These need refreshing," she announced, then looked up and noticed Ruby's layers. "Good heavens, Ruby, it's freezing in here! You'll have customers staging a rebellion."

Ruby grimaced. "Trust me, I'm already planning my escape to Aruba."

"You should ask Tommy to fix that radiator," Daisy said,

already pulling wilted blooms from the arrangement. "If he can't fix it, no one can. I'll bring fresh flowers later."

Ruby didn't have time to answer before the bell jingled again and Mrs. Patterson appeared in the doorway. She must have spotted Ruby through the window, bundled in multiple sweaters, because her expression was pure concern. "Ruby, dear, are you alright? I saw you through the window and thought—oh, it IS freezing in here! Your poor customers will turn into popsicles before they finish their cappuccinos."

"I'm ok, Mrs. Patterson. Thank you"

Ruby groaned. In Millbrook Falls, news traveled faster than espresso shots. She had no doubt half the town would know about her broken radiator before lunchtime.

Across the street, a pickup truck idled in front of Sullivan's Coffee while Tommy unloaded enough tools to renovate half of Main Street.

Ruby was still trying to guess the scope of whatever required that many power tools when her door chimed and Tommy strode in, grinning, a battle-scarred toolbox in hand.

"Morning, Ruby! Heard you're having a heating issue."

Ruby blinked. "How did you—"

"Small town. I ran into Daisy on her way out—she mentioned you looked dressed for the Arctic." He glanced at her layered sweaters and fuzzy slippers, grinning. "She wasn't exaggerating. Nice survival outfit."

"It's called layers. Very fashionable."

"If you say so." Tommy knelt by the radiator, already assessing the problem. "This thing hasn't been serviced in decades, has it?"

"Is that bad?"

"Let's just say I'm impressed it lasted this long."

"Jake's at grandma Rose today. Said he'd be back by early afternoon, but told me to get started on the shop anyway." Tommy grinned. "First time in fifteen years he's let me start work without supervising every single step."

Ruby raised an eyebrow. "So you're the Sullivan version of a handyman ninja."

"Exactly. Only with less stealth and more extension cords."

While Tommy worked, Ruby tried to focus on her morning customers, but her mind kept drifting across the street. Jake was visiting Rose today.

"So what's Jake having you do over there?" Ruby asked, trying to sound casual.

Tommy glanced up from the radiator, tools in hand. "Oh, the usual five-year backlog: fixing the wobbly table everyone pretends doesn't exist, replacing loose boards, updating the wiring so the lights don't flicker every time the grinder runs." He paused, then added with a knowing look, "And installing new lighting. Pendant lights. Warmer bulbs. The kind that make brick glow instead of look tired."

Ruby's cheeks warmed. "I haven't said anything to him about Sullivan's. That would be presumptuous and rude and I would never—"

"Maybe not out loud." Tommy winked. "But he notices. How you arranged this place. How you think about people feeling welcome. Ever since the festival, he's been looking at the shop like it's new." He returned to the radiator. "Yesterday he asked me what I thought about updating the lighting. Just like that. No debate, no five-year planning process. Just 'Tommy, what do you think about warmer lights?'"

Ruby's heart gave an unsteady flutter. "Really?"

"Really. You're good for him, you know. Makes him remember that the shop can evolve and still be Sullivan's."

Before Ruby could respond, Tommy had the radiator valve off, muttering something about "original parts" and "miracle it works at all."

In under an hour—with a mix of know-how and muttered curses—Tommy coaxed the system back to life. Heat began to hum through the pipes; Ruby could feel her toes again.

"There you go. Good for another few decades, probably."

A flutter rose in Ruby's chest—muscle memory, even if it was the wrong Sullivan brother. She smiled anyway. "Thank you. What do I owe you?"

"Nothing. Call it neighborly. Besides, Jake would revoke my brother privileges if I charged his business partner for basic maintenance."

Ruby looked up sharply. "Business partner?"

Tommy winced, recovering with a grin. "Business neighbor. Totally different."

But the slip landed squarely in Ruby's chest, making her heart trip.

Tommy hefted his toolbox. "Now I've got to get back before he returns and realizes I reorganized his storage room."

"You reorganized his storage room?"

"Someone had to. The man keeps coffee filters from three decades ago because 'they might be useful someday.'" Tommy shook his head with obvious affection. "Don't tell him I said that."

After Tommy left, Ruby tried to settle into her lunch routine, but she kept glancing across the street. Through Sullivan's windows, she could see Tommy moving around, testing lights, adjusting fixtures. The harsh fluorescents would flicker off, then warmer pendant lights would glow to life, and even from here Ruby could see how it transformed the space.

Around noon, Gladys Murphy appeared at Ruby's counter, lips pressed into a thin line of disapproval.

"Ruby, dear. I couldn't help but notice all the... activity at Sullivan's this morning."

Ruby's stomach sank. "Tommy's doing some maintenance work."

"Maintenance." Gladys made it sound like a euphemism for destruction. "I walked past earlier. He's changing the lights. Moving furniture. Making quite a lot of noise about it." She paused, her gaze pointed. "Frank mentioned at the post office this morning that Sullivan's is starting to look 'different.' Not in a complimentary way."

Ruby felt heat crawl up her neck—not embarrassment, but indignation. "Jake made his own decisions about what his shop needs—"

"Did he? Or has a certain newcomer's presence made him feel like Sullivan's wasn't good enough as it was?" Gladys's voice softened, but the edge remained. "You're young, Ruby. You haven't been here long enough to understand what Sullivan's means to this town. Jake's been running that shop perfectly well for fifteen years. His father ran it for thirty years before that. His great-grandfather built it from nothing." She collected her coffee with a sniff. "Some of us have been here long enough to know that not all change is improvement. And not everyone who arrives with new ideas understands what they might be disrupting."

The words stung more than Ruby expected. She'd thought the festival had proven she belonged here, that she understood Millbrook Falls. But Gladys's words made her feel like an outsider again—someone who'd swept in and disturbed a delicate balance without understanding the consequences.

After Gladys left, Ruby sank onto her stool, doubt creeping in. Was she the reason Jake was making changes? Had her presence —her modern shop, her different approach—made him feel like Sullivan's needed updating to compete? She'd never meant to make him feel inadequate. She'd thought they were just neighbors, each running their own businesses. But what if Gladys was right? What if she hadn't been here long enough to understand the weight of what Jake was risking?

The door chimed, and Daisy bustled in with fresh burgundy mums, already pulling the wilted arrangement from its vase. While Ruby recited Gladys visit.

"Don't listen to Gladys," Daisy said without preamble, arranging the fresh flowers with practiced efficiency. "That woman has been telling Jake not to change a single thing since the day he took over. Before that, she told his father the same thing."

"But what if she's right? What if I made him feel like Sullivan's needed fixing when it was fine the way it was?"

Daisy turned to face her fully, expression gentle but firm. "Ruby, dear. Jake's father told him, near the end, that his biggest regret was being too afraid to update the place. Said his own father—Jake's grandfather—would have been disappointed that Sullivan's stopped evolving."

Ruby looked up. "He did?"

"He did. Jake's been carrying that conversation around for three years, wanting to honor it but terrified of upsetting the town. You didn't make him feel like Sullivan's wasn't good enough. You made him feel brave enough to make it better." Daisy patted her hand. "There's a difference."

The afternoon crawled by with painful slowness. Ruby served customers, cleaned equipment that didn't need cleaning, and tried not to watch the clock. Tommy worked steadily across the street, and every time Ruby glanced over, Sullivan's looked more like the space she'd imagined—warm and welcoming instead of harsh and institutional.

At two-thirty, Jake's truck pulled up in front of Sullivan's.

Ruby watched him climb out, carrying a large box carefully in both arms. He paused on the sidewalk, looking at his shop's windows where the new lights glowed warm, then turned and headed straight for Scattered Beans.

The bell chimed. Jake stood in her doorway, the box in his arms, his expression unreadable.

"Hey," Ruby said, throat suddenly dry. "How was Rose?"

"Good. She sends her regards." Jake crossed to the counter and set the box down carefully. "She gave me something. Wanted me to see it. And I thought..." He paused, choosing his words. "I thought you should see it too."

Ruby looked at the box, then at Jake. His expression was serious but open, inviting. This was an invitation—into his family history, into something that mattered.

"What is it?"

"I'm not entirely sure yet. Rose has been cleaning out her attic —the old trunk that belonged to my great-grandfather. She found documents, photographs, things from the 1920s she'd forgotten existed." Jake rested his hand on the box. "She said there are stories here that even she didn't know the full truth about. Stories about how Sullivan's really operated back then."

Ruby's breath caught. "Can we look?"

"That's why I'm here."

They opened the box together, Jake carefully removing the packing materials to reveal Rose's note on top:

Dearest Jake,

Well, I finally tackled that attic trunk with Joanie's help, and Jake—I found things. Documents and photographs from the 1920s that I'd completely forgotten existed. Your great-grandfather kept records of everything, and some of what's in here... well, I think you need to see it for yourself.

I'm not entirely sure what it all means, but I have my suspicions, and I think you're going to find this fascinating.

All my love, Rose

Jake began removing items carefully, laying them out on Ruby's counter:

A leather-bound logbook, aged and worn, with "Sullivan's Coffee - Accounts 1922-1933" embossed on the cover in faded gold lettering.

A stack of sepia-toned photographs showing Sullivan's storefront looking almost the same but subtly different—the windows arranged differently, crowds of well-dressed people gathered outside.

Yellowed newspaper clippings in protective sleeves with headlines about "Social Clubs" and "Town Gatherings."

And finally, folded carefully at the bottom, what looked like a hand-drawn map or architectural sketch, the paper brittle with age, covered in faded ink annotations.

"Jake," Ruby breathed. "This is incredible."

Jake opened the logbook, his fingers gentle on the fragile pages. The entries were handwritten in neat, precise script—dates, names, orders. But as Ruby watched him scan the pages, she saw his brow furrow.

"These entries..." He traced a line with his finger. "Ruby, look at this."

Ruby leaned in. The handwriting was beautiful but the content was cryptic:

October 15, 1925 - Six cases special blend, under-ground storage
October 22, 1925 - Delivery to J.F. building, twelve units premium reserve November 3, 1925 - Main chamber stock replenished, notify J.F.

"What's 'special blend'?" Ruby asked. "And 'premium reserve'? Those don't sound like regular coffee orders."

"They don't." Jake turned more pages, revealing similar entries —always vague, always referencing storage, always mentioning " J.F. building." "And what's J.F. building?"

Ruby felt something click. "J.F. Could that be the building owner?"

"Possibly," Jake said slowly. "Rose might know. Or the histor-ical society."

They stared at each other, questions hanging in the air but not quite forming into answers yet.

"The map," Ruby said, reaching for the folded sketch.

Jake carefully unfolded the architectural drawing. They bent over it together, trying to make sense of the faded lines and nota-tions. It showed Sullivan's Coffee in detail—the layout Ruby could recognize from across the street, plus the basement. But there were other markings. Lines extending from the basement, annotations that were hard to read in the faded ink.

"What does this say?" Ruby squinted at a notation near the basement. "'Underground... something.' I can't make it out."

"'Storage,'" Jake read slowly. "I think it says 'underground storage.'" His finger traced one of the lines extending from the basement. "And this line goes... somewhere. But the paper's too faded here to see where."

"Ruby?" Tommy's voice came from the doorway. "Jake? I saw you come in and wanted to— whoa." He crossed to the counter, eyes widening as he took in the spread of documents. "What is all this?"

"Rose found it in Great-Grandfather's trunk," Jake said. "Records from the 1920s. But we can't figure out what they mean."

Tommy leaned in to examine the logbook, reading the cryptic entries. "'Special blend, underground storage.' 'Premium reserve.' 'Main chamber.'" He looked up, excitement sparking in his eyes. "Jake, this is Prohibition era. 1922 to 1933."

"I know, but—"

"What if 'special blend' isn't coffee?" Tommy's grin was widening. "What if our great-grandfather was hiding something?"

Ruby's breath caught. "You think Sullivan's was involved in something... illegal?"

"I think there's a reason Rose said these stories weren't what Jake might expect." Tommy picked up the map, studying it with the practical eye of someone who worked with buildings. "And this map is showing something underground. These lines, these notations about storage and chambers—" He looked at Jake. "I think we need to check the basement."

Jake was still staring at the documents, caught between fascination and uncertainty. "You think there's something hidden? After all this time?"

"Only one way to find out." Tommy was already pulling out his phone, probably making a list of equipment they'd need. "I'm working in your basement anyway for the electrical. I can look for unusual wall structures, hollow spaces, anything that doesn't match the current layout."

Ruby looked at the photographs again—the crowds of well-dressed people, the vague entries about "special blends" and "premium reserves." Her mind was spinning with possibilities, but nothing concrete yet. Just questions.

"What was your great-grandfather doing?" she asked softly.

Jake shook his head slowly. "I don't know. But Rose wouldn't have sent this if she didn't think it was important." He looked at Ruby, then at Tommy. "We need to figure this out. Carefully. Whatever this is—whatever he was doing—it's part of Sullivan's history. Part of the town's history."

"Tomorrow evening?" Tommy suggested. "After you close, Ruby. I'll bring proper equipment—moisture meter, stud finder, maybe some tools if we need to investigate walls. We'll start in your basement, Jake, since that's where the map focuses."

"And if we find something?" Ruby asked.

"Then we figure out what it means." Jake's hand rested on the logbook, protective. "But we do it right. Document everything, preserve whatever's there. This isn't just about satisfying curiosity. This is family history."

"Tomorrow evening then?" Tommy confirmed. "After closing?"

"After closing," Jake agreed. Jake carefully gathered the documents back into the box. "We should secure these. Maybe make copies before we do anything else."

"I can take photos," Ruby offered. "Document everything before we start investigating."

"Good idea." Jake's eyes held hers for a moment longer than necessary. "Thank you. For looking at this with me. For caring about it."

"Of course I care. This is your family's history."

After they left, Ruby stood in her quiet shop, looking at the photographs Jake had left temporarily on her counter. Sullivan's Coffee in the 1920s, looking almost the same as it did now. And somewhere in those cryptic entries and faded maps, a story waiting to be uncovered.

She thought about Gladys's words—*not everyone who suggests change understands what they're risking*. But mostly she thought about the careful way Jake had invited her into this mystery, trusting her with something precious.

What was "special blend"? Why the underground storage? What connected Sullivan's Coffee and the J.F. building?

And most intriguingly—what had Rose suspected when she'd packed up these documents and sent them to Jake?

Thursday evening, they'd start looking for answers.

CHAPTER *Nine*

THURSDAY OPENED IN THE USUAL RHYTHM—BEATRICE HISSED AWAKE, grounds bloomed, regulars filed in—but Ruby's mind kept drifting to Sullivan's basement and those cryptic 'special blends.'"

What had Jake's great-grandfather really been hiding?

She was arranging pastries in the display case when her phone buzzed with a text from

JAKE

Found something else in the documents.

Ruby stared at the message, her pulse quickening. Another discovery. Another evening alone with Jake, uncovering secrets in that quiet space between closing time and dawn.

RUBY

What did you find?

JAKE

Pattern in the dates. Easier to show you than explain.

Ruby was still staring at her phone, trying not to read too much into the casual intimacy of their evening plans, when the bell chimed and Zara breezed in, dropping onto her favorite stool with the dramatic sigh of someone who had Thoughts.

"Ruby Ashworth, we need to talk."

Ruby glanced up, slipping her phone into her apron pocket. "Good morning to you too. The usual?"

"Yes, and also I need you to stop pretending you're not completely gone for Jake Sullivan because it's getting painful to watch."

Ruby nearly dropped the milk pitcher. "I'm not—we're just—"

"You're 'just' neighbors who happen to have coffee together every morning. You're 'just' coordinating festival booths and sharing thermoses. You're 'just' looking at him like he hung the moon every time he walks into a room." Zara leaned forward, eyes dancing. "Text from Jake? I saw that little smile when you checked your phone."

"That was—he just texted about—" Ruby felt her face flame. "We're working on something together."

"Uh-huh. What kind of something makes you look all jittery?"

"Historical research! We found some old documents about his great-grandfather and tonight —" Ruby caught herself. She hadn't told anyone about Rose's package yet. "It's complicated."

"I bet it is." Zara's grin widened. "Ruby, the man could read the phone book and you'd find it fascinating."

"That's not—I don't—" Ruby grabbed the milk pitcher with more force than necessary. "Okay, so maybe I find his voice soothing. That's not a crime."

"Soothing." Zara laughed. "Is that what we're calling it?"

Ruby finished Zara's latte with more aggression than the poor espresso machine deserved. "Fine. Maybe I have feelings. Maybe I've had feelings since the festival, or maybe even before that. Happy now?"

"Deliriously. Continue."

"There's nothing to continue! We're neighbors. We're working on a project together. That's it."

"Right. And I'm sure all your neighborly projects involve

memorizing the exact shade of someone's eyes and noticing when they smile."

"I don't memorize—" Ruby stopped, caught. "They're amber. Kind of golden in the right light. And he doesn't smile often, but when he does—"

"Oh, you are SO far gone." Zara was practically bouncing on her stool. "This is amazing. My best friend is falling for the grumpy coffee hermit across the street."

"He's not a hermit! He's just... reserved. Thoughtful. He doesn't waste words on things that don't matter." Ruby grabbed a towel and started aggressively wiping the already-clean counter. "And his hands are very nice. Strong. He has calluses from years of working with coffee equipment, but they're not rough exactly, more like—why are you looking at me like that?"

"Because you just gave me a detailed analysis of Jake Sullivan's hands, complete with tactile review." Zara's grin was enormous. "Ruby. Honey. You need to tell him."

"Tell him what? 'Hi Jake, I've been cataloguing your physical attributes and also I think about you constantly and maybe want to kiss you'? That'll go over well."

"Yes! Exactly that! Maybe with slightly better phrasing, but yes!"

Ruby slumped against the counter. "What if I'm reading everything wrong? What if he just sees me as the rambling neighbor who never shuts up?"

"Have you seen the way he looks at you?"

"What do you mean?"

Zara pulled out her phone, tapped a few times, and turned it to show Ruby a photo. It was from the festival—Ruby mid-laugh, gesturing animatedly with a coffee cup, and in the background, Jake watching her with an expression so soft it made Ruby's heart skip.

"I took this by accident when I was trying to get a picture of the decorations. But look at his face, Ruby. That man is not looking at a rambling neighbor. That man is looking at someone he—"

"Don't say it."

"—is falling for just as hard as you're falling for him."

Ruby stared at the photo, her throat tight. "It's just a coincidence."

"Is it? The point is, he looks at you like this all the time. Yesterday I watched him stand in his doorway for five full minutes just watching your shop. I timed it."

"You timed it?"

"I'm thorough. It's what makes me good at my job." Zara pocketed her phone. "Speaking of watching people, Tommy Sullivan has very nice forearms. Have you noticed?"

Ruby seized the deflection gratefully. "Oh really? Have YOU noticed?"

Now it was Zara's turn to flush. "I'm just making an objective observation."

"Uh-huh. And how many objective observations have you made? From how close?"

"We've talked a few times. He's surprisingly easy to talk to. And he has really nice hands. Strong, you know? From all the construction work." Zara paused, then added in a rush, "And maybe he asked me to dinner next week."

Ruby squealed—actually squealed—making Zara laugh. "Zara Patel! You have a date with Tommy Sullivan!"

"It's not a date. It's just dinner. Two people eating food in the same location."

"That's literally the definition of a date."

"Okay fine, it's a date. But we're not talking about me!" Zara pointed accusingly. "We're talking about you and Jake and the fact that you're both clearly into each other but too stubborn to do anything about it."

"I'm not stubborn. I'm cautious. There's a difference."

"You're many things, but cautious about taking risks isn't one of them."

Ruby opened her mouth to argue, then closed it. "Okay, fair point."

"So what's really stopping you?"

Ruby leaned against the counter, her smile fading. "What if I mess this up? What if I'm not ready? Derek keeps calling about that Hartford job and I keep not answering and I don't know if that's because I'm sure about staying here or because I'm scared to close that door completely."

"Or maybe you're not answering because you already know the answer. You're just afraid to admit it." Zara's expression turned thoughtful. "What does your gut tell you?"

"That I want to stay here. That Scattered Beans feels more right than anything I did at BrewCorp. That Jake—" Ruby stopped, her cheeks warming. "That maybe I'm building something real here. Not just the business. Everything."

"Then trust that. And stop overthinking it." Zara stood, gathering her things. "Life's too short to waste time being scared of good things."

"When did you become a relationship expert?"

"Since I realized I'm falling for a guy who carries a tool belt and makes terrible puns about electrical current." Zara grinned. "We're both disasters, Ruby. Might as well be disasters together."

Ruby laughed, feeling lighter. "Fair enough."

Zara headed for the door, then paused. "And Ruby? Whatever you two are investigating tonight? I have a feeling it's going to be more romantic than you think. Historical research with the right person usually is."

"That's not—we're just—oh my god, you're impossible."

"I'm right. There's a difference." Zara's grin was wicked. "Just promise me you'll at least consider the possibility that Jake Sullivan might be falling for you too. And that maybe—just maybe—that's not something to be afraid of."

After Zara left, Ruby stood in the quiet of her shop, thinking about Jake's eyes in that photo, about the way he'd looked at her at the festival, about the text sitting in her phone promising another evening together.

Maybe Zara was right.

Maybe it was time to stop being afraid.

RUBY CLOSED SCATTERED Beans at six-thirty, her stomach fluttering with anticipation. She grabbed her jacket and the folder of photographs from Rose's package, then headed across Main Street.

Sullivan's was still open, Tommy's truck parked out front. Through the windows, Ruby could see the transformation nearly complete—the pendant lights casting warm pools of light over the refinished floors, the brick walls glowing instead of looking tired. It was beautiful. It was everything she'd imagined it could be.

Jake was behind the counter, wiping down the espresso machine with his usual methodical care. He looked up when she entered, and something in his expression made her heart skip.

"Hey."

"Hey." Ruby crossed to the counter, suddenly aware of how quiet the shop was without customers. "You found something?"

"Maybe. I was looking through the logbook again and noticed something about the dates." Jake pulled out the leather-bound book, opening it to a marked page. "These entries—they're all from weekends. Friday and Saturday nights specifically. And the quantities don't make sense for regular coffee orders."

Ruby leaned over the counter to look, close enough to catch that woodsy scent she'd come to associate with Jake. The handwriting was beautiful, the entries cryptic:

October 15, 1925 - Six cases special blend, underground storage.

October 22, 1925 - Delivery to J.F. building.

twelve units premium reserve. November 3, 1925 - Main chamber stock replenished, notify J.F.

Ruby pulled out the folder. "I've been thinking about those logbook entries. The ones about 'special orders' and 'underground storage.'"

Jake's attention sharpened. "And?"

Before Ruby could respond, Tommy emerged from the back room, tool belt slung over his shoulder and a satisfied expression on his face.

"Electrical's done. Want to see the final result?"

He flipped a switch, and the new pendant lights blazed to life with perfect, warm illumination. .

"Tommy, it's perfect."

"It really is." Jake was staring around his shop like he was seeing it for the first time. "Thank you. Both of you."

"Don't thank me yet. I still need to run one more check on the basement wiring." Tommy grabbed his flashlight. "Actually, perfect timing. Want to come look at that mysterious wall section while I'm down there?"

Ruby and Jake exchanged glances.

"The map," Ruby said.

Jake grabbed the architectural sketch from behind the counter. "Let's go."

The basement smelled of damp earth and old wood. Ruby shivered as her sneakers scuffed against the stone floor, spider-webs strung across support beams.

Tommy moved efficiently along one wall, checking his electrical work. "Everything looks good down here. Should be solid for another fifty years at least."

Jake unfolded the map. "According to this, there should be something along the northwestern wall. A section marked differently—like it was sealed or hidden."

Jake moved methodically along the perimeter. The brick was old, darkened with age, but mostly uniform in appearance.

"Here." Jake stopped at a section where the mortar looked slightly different—lighter in color, newer. "This was patched. Maybe eighty, ninety years ago?"

Tommy came over, running his hands along the brick. "Definitely different from the rest. See how the mortar's lighter? Someone sealed something up."

Jake knocked on the wall with the flat of his hand. The sound echoed differently than the solid sections—hollow, promising.

Ruby's breath caught. "There's something behind it."

"Could be an old storage area they closed off. Happens sometimes when buildings get renovated." Tommy knocked a few more times, tracing the hollow section. "It's pretty big, though. Maybe six-feet wide, goes floor to ceiling."

Jake studied the map, comparing it to the wall. "The drawing shows something here—looks like it might be a passage or access point. But there's another notation... under Main Street between our buildings. That's labeled 'main chamber, brick-lined.'"

"So our great-grandfather definitely built something here." Tommy stepped back, examining the wall with professional interest. "Question is, what?"

Ruby thought about the logbook entries—the special blends, the underground storage, the weekend deliveries. "I think we need to look inside."

"We could break through," Tommy said, already assessing the best approach. "Wouldn't take much—this patching job isn't structural. Just cosmetic sealing."

Jake was quiet, staring at the wall like it held answers to questions he'd been asking his whole life.

"Jake?" Ruby touched his arm gently. "What do you think?"

"I think..." He paused, choosing his words carefully. "I think my great-grandfather hid this for a reason. And I think we need to find out why."

They spent the next hour examining every inch of the sealed

section. Tommy showed them where the mortar was weakest, where they could potentially remove bricks without damaging the surrounding structure. Jake cross-referenced the map with the physical space, noting measurements and details.

Ruby photographed everything with her phone—the wall, the map, the mortar differences. Evidence before they changed anything.

"We could start tomorrow," Tommy suggested, checking his watch. "Bring proper equipment, do this carefully. Document everything as we go."

Jake ran his hand along the sealed bricks one more time, as if trying to feel what lay beyond them. "Tomorrow," he agreed.

But Ruby saw the way his hand lingered on the wall, the tension in his shoulders. This wasn't just curiosity for Jake—this was family, legacy, the weight of inheriting a story he hadn't known existed.

Tommy packed up his tools, yawning. "I'm beat. Been here since six this morning, and I promised Zara I'd help her move some boxes at the bookstore early tomorrow." He headed for the stairs, then paused. "You two take your time down here. Just lock up when you're done, yeah?"

"We're good," Jake said.

After Tommy's footsteps faded and the basement door closed above them, the space felt smaller, quieter. Just Ruby and Jake and the sealed wall between them and the past.

Ruby checked her phone—2:03 AM. "Oh my god. How is it two in the morning?"

Jake looked equally surprised. "We've been down here for hours."

"We should probably call it a night." But neither of them moved toward the stairs.

Jake was staring at the wall again, his expression caught between anticipation and something that looked like apprehension. "Once we break through, everything changes."

Ruby understood immediately. "You're worried about what we'll find."

"I'm worried about what it means. My great-grandfather—everyone remembers him as this upstanding businessman, pillar of the community. What if we find proof he was breaking the law? What if it changes how people see Sullivan's?"

Ruby moved closer, near enough to feel his warmth in the cool basement air. "Or what if we find proof he was brave? Resourceful? That he took care of his community during impossible times?"

"That's one way to look at it."

"Jake." Ruby waited until he looked at her. "Whatever we find tomorrow, it's still your family's story. It doesn't erase the hundred years of Sullivan's Coffee being part of this town. It just makes the story more complete."

In the flashlight beam, Jake's eyes were dark, unreadable. "When did you get so good at making me see things differently?"

"I don't know. When did you get so good at letting me?"

The air between them felt thick with possibility, weighted with unspoken things. They were standing so close Ruby could see the dust in Jake's copper hair, could count his heartbeats in the pulse at his throat. His gaze dropped to her mouth for just a second before snapping back up.

Jake's hand lifted slightly, as if he might reach for her, then fell back to his side. His jaw tightened.

Ruby's pulse raced. This was it—the moment she'd been dancing around for weeks, maybe months. All she had to do was close the distance, lean in, let whatever was building between them finally happen.

But Jake looked so vulnerable, so uncertain about what tomorrow's discovery might mean. And Ruby realized that kissing him now, in this moment of apprehension and exhaustion, wouldn't be fair to either of them.

"We should go," she said softly, even though leaving was the last thing she wanted. "It's late. We're both exhausted. And tomorrow—"

"Tomorrow we find out the truth."

"Together?"

"Together."

They made their way upstairs, both moving slowly, reluctantly. At the front door, Jake turned to face her.

"Thank you. For being here. For caring about this."

"It's nothing." She smiled softly.

Jake's expression gentled in a way that made her breath catch. For a moment, she thought he might kiss her—hoped he might kiss her—but instead he just said, "Goodnight, Ruby."

"Goodnight, Jake."

Ruby crossed Main Street alone, the October night crisp and clear around her. She could feel Jake watching from his doorway, making sure she got safely inside, and the knowledge made her heart warm despite the cold air.

Upstairs in her apartment, she was brushing her teeth when her phone buzzed with a text from Vi:

VI

Guess what! I got Friday off and I'm driving up to see your small-town adventure! Can't wait to meet the mysterious Jake Sullivan!

Ruby stared at the message, her mind spinning. Vi was coming tomorrow. Vi, who had no filter and would immediately see what was happening between Ruby and Jake. Vi, who would probably corner Jake and interrogate him about his intentions within five minutes of meeting him.

But also—Vi would be here when they broke through the wall. When they discovered whatever Jake's great-grandfather had been hiding for nearly a century.

Ruby typed back quickly:

RUBY

Perfect timing. You're not going to believe what we just found. Also he's not grumpy. Mostly.

VI'S RESPONSE WAS IMMEDIATE:

"Mostly" is doing a LOT of work in that sentence.
Tell me EVERYTHING.

RUBY

Can't text it. Too weird. Too big. Just trust me - you're arriving at exactly the right moment.

VI

Now I'm VERY intrigued. See you tomorrow! And Ruby? Whatever it is, I'm glad you're not doing it alone.

Ruby set down her phone, Vi's words staying with her. She wasn't doing this alone. She had Jake, Tommy, and in less than twelve hours, Vi would be here too.

She looked out her window at Sullivan's Coffee across the street, its new lights glowing warm through the windows. Somewhere beneath that building, behind a sealed brick wall, Jake's great-grandfather's secrets were waiting.

And tomorrow—today, really, given the time—they'd finally uncover the truth.

Ruby climbed into bed, exhausted but too wired to sleep. Her mind kept replaying the moment in the basement, the way Jake had looked at her, the almost-kiss that hung between them like a promise.

Tomorrow: the wall, and Vi. Everything might change.

Ruby closed her eyes, thinking about Zara's words: *Life's too short to waste time being scared of good things.*

She was falling. Had been falling for weeks, maybe since that first festival when Jake had handed her a thermos and said, " There you go" like it was the most natural thing in the world to take care of her.

The question was: what was she going to do about it?

Tomorrow, she decided. Tomorrow she'd figure it out.

For now, she'd let herself fall asleep thinking about basement discoveries and almost-kisses and the way Jake Sullivan looked at her like she was the answer to a question he'd been afraid to ask.

CHAPTER
Ten

Ruby's morning was already running on espresso fumes when the café door flew open and Vi Torres breezed in like she owned the place. A red scarf trailed dramatically behind her, her sunglasses still perched on her nose despite the October clouds, and she grinned as if she'd just caught Ruby in the act of doing something scandalous.

"Ruby Ashworth!" she announced, loud enough for the entire block. "This town is adorable. Stars Hollow meets Pinterest board. And please tell me that's Sullivan's Coffee across the street, because if your mysterious poetry-reading grump works there, I have questions."

Ruby's face broke into a huge smile. "Vi!" She rushed around the counter and threw her arms around her best friend, squeezing tight. "Oh my god, I missed you so much! You're actually here! I can't believe you drove all the way up and the timing is perfect because we're investigating the basement tonight and I have so much to tell you and—wait, did you eat? You must be starving. Let me make you something. Coffee, obviously, but also I have these amazing cranberry scones that Daisy—she's this wonderful woman who runs the flower shop—anyway, she brought in fresh cranberries and I've been experimenting with—"

Vi hugged back just as fiercely, laughing. "Ruby. Breathe. I'm here, I'm not going anywhere, and yes, I would love coffee and a scone and all the details you're currently trying to tell me at once."

When they finally pulled apart, Vi kept her hands on Ruby's shoulders, studying her face with the sharp attention only a best friend could manage.

"Look at you," Vi said softly. "Ruby, you're glowing. Like actually glowing. Hartford Ruby never glowed."

Ruby felt tears prick her eyes. "I am, aren't I? It's so weird, Vi. Like I didn't even realize I wasn't happy before until I got here and suddenly everything just—I don't know, it feels right? Does that make sense? The shop, the people, even the weird drafts in my basement that I probably need to get checked out but haven't because I've been so busy with the festival and helping Jake with his renovation and—"

"Ruby." Vi smiled. "You're rambling. I love it. Keep going."

Ruby laughed, wiping at her eyes. "Sorry. I'm just really happy you're here."

"Good. So this is the famous coffee that made you trade a corner office for Main Street charm?"

Ruby gestured around Scattered Beans with obvious pride. Exposed brick, mismatched chairs, Daisy's thriving mint on the sill—it was all hers, every choice intentional. Vi walked through like a seasoned investor, heels clicking on the hardwood, but Ruby could see the warmth beneath the professional assessment.

"This is actually incredible," Vi said, running a hand along the counter. "Like you took everything BrewCorp tried to flatten out of you and just let it loose."

Ruby felt a glow of pride as she started pulling Vi's usual order—a double shot latte with an extra pump of vanilla because Vi claimed it helped her think. "So no lecture about financial responsibility? Career suicide? The statistical likelihood of small business failure in rural areas?"

"Not today." Vi smiled slyly. "Today I'm too busy being impressed."

As if to punctuate her point, a faint draft curled around Ruby's ankles. She bent, frowning at the floorboards. "See? That's what I mean about the drafts. It's like the place is breathing. Which is probably not structurally great, but also kind of charming? Or maybe I'm just trying to make my potentially faulty foundation sound romantic—"

Vi arched a brow. "Haunted small-town café? Excellent marketing angle."

Ruby straightened, shaking her head, but the chill lingered. Millbrook Falls was cozy enough on the surface, but sometimes the past pressed closer than people wanted to admit.

The bell chimed. Jake walked in, and Ruby's pulse did its usual traitorous leap. He wasn't in his usual work clothes—instead he wore jeans and a flannel shirt, and he carried a leather messenger bag that looked like it had seen better decades. His dark hair was slightly disheveled, and there was an energy about him that Ruby recognized: the restless focus of someone who'd been up half the night thinking.

"Morning," Jake said, pausing when he noticed Vi.

"Jake! This is Vi—my friend Vi—she just got here from Hartford and I was just telling her about the documents and—" Ruby caught herself, took a breath. "Jake Sullivan, this is Vi Torres. Vi, Jake."

"Vi Torres." She offered her hand with boardroom polish. "I've heard a lot about you."

"Nice to meet you." Jake's handshake was steady, his expression polite but distracted. "Ruby mentioned you were visiting."

"I had to see what convinced my best friend to abandon Hartford for—" Vi gestured broadly, "—all this small-town charm. And I have to say, she undersold it."

Ruby felt her cheeks warm. "Vi—"

"Actually," Jake interrupted, his attention shifting to Ruby, "I was hoping we could go over those documents today. I couldn't sleep last night—kept thinking about the map and the logbook entries. Sullivan's is closed for the day anyway. Tommy's done with the electrical work and has started on some of the heavier construction, so I figured..." He trailed off, glancing at Vi. "Sorry, you just got here. This can wait."

"Are you kidding?" Vi's eyes lit up with interest. "Historical mystery? I'm absolutely in. What kind of documents are we talking about?"

Jake looked at Ruby, a question in his amber eyes. Ruby nodded enthusiastically, words tumbling out. "We should definitely tell her. I mean, if we're going to investigate the basement after closing tonight, which we are—at least I think we are, we said we were last night—then Vi should know what we're looking for. Plus she's amazing at patterns and analysis and she used to help me decode corporate financial reports which is basically the same as speakeasy logbooks, right? Just with less illegal alcohol and more questionable accounting practices—"

"Ruby," Jake said, but there was warmth in his voice. "Yes. We're still investigating tonight. And yes, Vi should know."

Ruby beamed at him, then turned to Vi. "Okay, so Jake's grandmother Rose—who is amazing, by the way, I haven't met her yet but she sounds incredible from everything Jake says—she gave him this package full of historical documents. Letters, photographs, a hand-drawn map, and this leather logbook from the 1920s. We think his great-grandfather might have been running a speakeasy during Prohibition. Like, an actual secret bar where people gathered and drank illegal alcohol and probably listened to jazz and—"

"A speakeasy?" Vi's expression shifted from curious to fascinated. "In his building?"

"Possibly. The evidence is pretty compelling, but we haven't confirmed anything physical yet." Jake pulled out his phone and checked the time. "Ruby, if you're not too busy, could we spread everything out here? Go through it more carefully?"

Ruby glanced around Scattered Beans. It was Friday morning, usually steady but not overwhelming. Mrs. Patterson was in her corner with her romance novel, and a couple of regulars sat by the windows, but there was plenty of room at the large table near the back.

"Absolutely! Yes! Let me just make Vi's coffee first—she gets dangerously cranky without caffeine. Not cranky exactly, more like hyper-focused in a slightly terrifying way, but the coffee helps with—Vi, stop laughing at me—"

"I prefer 'efficiently focused,'" Vi corrected, but she was already eyeing the table like a general surveying a battlefield.

Twenty minutes later, the table was covered in carefully arranged documents. Jake had organized everything into categories: the logbook, Rose's letters, the photographs, and the hand-drawn map spread out flat across the center.

Ruby moved between the table and the espresso bar, pulling shots and steaming milk for the steady trickle of customers while keeping one eye on the historical treasure spread before them. She kept drifting back to the table between orders, unable to stay away.

"Okay," Vi said, pulling the logbook closer. "Walk me through what you know."

Jake sat across from her, his elbows on the table, hands clasped. "The logbook covers 1922 to 1933—the entire Prohibition era. Most entries look like normal coffee shop business, but then there are these." He flipped to a marked page. "Special orders. Weekend deliveries. References to 'underground storage' and 'special blends.'"

Vi scanned the entries, her finger tracing down the page. "These aren't coffee orders."

"Right? That's what we thought!" Ruby said, delivering another latte to Mrs. Patterson before rushing back. "Because the quantities don't make sense for coffee, and the timing is all wrong —mostly weekends, mostly late at night—and the codes are so obvious once you start looking at them, but I guess back then if federal agents came by they'd just see normal business records unless they really knew what to look for, which is actually kind of brilliant when you think about it—"

"Because you're not thinking like smugglers," Vi interrupted gently, grabbing a napkin and starting to make notes. "In the 1920s, speakeasies used customer codes constantly. Look—'special blend' probably means a specific type of alcohol. 'Case' is self-explanatory. 'Premium reserve' might be top-shelf stuff." She tapped another entry. "'Underground storage'—that's not metaphorical, is it?"

"We don't think so," Jake said quietly. "The map shows something in Sullivan's basement. A section that looks different, like it was sealed off."

Vi leaned forward, studying the hand-drawn sketch more carefully. "Wait, this is the actual map? Let me see this more closely." She traced the lines with her finger, her analytical mind clearly working. "This shows a complete cross-section. Your great-grandfather was meticulous."

The map showed Sullivan's Coffee in detail—the main floor, and below it, the basement. But one corner of the basement was marked differently.

"Holy shit," Vi breathed. "This is incredible. Your great-grandfather documented his own speakeasy?"

"Rose thinks he made the map later, maybe in the 1950s or 60s," Jake explained. "Like he wanted someone to know eventually, but not while he was alive." His voice was thick with emotion. "She said in her letter that she always suspected there was more to the story. That great-grandfather would disappear for hours on weekend nights, that there were whispers in town, but no one ever got caught."

Ruby set down three fresh coffees—they were going to need them—and pulled up a chair beside Jake, her words tumbling out with excitement. "And look at the dates, Vi. The logbook entries cluster around Friday and Saturday nights, which makes sense for a speakeasy, right? And then look here—" She pointed to a series of entries from November 1925. "They almost stop completely this week, then pick up again the following Monday. We think federal agents were in town and he had to shut everything down temporarily, which means he was smart about it, careful, not just some reckless bootlegger but someone who really thought things through and—"

Vi leaned in, catching Ruby's enthusiasm. "Federal agents in town?"

"Look at this." Jake pulled out his phone and showed her a photograph. "This is from a newspaper clipping Rose sent. 'Federal Officers Investigate Local Establishments.' It's dated November 18, 1925—right in the middle of that gap."

"So he knew when to lay low. That's actually brilliant." Vi sat back, her analytical mind clearly piecing together the operation. "Smart. What else do the letters say?"

For the next hour, between customers and coffee orders, they worked through Rose's correspondence. Ruby kept bouncing between the espresso bar and the table, adding observations and questions that came faster than she could organize them.

"Oh! What about this notation here—'midnight delivery'—that has to mean alcohol, right? Because who delivers coffee at midnight? Although actually, now that I think about it, some of those Silicon Valley startups probably would, but that's different—"

"Ruby," Jake said, but he was smiling. "Focus."

"Right. Sorry. It's just so exciting! Your great-grandfather was like an entrepreneurial genius. Taking a legitimate business and using it as cover for community service, basically, because that's what it was, right? Providing a service people wanted during an impossible time? It's actually kind of beautiful when you think about it, even though it was technically illegal, but unjust laws and civil disobedience and—okay, I'm rambling again."

Vi's fresh perspective helped them see patterns they'd missed—the careful way great-grandfather Sullivan had documented everything in code, the timing of deliveries, the network of trusted customers.

"Here's what I think happened," Vi said finally, studying the documents with her sharp analytical gaze. "Sullivan's was the front—the legitimate business, the public face. But behind that, your great-grandfather was running a sophisticated operation. He wasn't just storing alcohol. He was creating a gathering place."

Jake looked at the documents with new understanding. "Rose mentioned that in one of her letters. She said great-grandfather always talked about 'serving the town,' but she thought he meant more than just coffee."

"Exactly!" Ruby jumped in. "He was providing something people wanted during impossible times. A place to gather. To feel normal when everything else was restricted. It's like what coffee shops do now, actually—creating third spaces where people can just be—except with more illegal alcohol and probably less wifi, obviously, although the wifi in Millbrook Falls isn't great either, I keep meaning to upgrade my router—"

The bell chimed, and a small rush of lunch customers flooded in. Ruby jumped up to handle orders, but she kept glancing back at the table, clearly torn between her café responsibilities and the historical mystery unfolding across the room. Vi and Jake continued working, Vi asking sharp questions while Jake provided historical context.

Ruby delivered orders with slightly more chattiness than usual, her excitement bubbling over. "Mrs. Martinez, you will not believe what we're discovering—oh, you want your usual? Of course, one decaf latte coming right up—but seriously, Jake's great-grandfather might have run a speakeasy and we're investigating the basement tonight and—yes, extra foam, I remember—"

By two o'clock, the lunch rush had cleared, and they'd gone through every document twice. Ruby was wiping down tables, her mind still spinning with everything they'd learned, when she noticed Jake and Vi had their heads together over one particular set of entries.

"What did you find?" she asked, abandoning her cleaning cloth.

"A pattern," Vi said, tapping her notes. "Look—every single weekend entry mentions 'special service.' But on holidays—

Christmas, New Year's, Fourth of July—the entries say 'premium service' instead."

Jake leaned forward. "Premium versus special. Different products? Different clientele?"

"Or different prices," Vi suggested. "Special occasions, premium alcohol. Your great-grandfather was running a full business operation, not just slinging bootleg whiskey in a basement."

Ruby felt a thrill run through her. "He was creating experiences. Special nights, holiday celebrations—giving people a reason to gather and celebrate even when the law said they couldn't."

"Exactly." Vi sat back, looking satisfied. "This wasn't just about breaking the law. This was about maintaining community and normalcy during a time when both were under attack."

Jake was quiet for a moment, staring at the documents with an expression Ruby couldn't quite read. "I keep thinking about what it must have been like. Building something like this, risking everything to give people a place to feel human."

"Kind of like what you're doing now," Ruby said softly. "Renovating Sullivan's, honoring the past while building something new. Taking risks to create something meaningful."

Jake looked up at her, and something in his amber eyes made her breath catch. "I couldn't do it without you."

"Jake—"

Before she could finish, Jake's phone buzzed. He glanced at the screen, and his expression shifted to anticipation mixed with nerves. "It's Tommy. Says everything's safe and secure. Wants to know if we're still planning to investigate after you close."

Ruby's heart skipped, and words tumbled out before she could stop them. "Oh my god, we're really doing this. We're actually going to break through that wall and find out what's behind it and what if there's nothing there? What if we're completely wrong and it's just an old storage closet with like, ancient coffee beans or broken furniture? Or what if there's something there but it's not what we think and—"

"Ruby," Jake said gently. "Breathe."

She took a breath, but couldn't stop the flow of thoughts. "You're right. Sorry. I'm just nervous and excited and terrified all at once and I really want us to find something because this means so much to you and Tommy and your family and—"

"We have to know," Jake said simply. "One way or another, we need to know what's behind that wall."

Vi was practically vibrating with excitement. "I assume I'm invited to this historical excavation?"

Jake smiled—a real smile that made Ruby's stomach flip and her thoughts scatter. "You helped decode half of this. You've earned it."

"What time?" Ruby asked, then immediately continued without waiting for an answer. "I close at six-thirty but I could close earlier if we wanted to start sooner, or we could wait until it's fully dark for atmosphere, although that might be too dramatic and also impractical because basements are already dark and—"

"Six-thirty sounds perfect," Jake said, and Ruby caught the warmth in his amber eyes.

"Six-thirty. Right. Good. I can do six-thirty." Ruby's hands trembled slightly as she looked around at the café that still needed closing tasks. "This is really happening. In a few hours we're going to find out if the map is accurate, if your great-grandfather really hid something down there for nearly a century, and Vi, you have to promise not to judge me if I get too excited because I have a tendency to ramble when I'm nervous and—"

"Ruby," Vi said, grinning. "I know. It's one of your most endearing qualities."

Jake stood, carefully rolling the map and tucking it into his messenger bag along with the other documents. "Thank you. Both of you. For caring about this. For helping me understand what great-grandfather might have been trying to preserve."

"Of course we care!" Ruby said, the words rushing out. "This is incredible, Jake. Your family's history, this town's history—it all matters. And the fact that your great-grandfather documented everything means he wanted someone to find it eventually, wanted the story told, and now we get to be the ones who tell it and that's just—it's really special. Important. I'm so glad you're letting us be part of it."

Something warm flickered in Jake's amber eyes as he looked at her. "Six-thirty, then. I'll see you across the street."

After Jake left, Vi turned to Ruby with an expression that could only be described as gleeful. "Ruby Ashworth, you are in so deep."

"I don't know what you're talking about."

"The way you look at him. The way you ramble even more than usual when he's around. The way he looks at you like your chattiness is the best part of his day." Vi grinned. "And we're about to go crawling around in a basement together looking for bootleg evidence. This is better than any romance novel I've read."

Ruby felt her cheeks burn, and her words tumbled out defensively. "We're just neighbors working on a historical project. I ramble at everyone, that's not special. And he doesn't look at me like—I mean, maybe he tolerates my rambling because we're friends and neighbors and working together on the renovation, but that doesn't mean—"

"Yeah. Sure. And I'm just a casual observer with no opinions." Vi's expression softened. "But seriously, Ruby—he's good for you. I can see it. You're different here. Lighter. More yourself."

Ruby didn't know how to respond to that, so she just started cleaning up the table, carefully stacking coffee cups and wiping away napkin notes. But Vi's words stayed with her, settling warm and true in her chest.

The afternoon passed in a blur of customers and anticipation. Ruby kept glancing at the clock, watching the minutes crawl toward closing time. She over-explained drinks to customers, recommended pastries with more enthusiasm than necessary, and generally couldn't keep her nervous energy contained.

"Yes, the cranberry scone is amazing—Daisy brought the cranberries and they're so tart and perfect and I've been experimenting with the glaze recipe and—oh, you just wanted a black coffee? Right. Sorry. One black coffee coming right up."

Across the street, she could see lights on in Sullivan's basement windows—Tommy still working, preparing the space for their investigation.

At six o'clock, Ruby started her closing routine early, too anxious to wait any longer. Wiping down the espresso machine, counting the register, stacking chairs. Vi helped, moving with surprising efficiency for someone in designer heels.

"You know," Vi said as she wiped down tables, "I came up here expecting to find you stressed and second-guessing your decision to leave Hartford. Instead, I find you completely in your element, about to go on a historical adventure with a guy who's clearly falling for you."

"Vi—"

"I'm just saying, Ruby. Whatever you're building here—the café, the friendships, this thing with Jake—it's real. It's good. And I'm really proud of you for taking the risk."

Ruby felt tears prick her eyes. "I'm terrified I'm going to mess it up."

"You won't. And even if you stumble, you've got people here who care about you. That's what matters." Vi pulled her into a quick hug. "Now come on. Let's go find out what's behind that wall."

Ruby finished the last of her closing tasks, her hands shaking slightly as she locked the cash register. At six-fifteen, she flipped the sign to "Closed" and grabbed her jacket.

"You nervous?" Vi asked.

"Terrified," Ruby admitted, words spilling out. "What if we don't find anything? What if the map is wrong, or everything was cleared out decades ago, or we're completely misinterpreting the evidence? What if we break through that wall and disappoint Jake and Tommy because there's nothing there and they've built up all these hopes about understanding their great-grandfather and—"

"Or," Vi countered gently, "what if you find exactly what you're looking for? What if their great-grandfather really did leave something behind, and you're about to uncover a piece of history that changes how this whole town understands itself?"

Ruby took a deep breath, looking out at Sullivan's Coffee across the street. The lights were on, warm and inviting in the October evening. Jake was probably already there, waiting for them. Tommy too. Both of them nervous and excited and hoping for answers to questions that had been hidden for nearly a century.

"Okay," Ruby said, squaring her shoulders. "Let's go find out what's behind that wall."

They stepped out into the cool October evening, and Ruby locked the door behind them. As they crossed Main Street, Ruby's heart hammered with anticipation and nervousness and hope.

Whatever they found in that basement—whatever secrets great-grandfather Sullivan had hidden away—they were about to uncover them together.

And somehow, that felt like the most important part of all.

CHAPTER
Eleven

SULLIVAN'S COFFEE FELT DIFFERENT IN THE EARLY EVENING LIGHT. The construction dust had settled, and Tommy's work had transformed the space—the new pendant lights cast warm pools of light over the exposed brick, making everything feel both historic and welcoming.

Tommy was in the back, packing up his tools. He looked up when they entered, his grin easy despite the long day of work evident in his dusty clothes.

"Hey," Tommy said, wiping his hands on his jeans. "Ready for some historical detective work?"

"Is that what we're calling it?" Vi asked, extending her hand. "Vi Torres. Ruby's friend and apparently tonight's expedition member."

"Tommy Sullivan. Jake's brother and your friendly neighborhood electrician." His handshake was firm, his grin easy. "Fair warning—the basement's a mess. I've been down there all day fixing shelves, and it's dusty as hell."

"Speaking of messes," Ruby said with a mischievous smile, "how did moving boxes at the bookstore go this morning? Zara mentioned you were helping out."

Tommy's ears turned slightly pink. "It went fine. Zara had a lot of boxes. Like, a concerning number of boxes for one person. I think she might be a book hoarder."

"A book hoarder who you're helping early in the morning, before work," Ruby teased. "That's very neighborly of you."

"I'm a helpful guy," Tommy said, but his smile suggested there might be more to the story.

Jake emerged from the back room carrying flashlights and the pry bar. "Tommy's got the section all marked. We're ready whenever you are."

Ruby noticed Jake's hands weren't quite steady as he distributed the flashlights, and her nervous chatter returned. "Okay, so we're really doing this. We're going down into the basement and breaking through a wall that's been sealed for like ninety years and hopefully finding something amazing and not just discovering that your great-grandfather was really into brick-sealing as a hobby—"

"Ruby," Jake said, but his voice was warm. "It's going to be fine."

"Right. Fine. Totally fine. Let's go break through some historically significant bricks."

They made their way to the basement door. The stone steps solid under their weight as they descended into the coolness below. Ruby shivered, partly from the temperature and partly from anticipation, her words coming faster as they descended.

"Is it always this cold down here? It feels like a refrigerator, which I guess makes sense for a speakeasy because you'd want to keep the alcohol cool, although I don't know if they had refrigeration in the 1920s—did they? They must have, right? Or maybe they used ice blocks like in old movies where people had ice boxes instead of—"

"Ruby," Vi said gently. "You're nervous-rambling."

"I know. Sorry. I do that."

Tommy had set up a some extra work light in the corner, illuminating the northwestern wall where the different mortar was clearly visible in the bright light.

"There it is," Tommy said, gesturing to the sealed section. "I've been staring at it all day, thinking about what might be back there."

Jake pulled out the map one more time, comparing it to the physical space. "If the map is accurate, there should be a room behind this. Not just a storage closet—an actual room."

"Then let's find out." Tommy grabbed the pry bar, his expression determined but emotional. "Ready, brother?"

Jake nodded, moving to stand beside Tommy. "Let's do this."

Ruby watched as the two brothers worked side by side, carefully prying loose the first brick. Her hands twisted together nervously, and she couldn't keep quiet. "Be careful with that brick—it looks loose but you never know—oh, that one came out easily—is that good or bad? That's probably good, right? It means the mortar isn't too strong, which makes sense if it was done in a hurry—"

"Ruby," Vi whispered. "They've got this."

"I know. I just—what if there's nothing there? What if—"

Then Tommy removed another brick, creating an opening, and a draft of stale air escaped.

"There's definitely space back here," Tommy said, his voice tight. He removed another brick, then another, creating an opening large enough to shine a light through.

Jake aimed his flashlight beam into the gap, and Ruby heard his sharp intake of breath.

"What is it?" she asked, moving closer. "What do you see? Is it something? Please tell me it's something—"

"Glass. Shelves. And—" Jake's voice cracked. "There's more. So much more."

Tommy worked faster now, and Ruby could see his hands shaking as he widened the gap. When it was large enough to see through clearly, all four of them crowded around, their flashlight beams illuminating what lay beyond.

Ruby gasped, and for once, words failed her completely.

It wasn't just a storage closet. Through the opening, they could see what had clearly been a complete room—roughly twelve feet by fifteen feet. Wooden shelving lined two walls, still holding dozens of bottles in careful rows, their glass catching the light. Against the back wall stood what had definitely been a bar counter, simple but functional, with more bottles arranged behind it. Scattered around the space were the remains of small tables and chairs, some collapsed with age but still recognizable. And in the corner, barely visible in the flashlight beams, was an old gramophone, its brass horn dulled but intact.

"Oh my god," Vi whispered. "It's not just storage. It's an actual speakeasy."

"He built a whole room," Tommy breathed, his voice thick with emotion. "A place where people could gather. Drink. Feel normal."

Jake reached carefully through the opening and pulled out one of the bottles from the nearest shelf. His hands shook as he examined it, and Ruby could see tears tracking down his dusty cheeks.

The bottle was intact, with a hand-written label that read "Sullivan's Special Reserve - 1927."

Ruby's heart felt like it might burst. All her nervous energy, all her worry, all her anticipation crystallized into pure joy. This wasn't just history—this was Jake's family, his legacy, proof that his great-grandfather had built something remarkable.

"Jake!" The word came out as a squeal, her voice echoing in the basement as every professional filter she possessed evaporated. "This is incredible! This is actual history! Your great-grandfather didn't just bootleg, he created a whole gathering place and you found it and this changes everything about how we understand his legacy and the town's history and it's so much better than we imagined and—"

Before her brain could catch up with her heart, before logic could override the pure joy of discovery, Ruby threw her arms around Jake and planted a kiss on his cheek.

The moment her lips touched his skin, everything else fell away. She felt the warmth of his cheek, the slight roughness of stubble, the way he smelled like coffee and sawdust and something fundamentally him. Jake went very still, and Ruby became acutely aware of how close they were, how her hands were pressed against his chest, how his heart was beating just as fast as hers, how he wasn't pulling away.

Time seemed to suspend itself in the dusty basement air.

Then reality crashed back in, and Ruby jerked backward, words tumbling out in a mortified rush. "Oh my god, I'm so sorry, I just got excited about the discovery and the room and your face was right there and I didn't think, I never think, I just do things and then realize maybe I shouldn't have done them and now I've made everything weird and—"

"Ruby." Jake's voice was rougher than usual, deeper, and when she dared to look at him, his amber eyes were darker than she'd ever seen them, focused entirely on her face with an intensity that made her forget how to breathe. "You don't need to apologize."

"I don't?" Her voice came out as a whisper.

"No. You don't."

The air between them felt charged, impossibly heavy with something Ruby didn't have words for. She was vaguely aware of Vi and Tommy suddenly finding the far wall extremely interesting, their backs diplomatically turned to give them a moment of privacy in the crowded basement.

Ruby opened her mouth, closed it, opened it again. "So I didn't just completely—I mean, that wasn't too—you're not upset that I—"

Jake's mouth quirked into something that was almost a smile. "Ruby. It's fine. Better than fine."

"Better than—okay. Good. That's good. Great, actually. Not that I was planning to make a habit of randomly kissing people, even on the cheek, because that would be weird and also probably inappropriate in most professional contexts, although this isn't exactly a professional context, more like a historical excavation with friends, which is different, but still—"

"Ruby," Vi called from where she was very deliberately examining the hidden room. "You might want to see this. There's more back here."

Ruby gratefully seized the interruption, even as her cheeks burned hot enough to probably be visible in the dark basement. "Right! Yes! More historical evidence! That's why we're here!"

Jake and Tommy worked to widen the opening further, and Ruby tried to focus on the discovery rather than the fact that she'd just kissed Jake Sullivan and he'd said it was "better than fine" and what did that even mean?

As they removed more bricks, the full scope of what great-grandfather Sullivan had built became visible.

The room was complete, preserved by accident behind its sealed wall. The bar counter had shelves behind it, still lined with bottles. The small tables, though aged and fragile, were arranged as if waiting for customers. Ruby could almost imagine what it had looked like—candlelight, quiet conversations, the scratch of the gramophone playing jazz while people gathered to forget the world outside for a few hours.

Jake carefully reached through the opening and retrieved a wooden box. When he opened it, his expression transformed into pure wonder.

"What is it?" Ruby asked, moving closer, her embarrassment momentarily forgotten in the face of new discovery. "More bottles? Records? A secret diary? Oh my god, what if he kept a diary and it's full of speakeasy gossip and—"

"Recipe cards," Jake said, his hands trembling as he lifted them out. The cards were wrapped in oiled cloth that had protected them from decades of moisture. "Look at this—'Sullivan's Special Blend: Equal parts imported whiskey and locally sourced corn spirits, aged in oak barrels behind the coffee roaster.'"

Tommy leaned over his brother's shoulder, reading another card. "'Morning Revival: coffee, Irish whiskey, brown sugar, and fresh cream. Serve hot before dawn patrol.'" He looked up, his eyes bright with unshed tears. "He was mixing coffee with the alcohol. Creating specialty drinks."

"He was innovating," Ruby breathed, her words coming faster with renewed excitement. "Taking care of people. Making something special during a hard time. It's like what good coffee shops do now—creating experiences, building community—except he was doing it ninety years ago with illegal alcohol and probably significant risk of federal prosecution, which makes it even more impressive, actually—"

Jake nodded, sorting through more recipe cards with reverent care. "There's coffee cocktails here, specialty blends." His voice cracked. "He wasn't just breaking the law. He was creating."

"Just like you're doing now," Ruby said softly, and this time her words came slower, more deliberately. "Honoring what matters while building something new. Your great-grandfather would be so proud of what you and Tommy are doing with Sullivan's. I know I'm not family, but I'm proud too, if that counts for anything—"

"It counts," Jake said, and the way he looked at her made Ruby's breath catch. "It counts for a lot."

Tommy pulled out his phone and started taking photographs, documenting everything they could see. Jake and Ruby carefully catalogued items visible through the opening, and Vi organized their notes with her usual efficiency. The speakeasy revealed its secrets slowly—more bottles, more recipe cards, even a small ledger tucked behind the bar that detailed the operation with meticulous care.

"Look at this," Vi said, carefully extracting the ledger through the opening. She opened it gently, mindful of its age. "It's like a complete business record. Customer tabs, inventory, even notes about special events."

Ruby peered over her shoulder, reading aloud. "'New Year's Eve 1926 - Full house, premium blend only. J.F. brought cigars.' J.F. —that must be one of his regular customers. And look at this entry—'Mrs. Henderson's birthday celebration - reserved back table, special coffee service.' He was hosting parties. Private events."

"This wasn't just a speakeasy," Tommy said, his voice full of wonder. "It was a social club. A gathering place for the whole community."

Jake was quiet, running his fingers over one of the recipe cards with careful reverence. "He built something that mattered. Something that brought people together during one of the hardest times in American history."

"And he documented it all," Ruby added. "Made sure someone would know eventually. That the story wouldn't be lost."

They spent the next hour carefully examining everything they could reach through the opening. Tommy took dozens of photographs from every angle. Jake made detailed notes about the layout and contents. Vi catalogued the recipes with her typical efficiency. And Ruby couldn't stop marveling at the completeness of it all—the way great-grandfather Sullivan had created not just a business, but an entire experience.

Finally, when they'd documented everything accessible, they sat on the basement floor, dusty and exhausted and exhilarated.

"This is bigger than we imagined," Tommy said, wiping his eyes without shame. "Man, I wish I could have met him. Really understood what he was trying to do."

"You're honoring him now," Vi said gently. "Both of you. By uncovering this. By caring enough to tell the real story."

Jake looked at the sealed opening, at the glimpse of his great-grandfather's hidden world. When he spoke, his voice was thoughtful. "So what do we do with this?"

"We tell the story!" Ruby said, her enthusiasm returning in full force. "The whole story. We could incorporate some of the historical cocktail recipes into Sullivan's menu—not replacing the traditional coffee, obviously, because that's your foundation, but adding to it. Showing people that Sullivan's has always been about innovation. And maybe we could do tours? Let people see the actual speakeasy? I know that would require making it safe and probably getting permits and dealing with insurance, which sounds boring but it's important, and—"

"And we could display some of this stuff," Tommy added, his contractor mind already working. "Make the opening safe, install proper lighting. Let people see what great-grandfather built. Ruby's right about the permits, though. We'd need to do this carefully."

"You'd have to frame it carefully too," Vi cautioned, her marketing expertise showing. "Prohibition is far enough in the past to be historical rather than controversial, but you want to focus on the community aspect. How your great-grandfather created a gathering place during impossible times. Make it about connection and resilience, not just lawbreaking."

"Like speakeasy tours in other cities," Ruby jumped in, her words tumbling faster. "They're popular tourist attractions now—the history, the atmosphere, the sense of stepping back in time. And Sullivan's has something none of those places have—an actual, untouched speakeasy that's been sealed for ninety years. That's incredible! People would come from all over to see this. It could really help the town's economy, bring in tourists, and—"

"Ruby," Jake said, but his smile was warm. "Breathe."

She took a breath, grinning sheepishly. "Sorry. I get excited about possibilities."

"I know." Jake's expression softened. "It's one of the things I—" He paused, seeming to reconsider his words. "One of the things that makes you good at this."

Ruby felt her cheeks warm, but before she could overthink what he'd almost said, Tommy stood up, stretching.

"We should probably call it a night," he said. "It's getting late, and we need to think this through carefully. Figure out the best way forward."

Jake nodded slowly, his gaze moving from the hidden room to the recipe cards in his hands to Ruby's face. "You're right. This is too important to rush."

As they made their way back upstairs, Ruby's mind was already spinning with possibilities. The speakeasy tours, the historical recipes, the way this discovery could transform not just

Sullivan's but the entire town's identity. She could see it all so clearly—the warm lighting, the carefully curated displays, the way visitors would gasp when they first glimpsed the hidden room, just like they had.

They emerged into Sullivan's main floor, all four of them dusty and exhilarated. The new pendant lights cast everything in warm gold, and Ruby thought about how fitting it was—uncovering treasure, literally and figuratively.

Tommy stretched, grinning despite the emotion still visible in his eyes. "Well, this was definitely the most interesting Friday I've had in forever. Historical excavation beats drywall installation by a mile."

"Thank you," Jake said, and Ruby heard the depth of feeling in his voice. "For being part of this. For understanding what it means."

"Are you kidding? This is our great-grandfather, man. Our family." Tommy's voice was thick. "I wouldn't have missed it." He grabbed his tool bag, slinging it over his shoulder. "I'm going to head out—long day, and I'm exhausted. But let me know what you decide about the tours and displays. I can build whatever you need to make it safe and accessible."

"Will do," Jake said, pulling his brother into a brief hug. "Thanks for everything today."

After Tommy left, the three of them stood in the quiet of Sullivan's, the weight of the evening's discovery settling around them.

"So," Vi said, her eyes sparkling with barely contained delight. "What now?"

Jake looked at Ruby, and in his amber eyes she saw excitement, possibility, and something that made her pulse quicken. "Now we figure out how to honor the past while building the future."

"Together?" Ruby asked, the word catching in her throat.

"Together." The way he said it made Ruby think he might be talking about more than just coffee shops and historical discoveries.

Vi cleared her throat deliberately. "Well, I can see you two have things to discuss, and I desperately need a shower after crawling around in that basement. Ruby, I'll meet you back at your place?"

"Yeah, I'll be there soon." Ruby's cheeks burned, but she was grateful for Vi's discretion.

After Vi left, Ruby and Jake stood alone in the renovated space. The discovery sat between them—not just the physical evidence in boxes on the counter, but the emotional weight of what they'd uncovered together.

"Thank you," Jake said finally. "For helping me see this differently. For understanding what it means to my family. To me."

The words hung between them, loaded with meaning that went far beyond recipe cards and hidden rooms. Ruby felt hope bloom in her chest as she realized that this—the renovation, the discovery, the way Jake was looking at her like she'd just helped him solve the mystery of his own life—this was what she'd been searching for without even knowing it.

This was partnership. This was trust. This was the beginning of something that felt like it could last a hundred years, just like the Sullivan family legacy they'd just uncovered.

"Thank you for letting me be part of it," Ruby said softly, and for once her words didn't tumble over each other in a nervous rush. "For trusting me with something this important."

Jake stepped closer, and Ruby's heart hammered in her chest. For a moment, she thought he might kiss her—hoped he might kiss her—but instead he just smiled, a real smile that transformed his serious face into something that made her knees weak.

"Get some rest," he said. "Tomorrow we start figuring out how to tell this story."

Ruby nodded, not trusting herself to speak without launching into another rambling monologue about feelings and historical discoveries and the way his smile made her forget how words worked. As she crossed Main Street back to Scattered Beans, she could feel Jake watching from his doorway, making sure she got safely inside.

Upstairs in her apartment, Vi was already in pajamas, her designer clothes abandoned in favor of Ruby's spare sweats.

"So," Vi said without preamble. "You kissed him."

"On the cheek! It was just excitement about the discovery, it didn't mean—"

"Ruby." Vi fixed her with a serious look. "The man looked at you like you were his whole world and personally handed him the keys to his family's history. And you looked at him like he was the answer to a question you didn't know you were asking." She smiled softly. "Whatever this is between you two, it's real. And it's beautiful. Don't overthink it."

Ruby sank onto the couch, her mind spinning with the events of the evening—the documents, the discovery, the kiss, the way Jake had said "together" like it was a promise. "I think I'm falling for him," she admitted quietly.

"I know, sweetie. I could tell from your first texts about him." Vi sat beside her, pulling Ruby into a side hug. "The question is, what are you going to do about it?"

Ruby looked out her window at Sullivan's Coffee across the street, its warm lights glowing in the October darkness. Somewhere in that building, Jake was probably thinking about recipe cards and speakeasy history and the legacy his great-grandfather had left behind.

And maybe—hopefully—thinking about her too.

"I don't know yet," Ruby said, leaning her head on Vi's shoulder. "But I think I want to find out."

Vi squeezed her hand. "Good. Because that man is clearly already gone for you, and watching you two dance around it was starting to give me anxiety."

Ruby laughed, feeling lighter than she had in months despite the weight of uncertainty still sitting in her chest. "You know what's crazy? A year ago I was in Hartford, miserable in a corner office, thinking that was what success looked like. And now I'm in Millbrook Falls, covered in basement dust, having just kissed a man on the cheek in front of my best friend, and I've never been happier."

"That's not crazy," Vi said gently. "That's called finding where you belong."

Ruby let those words settle over her like a warm blanket. Where she belonged. Not just Millbrook Falls, not just Scattered Beans, but here—in this moment, in this life she was building, with these people who were becoming more than just neighbors and customers and business associates.

They were becoming family.

"I'm really glad you came," Ruby said softly.

"Me too, sweetie. Me too." Vi yawned. "Now can we please sleep? Because tomorrow I want to hear every single detail about how you and Jake are going to turn a bootleg speakeasy into the most romantic historical attraction in Connecticut. Before I have turned rush back."

"It's not romantic! It's historical!"

"Uh-huh. Keep telling yourself that."

Ruby laughed and didn't argue, because maybe Vi was right. Maybe everything about this—the discovery, the partnership, the way Jake looked at her—was a little bit romantic and a little bit historical and entirely, wonderfully real.

Ruby let herself fall asleep thinking about hidden rooms and cheek-kisses and the way Jake Sullivan looked at her like she was part of something bigger than herself—part of a story that had been waiting a hundred years to be told.

And maybe, just maybe, part of a new story that was only just beginning.

CHAPTER *Twelve*

Derek Castellano arrived in Millbrook Falls on Monday evening, December 2nd, in a black BMW as out of place on Main Street as he was about to be in her shop.

Ruby stood at her apartment window, watching him parallel-park with the kind of aggressive precision that turned every maneuver into a competition. Sharp suit, expensive shoes, the confidence of someone who'd never questioned whether career advancement was the only measure of success.

She'd been dreading this moment for days. But seeing him now—so clearly a corporate transplant, so obviously uncomfortable in a town with actual charm—Ruby felt something unexpected.

Clarity.

She grabbed her keys and headed downstairs.

Her boots thudded on the stair treads, each step knocking loose a little of the calm she'd felt at the window. Resin and pine from the garland met the sharper scent of fresh espresso—home crowding out doubt, if only for a breath.

The shop was already closed for the evening, but Ruby unlocked Scattered Beans and flipped on the lights.

The room answered in twinkle and color: reflections skittered across the pastry case; a strand of bulbs blinked to life like a slow intake of breath. For a heartbeat she just stood there, hands on the counter, remembering laughter around the Thanksgiving table.

The Christmas decorations she'd spent Thanksgiving weekend installing glowed warm—colored lights framing the windows, garland draped over the counter, three trees filling corners with cheerful chaos. The warmth of Thursday's dinner—Jake's quiet smile across the table, Zara's wine-fueled storytelling, Tommy's insistence on making three kinds of pie—felt like it belonged to a different world than the one about to walk through her door.

Across the street, Sullivan's Coffee glowed under Jake's pendant lights, white lights and garland wrapped around exposed brick. Ruby could see movement behind the windows—Jake closing up, unaware that her entire future was about to demand an answer.

The bell chimed.

"Ruby!" Derek's smile was polished, practiced. "This place is... exactly what I expected." His gaze swept the Christmas decorations. "Very festive. The gingerbread latte thing is a bit on-the-nose for December, though."

Ruby felt the old conference-room reflex—explain, justify, smooth—rise to her throat and made herself swallow it. Not here. Not anymore.

Ruby bristled. "Hello, Derek. Thanks for making the drive."

"Wouldn't miss it." Derek settled onto a stool, somehow making it look uncomfortable. His attention snagged on one of her trees—coffee-themed ornaments, colored lights twinkling. "Very authentic. I can see the appeal of playing coffee shop for a while."

"I'm not playing. This is my business."

"Right, of course." Derek waved a hand. "Can I get coffee? Nothing fancy—just regular."

Ruby moved to Beatrice, who'd been purring along beautifully for weeks, and tried to center herself. This was just coffee. Just a conversation. It didn't have to change anything.

She made his Americano with the same care she brought to every drink and set it in front of him.

Derek sipped without really tasting. "So. Let's talk about your future." His impatience was familiar. "I've got exciting numbers to show you, and I'd hate for you to miss this opportunity because we got distracted."

Ruby's stomach tightened, but she stayed quiet.

"Regional manager position. Sixty percent salary increase from BrewCorp. Company car, full benefits, stock options."

He slid his phone across the counter, columns and charts bright as a runway. Ruby didn't touch it. The glossy screen reflected her garland instead of her face.

"And here's the kicker—you'd oversee our new 'artisanal experience' initiative. Doing what you're doing here, but at a scale that matters."

"A scale that matters?"

"Come on, Ruby. You know what I mean. This is cute, but how many people are you reaching? Maybe a hundred customers a day? With BrewCorp, you'd impact thousands across three states. Real change in the industry."

Ruby looked around her shop, at what she had accomplished. "The people here aren't statistics. They're my neighbors."

"And that's sweet. But let's be practical." Derek took his phone and started scrolling. "I've been tracking your Instagram. Busy, sure. Lots of engagement. But busy doesn't mean profitable. What are your actual margins? Monthly overhead? In towns this size, even successful shops barely scrape by."

Ruby's throat went dry. She'd been so focused on building relationships that she hadn't examined her profit margins in weeks.

"I'm not saying you'll fail. You're talented. But talent isn't enough when you're dealing with overhead costs, seasonal fluctuations." Derek's voice softened, almost kind. "How many lavender lattes can three thousand people really support?"

Before Ruby could answer, the bell chimed.

Jake stood in the doorway, snowflakes dusting his hair. Derek's cologne—clean, expensive—met the simple warmth of coffee and wool from Jake's coat. Two lives, two futures, sharing the same square of floor. His eyes found hers immediately, and Ruby's heart skipped. In the warm glow of Scattered Beans, Jake's quiet strength made Derek's polished charm look hollow.

"Sorry. Didn't mean to interrupt. Just wanted to check if you needed anything before I head up."

"Not interrupting." Derek stood, extending his hand. "You must be the local competition. Derek Castellano, BrewCorp Regional Development."

Jake shook his hand, wariness flickering across his face. "Jake Sullivan. Sullivan's Coffee."

"Ah, the family business Ruby mentioned. Very... traditional." Derek made it sound like an insult. "I was just telling Ruby about opportunities in the real world. Corporate coffee—where the money actually moves."

Jake's jaw tightened. "The real world?"

"Major markets. Growth potential. Career advancement." Derek gestured vaguely at the shop. "This small-town thing is charming, but eventually reality sets in. Limited customer base, no expansion room. Not sustainable long-term."

"Sullivan's has been here almost a hundred years."

Derek laughed, and the sound scraped against Ruby's nerves. "Exactly. A hundred years of the same menu, same customers, same limited vision. That's not growth—that's survival."

Ruby opened her mouth, but Derek kept going.

"I'm not criticizing. I'm saying there's a difference between maintaining status quo and building something that matters. Ruby has talent to impact thousands, not just serve the same fifty people daily."

The silence was thick. Ruby watched Jake process Derek's words, saw hurt flicker across his face before he shut it down. He reached for the handle like it weighed more than it should.

"Good luck with whatever you decide, Ruby." His voice was careful, neutral. "I'm sure you'll make the right choice."

The door chimed behind him.

Ruby stared at the space where he'd been, anger building in her chest.

"Nice guy. Very local." Derek sat back down. "Anyway, where were we?"

"You were dismissing everything I've built here like it doesn't count."

Derek blinked. "Ruby, I'm trying to help you see—"

"See what? That Main Street doesn't matter? That Jake's family legacy is just survival?" Ruby's voice shook. "You know what I've built here, Derek? Relationships. Community. A place where what I do actually matters to the people I serve."

"That's nice, but—"

"That's everything." Ruby gripped the counter. "Mrs. Patterson stops by every morning not for coffee, but because she needs someone to ask about her grandchildren. Zara writes here because the atmosphere helps her think. Frank Kowalski—who hasn't tried anything new in fifteen years—ordered a specialty drink because he trusted me. That's the point, Derek. They trust me. I don't get that in a rollout deck."

Derek waited, like she was listing quaint anecdotes before getting back to business.

"You're talking about maybe fifty regulars. I'm talking thousands—"

"Thousands of strangers who'll never know my name." Ruby took a breath. "I don't want to impact anonymous customers. I want to matter to people who matter to me."

Derek recalibrated. "Okay. I see you're attached. But Ruby, be practical. What happens when the novelty wears off? When you can't make rent? This little shop can't support real life goals—travel, a house, a family."

A draft slipped under the door. For an instant she saw the line item she always skipped: ***Emergency Fund: $0.***

The doubt crept in. Derek wasn't wrong about financial realities. Independent shops were risky. One equipment failure could sink her.

But then she thought about Jake. The Festivals.The discoveries they'd done together. The way he'd looked at her in the basement when she'd kissed his cheek.

"What if the life I want is here?"

"Then you're settling. You have too much talent to waste serving lattes to farmers."

Something snapped. "Waste it? Do you hear yourself?"

"I'm being realistic—"

"You're being condescending." Ruby stood. "You've spent twenty minutes telling me nothing I've built matters because it's not big enough or profitable enough for your standards. But I've never been happier than in this little shop, in this little town, serving people you think don't matter."

Derek held up his hands. "Ruby, I'm trying to help you see the bigger picture."

"Your bigger picture is a corporate bubble where success is quarterly reports and market penetration. My bigger picture is Jake trusting me with his family's legacy. Daisy bringing me mint because she believed I could keep something alive. Frank trying something I created."

Derek looked at her like she'd confessed to believing in unicorns. "Ruby—"

"I appreciate the offer. I do." Ruby's certainty wavered. "But I need time to think."

Derek blinked, clearly not expecting that. "Time? What's there to think about? Financial security, career growth—"

"Leaving everything I've built." Ruby gestured around.

"I'm not saying it's less important. I'm saying you have bigger potential—"

"Than what? Making Mrs. Patterson's day better? Giving Zara inspiration?" Ruby's throat ached. "You're asking me to choose between two definitions of success, and I can't decide while you're standing here telling me everything I love isn't enough."

Something shifted in Derek's expression. The aggressive pitch softened.

"I'm not attacking what you built. I'm trying to help." He set down his cup. "Look, I can see this matters more than I realized. And I'm sorry I didn't stand up for you when you got fired. I'm trying to rectify my mistake. The offer's real, and it's good—better than anything else available. But I get it. You're invested."

"I'm home. There's a difference."

"Maybe." Derek gathered his things, less aggressive now. "Think about it. Really think—not just warm feelings, but practical realities. Margins, overhead, long-term sustainability."

The cold settled in Ruby's chest. He wasn't wrong about the risks.

"I'll come back after Christmas," Derek continued, pulling on his coat. "That gives you a few weeks without pressure. Think about where you want to be in five years. Ten. Think about what happens if this doesn't make it—because, Ruby, independent shops in towns this size struggle."

"Derek—"

"I'm not trying to scare you. I'm being realistic. You're talented. Too talented to let stubbornness or feelings cost your future." He paused at the door. "The offer stands until I come back. After Christmas. That's your deadline. But if you say no..." He shrugged. "These opportunities don't come twice."

The door chimed.

Ruby stood alone, Derek's words echoing.

What are your actual margins? Even successful shops barely scrape by.

She looked across Main Street. Sullivan's lights were still on, but Jake was gone. Tommy was cleaning up, probably getting ready to close.

She'd defended this place with everything she had. Meant every word about relationships mattering more than corporate success. But Derek had given her time to think, and that time felt terrifying.

Because what if he was right? What if her feelings for Jake were clouding judgment about business realities? What if staying was stubbornness dressed as authenticity?

Ruby locked up, hands shaking, then stood on the sidewalk between her shop and Jake's, trying to decide.

She needed to talk to Jake. Explain that Derek's dismissiveness didn't reflect her feelings. That she wasn't planning to leave.

But *I haven't decided yet* sounded like *I might leave* from Jake's perspective.

She crossed Main Street anyway, breath forming clouds in December cold. Sullivan's was dark, but light glowed from Jake's apartment. She climbed the steps and knocked.

Her knuckles hovered a second too long. She wasn't sure if she wanted him to open the door or buy her time not to.

Jake answered in flannel pants and a faded t-shirt, hair messed like he'd been running his hands through it. His guarded expression made her chest ache.

"Ruby. Everything okay?"

"No. Can we talk?"

He stepped aside, gesturing her into his apartment—clean lines, comfortable furniture, poetry collections lining the shelves. It was him, and Ruby's uncertainty deepened. This man, this life, this place—it felt right. But Derek's questions kept echoing.

"About Derek," Jake started, voice careful. "You don't need to explain. Corporate opportunity, better money, security—"

"Jake, stop." Ruby held up a hand. "I didn't accept his offer."

"Okay."

"But I didn't say no either." The words rushed out. Jake's expression shuttered. "He's giving me until after Christmas. And Jake, I know what I want emotionally. I want this. I want Millbrook Falls and Scattered Beans and everything I've built and..." She couldn't say *you*, not when admitting she might leave. "But

Derek asked about my margins, my overhead, my profitability, and I—"

"You're considering it."

"I don't know." Ruby ran a hand through her hair. "I came to apologize for how he dismissed Sullivan's. How he dismissed you. But I can't pretend I'm not scared about what he said."

Jake was quiet, choosing words. When he spoke, his voice was steady but distant.

"You should think about it. Derek's not wrong about the risks. Independent shops are hard. Slim margins, slow winters. One bad season can sink you." He met her eyes. "I can't ask you to risk your financial future, even if this feels right."

"That's not fair. It's more than—"

"Is it?" Jake's question was gentle but piercing. "Four months ago you didn't know this place existed. You had a life in Hartford, a career, plans. Derek's offering you that back, but better. More secure. More successful by any measure."

Tears pricked Ruby's eyes. "You're telling me to take it?"

"I'm telling you to make the decision that's right for your life. Not romantic or adventurous or rebellious. The decision that makes sense."

"What about us?" Her voice was small, trembling despite her effort to sound steady. "What about what we've been building?"

Pain flickered across Jake's face—quick, contained, but unmistakable. "Ruby, we've been neighbors for four months. We've flirted, worked side by side, shared a few near-disasters with that espresso machine. And yeah—there's something here." He hesitated, his jaw tightening. "But is that enough to base your life on? Is it fair to either of us if you stay because of feelings that might fade once the newness wears off?"

"That's not fair."

"Maybe not. But it's honest." He raked a hand through his hair again, leaving it messier than before. "I care about you. More than I should. But this—" He gestured vaguely between them, his voice rough. "This life isn't easy, Ruby. My great-grandfather built this place during the hardest years anyone could imagine. My family kept it going when every number on paper said it shouldn't have survived. I know exactly what it takes. And I know it's not for everyone."

"So you think I should leave," she whispered.

"I think you should do what's right for you." His voice softened, but the distance stayed. "Not for me. Not for Millbrook Falls. Not because of anyone else's expectations. Just you."

He stepped back, the space between them stretching wider than the tiny apartment could contain. "Take the time Derek gave you. Think about where you really want to be. Whatever you decide..." He swallowed hard, eyes dark with something she couldn't read. "I'll understand."

Ruby stood there, the quiet hum of the heater filling the silence he left behind. She'd come hoping for reassurance—for him to tell her she was right to stay, that love and belonging were enough. Instead, he'd handed her space to doubt. Permission to walk away.

And somehow, that hurt more than anything Derek had said.

"I should go," she said softly, even though she didn't want to.

"Yeah," he murmured. "Probably."

Ruby turned toward the door, her hand on the knob, then hesitated. "Jake, I—"

But the words tangled. *I love you* felt reckless. *I want to stay* felt untrue while fear still knotted in her chest. *I don't know what to do* felt too small for the storm inside her.

Jake's voice broke the silence first. "Good night, Ruby."

She turned back once, just long enough to see the tired kindness in his eyes. "Good night."

Ruby crossed Main Street in the biting December cold, the snow falling in soft, unhurried flakes that melted against her cheeks. Upstairs in her apartment, she dropped her keys on the counter and went straight to the window.

Below, her shop and Jake's faced each other across twenty feet of asphalt that suddenly felt like miles. The Christmas lights on both storefronts glowed softly through the snowfall, twin halos in the dark.

Derek had given her until after Christmas. Three and a half weeks to decide if she was brave enough to risk everything on a dream that might fail—or sensible enough to walk away before it did.

She looked at her phone, Derek's contact still glowing on the screen. Then across the street at Sullivan's, dark and still, a single light burning in the apartment above.

Snow stitched the two buildings together in thin white threads, fragile and fleeting.

And she had absolutely no idea what she was going to do.

CHAPTER *Thirteen*

Three days after Derek Castellano left Scattered Beans with his job offer and his spreadsheets full of failure statistics, Ruby Ashworth found herself standing outside Sullivan's Coffee at 9 pm, mail tucked under her arm, staring at the light in Jake's window.

She'd been avoiding him. Not obviously—they still exchanged polite waves across Main Street, still maintained the careful choreography of small-town neighbors who happened to run competing businesses. But the easy collaboration they'd built over time, the comfortable silences and shared glances and moments when their hands brushed while reaching for the same equipment—all of that had vanished the moment Derek walked through her door.

Ruby hadn't meant for it to happen. Hadn't planned to create distance between them. But Derek's offer sat on her kitchen counter like a ticking bomb, and every time Ruby looked at Jake, she felt the weight of a decision she wasn't ready to make.

The mail had been sitting on her counter for two days—three pieces addressed to Sullivan's Coffee that the postal carrier had mistakenly delivered to Scattered Beans. Ruby had meant to bring it over. Had picked it up a dozen times, fully intending to cross the street. But each time, she'd set it back down, not ready to face whatever careful politeness or, worse, hurt she might find in Jake's eyes.

Tonight, though, she'd run out of excuses. The mail was a reason. A good reason. A reason that had nothing to do with the fact that she missed him.

Ruby took a breath of cold December air and pushed open the door before she could talk herself out of it.

The bell chimed when she entered Sullivan's, and Jake looked up with an expression that cycled through surprise, caution, and something that might have been relief before settling into careful neutrality. Behind him, white Christmas lights gleamed against the exposed brick, the renovation work now framed by holiday warmth.

"Ruby. Hi."

"Hi." Ruby held up the envelopes like a shield. "The mail carrier mixed up our deliveries again. Thought you might need these."

Jake took the mail, his fingers carefully avoiding hers. "Thanks. Could have waited until morning, though."

"I know. I just—" Ruby shoved her free hand in her pocket, suddenly uncertain. "I saw your light on. Thought you might be looking at those documents again."

Jake glanced down at the map spread across the table, his great-grandfather's careful handwriting marking mysterious notations and measurements. "Can't stop thinking about them. There's something here I'm missing. Something important."

Ruby crossed to the table, and Jake shifted slightly, making room for her without quite meeting her eyes. The careful distance felt wrong, like something precious had been damaged and neither of them knew how to fix it.

"Can I see?" Ruby asked quietly.

Jake nodded, pushing the map toward her.

Ruby studied the brittle paper, taking in the layout she'd

memorized weeks ago. Sullivan's Coffee, clearly marked. The basement, with its careful measurements.

"I've been thinking," Ruby said slowly, tracing one of the lines with her finger. "What if we've been reading this wrong?"

Jake leaned closer, his shoulder almost touching hers. "What do you mean?"

"This notation here—'main chamber, 12x15, brick-lined.' We assumed it was in your basement, right? Part of the speakeasy operation."

"Right."

"But look at the measurements." Ruby pointed to the scale notation at the bottom of the map. "If this chamber was in your basement, it would take up almost half the space. And you've been down there. Tommy's been working on renovation. There's no twelve-by-fifteen chamber."

Jake went very still, processing. "So where is it?"

Ruby's finger traced the line that had been bothering her for weeks—the one that connected Sullivan's Coffee to another building. "What if it's not in your building at all? What if it's between our buildings?"

The silence stretched long enough that Ruby looked up, finding Jake staring at her with an intensity that made her breath catch.

"Under Main Street," Jake said quietly. "The sewer junction chamber Rose mentioned in her letter. The abandoned infrastructure from when they rerouted the system."

"Your great-grandfather didn't just run a speakeasy," Ruby continued, excitement building despite the complicated feelings between them. "He had access to an underground chamber that connected to—" She stopped, reading the faded notation "J.F. Building. Wait I seen this before. Ohh my god I can't believe I didn't connect it until now. John Fairfield. That's my building. I remember it now from the deeds. It's my building Jake."

Jake reached for one of Rose's letters, flipping through pages until he found what he was looking for. "Listen to this. 'Your great-grandfather always said the operation worked because of partnership. Two buildings, two purposes, one goal.' I thought she meant partnership with the community. But what if she meant literal partnership? With the building across the street?"

Ruby's heart raced. "Sullivan's was the distribution point. The public face. But the storage, the receiving—"

"That was your building." Jake's voice carried a mixture of wonder and something else, something that made Ruby's chest tight. "Ruby, you didn't just buy any foreclosed property. You bought the other half of the operation."

They stared at each other across Rose's documents, the implications settling between them like snow falling on Main Street.

"We need to look," Ruby said finally. "If there's access from your basement, and access from mine—"

"We must find the chamber." Jake stood up abruptly, the careful distance forgotten in the face of historical discovery. "Now. Before we lose our nerve."

"Tommy's still here, right?"

"Putting in some extra shelves in the basement." Jake was already gathering the documents, his movements quick with purpose. "He'll have the tools we need."

Ruby followed Jake toward the basement stairs, and for the first time in three days, the awkwardness between them felt secondary to something bigger. This wasn't about Derek's offer or impossible decisions or feelings they couldn't act on. This was about uncovering a truth that had been buried for ninety years.

This was about understanding what their buildings were always meant to be.

The basement smelled of fresh lumber and Tommy's seemingly inexhaustible supply of energy drinks. Ruby found him in the northwest corner, wrestling with a heavy-duty shelf bracket.

"Tommy," Jake called down the stairs. "We need your help with something."

Tommy looked up, taking in Jake's intensity and Ruby's presence with a grin that suggested he was reading way too much into the situation. "Finally making up after whatever weird thing has been happening with you two?"

"We're not—" Ruby started.

"There's no weird thing—" Jake said at the same time.

Tommy's grin widened. "Right. Sure. What do you need?"

Jake spread the map on Tommy's work table, pointing to the section that showed the mysterious chamber. "We think there's a sealed access point somewhere in this corner. Something that leads to an underground space beneath Main Street."

Tommy studied the map, his expression shifting from amused to professionally intrigued. "Huh. You know, I was just trying to anchor this bracket, and my anchor bit won't catch. Keeps drilling into nothing." He gestured to the wall. "Like there's empty space behind here."

"Can we open it?" Ruby asked.

"Legally or practically?"

"Both?"

Tommy walked to the wall, running his hands over the surface with the practiced touch of someone who understood buildings the way Ruby understood coffee. "This section was definitely sealed later. Plastered over, probably decades ago." He tapped it with his knuckles, and the hollow sound echoed. "Yeah, there's definitely space back here."

"Can you open it without bringing down the ceiling?" Jake's voice was carefully steady, but Ruby caught the excitement underneath.

"Oh, I can open it." Tommy grabbed a pry bar from his tool belt. "Whether you're ready for what's behind it—that's the real question."

Ruby and Jake exchanged glances, and something passed between them that felt like the old understanding, before Derek and corporate offers and impossible choices had complicated everything.

"Open it," they said together.

Tommy started carefully chipping away at the plaster, working to avoid damaging the surrounding wall. "You know, when I signed up to help with this renovation, I figured I'd be dealing with old wiring and maybe some questionable plumbing. This is way more interesting."

"Consider it a bonus feature," Ruby said, though her attention was fixed on the wall Tommy was systematically revealing.

THE PLASTER CAME AWAY in chunks, and behind it, Ruby could see older brick. Tommy kept working, and soon he'd exposed a small wooden door, maybe four feet high, built directly into the wall. The wood was dark with age but surprisingly intact, hinges rusted but still attached.

"Should I?" Tommy asked, hand on the rusted handle.

Jake handed Ruby a flashlight, then took one for himself. "Yeah. Open it."

The door protested, hinges shrieking after decades of disuse, but Tommy's strength won the battle. The door swung inward, revealing a passage that shouldn't exist—brick-lined, maybe three feet wide, disappearing into darkness.

"Holy shit," Tommy breathed. "There's actually a tunnel under Main Street."

Ruby felt Jake's presence beside her, both of them staring into the darkness that connected their buildings. Literally connected them, through earth and brick and ninety years of hidden history.

"We're going in," Jake said quietly.

"Obviously," Ruby agreed.

"Obviously?" Tommy looked between them. "This is either really cool or really stupid. Maybe both."

"Very on-brand for me," Ruby said but her hand found Jake's in the darkness, holding on like he was the only solid thing in a shifting world.

Jake's fingers closed around hers, steady and warm. "Together?"

"Together."

The passage was narrow enough that they had to go single file, Jake first with his flashlight, Ruby close behind, Tommy bringing up the rear with his phone light and running commentary about structural integrity.

"The brickwork is actually pretty good," Tommy observed. "Whoever built this knew what they were doing. This isn't just some hastily dug tunnel—this is engineered."

Ruby's flashlight beam caught mortar lines, careful construction, evidence of planning and skill. "Your great-grandfather did this?"

"Maybe. Or maybe he found it and adapted it." Jake's voice echoed slightly in the confined space. "Rose said the sewer system was rerouted in the 1910s. If they abandoned this section, it would have been perfect for—"

The tunnel widened, and they stepped into a chamber that took Ruby's breath away.

It wasn't large, but it *felt* vast — the ceiling arched high above them in perfect symmetry, brickwork forming ribs like a cathedral nave. Their flashlights swept upward, tracing those curves until they vanished into darkness. Every surface seemed to hold the hush of time, the reverence of a place that had once meant something.

Dust motes drifted in their beams like incense smoke. The walls were lined with old barrels and crates, their stenciled lettering faded to ghosts. Along the far wall, an inscription carved into the brick caught the light: *Together we serve the town.*

Ruby stared, throat tight. "It's beautiful," she whispered.

"It is," Tommy said, his voice was hushed, as he too felt the weight of it.

Jake's beam swept over the arching ceiling again, reverent. "No," he said softly. "It's more than that. It's a monument. To what they built together."

"This is it," Jake whispered, and Ruby heard the awe in his voice. "This is the main chamber. This is where it all happened."

Ruby moved deeper into the space, her flashlight catching

details that made her heart race. Dates carved into the wall—1922 through 1933. Names she didn't recognize. And in the corner, careful handwriting that looked like the same script from Rose's documents: "Partnership with J. Fairfield—Sullivan serves, Fairfield stores. Together we serve the town."

Tommy had gone quiet, his phone light steady on the carved words. When Ruby glanced at him, she saw his jaw working, eyes bright. "He didn't just survive Prohibition," Tommy said quietly. "He built something that mattered. With a partner. With trust." He looked at Jake, his voice thick with emotion. "This is what it means to be a Sullivan. Building something bigger than yourself."

"Jake," Ruby said, her voice breaking slightly. "Look at this."

Jake joined her at the inscription, his flashlight illuminating words that had been hidden for ninety years. Ruby watched his expression shift as he read, understanding dawning in his eyes.

"My great-grandfather and John Fairfield. They weren't just neighbors. They were partners."

"Your building was the front," Ruby said quietly, pieces clicking into place. "The legitimate business, the public face. But my building—Fairfield's building—that was the storage facility. The warehouse."

Tommy had moved to the metal shelf, carefully unwrapping an oilcloth to reveal a leather-bound ledger. "Guys? You're going to want to see this."

The ledger was remarkably well-preserved, the oilcloth having protected it from the worst of the moisture. Tommy held it gently while Ruby shone her light on the pages, and Jake read aloud:

"'July 15, 1925. Delivery to J.F. Building, rear entrance. 6 cases, special blend. Stored underground, distributed as needed.'" Jake flipped through pages, his voice growing more certain with each entry. "'August 3, 1925. Partnership meeting with J. Fairfield. Agreed on new distribution schedule. His building receives and stores, mine serves and sells. System working well. Customers satisfied.'"

Ruby felt something shift in her chest, a realization so profound it almost hurt. "I bought half of a legacy."

Jake looked at her across the ledger, his face illuminated by the flashlight glow, and Ruby saw her own wonder reflected in his expression. "These buildings were never supposed to work alone. They're two halves of the same operation."

"Two halves of the same story," Ruby corrected softly.

Jake was quiet for a moment, studying the dates carved into the wall. "1922 through 1933. The partnership lasted through all of Prohibition."

"What happened after?" Ruby asked. "After it ended?"

Jake shook his head slowly. "I don't know. Rose never mentioned what happened to Fairfield's side. The building must have changed hands dozens of times over ninety years."

Tommy cleared his throat. "Not to interrupt this moment, but should we check if there's access from Ruby's side? Complete the circuit?"

The passage continued beyond the chamber, narrower but clearly leading toward Scattered Beans. They followed it in silence, Ruby's mind racing with implications. The tunnel curved slightly, following what must have been the original sewer line, until it reached another door.

"This should open into your basement," Jake said, trying the handle. It didn't budge. "Stuck. Probably swollen with age."

"Let's go upstairs and check from my side," Ruby suggested.

They retraced their steps through the chamber and passage, emerged into Sullivan's basement, and climbed back to street level. The December cold hit them as they crossed Main Street, snow falling softly under the streetlights.

In Scattered Beans' basement, Ruby led them to the back corner, behind the shelving unit she'd been meaning to organize for weeks. "I never really looked back here closely," she admitted.

Tommy and Jake moved the shelves aside, revealing the wall behind. And there it was—a door, identical to the one in Sullivan's basement, just barely visible under years of dust and neglect.

"It's here," Ruby breathed. "It's actually here."

Tommy tried the handle from this side, and with some effort, the door creaked open, revealing the passage beyond.

Ruby stared at the open doorway. The passage she'd just walked through with Jake, the chamber they'd discovered together, the partnership that had been hidden for ninety years—it all connected to her building. Her basement. Her dream.

"The whole operation depended on both buildings working together," Jake said quietly. "When Fairfield's business ended and this building changed hands over the years, the partnership broke. And stayed broken."

"Until now," Ruby whispered.

Tommy's phone buzzed, breaking the moment. "That's Zara. I promised I'd meet her for dinner." He looked between them, grinning. "You two going to be okay exploring the rest of this without me?"

"Yeah," Jake said. "We're good."

After Tommy left, Ruby and Jake stood in her basement, the open passage between them, surrounded by evidence of a partnership that predated their conflict by a hundred years.

"I need to tell Rose," Jake said finally. "She sent those documents because she knew there was more to find."

Ruby looked at the passage, the careful construction, the evidence of collaboration, trust and two people who'd found a way to build something meaningful by working together.

"This changes everything," she whispered.

Jake was quiet for a long moment. When he spoke, his voice was carefully neutral, that protective distance settling back between them. "Does it?"

Ruby understood what he was asking. Does it change your decision about Derek? Does it change whether you're staying or leaving? Does it change us?

"I don't know," she admitted, and watched something flicker across Jake's expression—disappointment, maybe, or resignation.

"Jake, this isn't just my building anymore. It's part of your family's history. Part of the town's history. If I leave—"

"It's still your building, Ruby. Your choice." Jake stepped back, creating physical distance that felt like emotional walls going up. "We can figure out the historical preservation stuff regardless. The chamber, the documents, the tours—none of that depends on you staying."

But his eyes said: Everything depends on you staying.

Ruby felt tears prick at her eyes, frustrated and overwhelmed and impossibly torn. "That's not fair."

"What's not fair?"

"You being understanding. You giving me space. You acting like this doesn't matter when I can see—" Ruby gestured helplessly between them. "When I can see it matters to you."

Jake's jaw tightened. "Of course it matters. Ruby, it all matters. This discovery, the history, what we've built together. You—" He stopped, running a hand through his hair. "But I'm not going to pressure you to stay because of historical significance or family legacy or —" His voice cracked slightly. "Or feelings that might not be enough."

"That's not what I—" Ruby started, but Jake held up a hand.

"You asked for time to think. Take it. Think about what you want, where you want to be, what kind of life you want to build. Not for me. Not for Millbrook Falls. For you." He moved toward the passage, pausing at the entrance. "I'll be at Sullivan's if you need me. For the historical stuff. For documenting the discovery. For anything that doesn't involve making your decision harder."

Jake disappeared into the passage, leaving Ruby alone in her basement with the weight of ninety years of history and two weeks until Derek wanted her answer.

Ruby stood in her apartment window that night, looking down at both buildings—hers and Jake's, separated by Main Street but connected underneath by brick and history and something that felt like fate.

Her phone sat on the counter next to Derek's offer, his statistics and questions. What are your actual margins? Even successful shops barely scrape by. The numbers made logical sense. The safe choice made logical sense.

But Ruby's eyes kept drifting to the street below, to the buildings that had been designed to work together, to the partnership that had been broken for ninety years until she'd stumbled into Millbrook Falls with seventeen syrups and a moving truck full of chaos.

Her phone buzzed with a text from Jake:

JAKE

Thank you for today. For finding this with me. Whatever you decide about Derek, I'm glad we discovered this together.

Ruby stared at the message, her thumb hovering over the reply button, but couldn't find words that felt adequate. What could she say? 'I'm glad too' felt hollow. 'I don't want to leave' felt premature. 'I think I'm falling in love with you' felt terrifying.

She set down the phone and looked at her grandmother's photo instead, the one she'd placed in her kitchen window the day she moved in.

"What do I do?" Ruby whispered to the photo, to the memory of the woman who'd believed she could do anything. "How do I choose between security and faith? Between what makes sense and what feels right?"

Her grandmother smiled back from the frame, silent and patient, offering no answers.

Ruby's gaze shifted to the street below again. Through Jake's window, she could see him in Sullivan's, cleaning up, probably processing everything they'd discovered.

Two buildings. One partnership. Ninety years of waiting for someone to complete what had been broken.

Ruby knew one thing with certainty: whatever she decided, nothing would ever be the same after today. They'd uncovered more than just a hidden chamber or historical artifacts. They'd uncovered the truth about what their buildings were meant to be.

Now Ruby just had to decide if she was brave enough to be part of completing that story, or smart enough to walk away before the odds caught up with her.

Outside, snow continued to fall on Main Street, covering both buildings in pristine layers, making everything look clean and possible and new. Ruby pressed her palm against the cold window glass and whispered to the silence:

"Two weeks. I have two weeks to figure out the rest of my life."

CHAPTER
Fourteen

The speakeasy discovery hadn't left Ruby alone for a single minute. Every sound in Scattered Beans—the hum of the espresso machine, the clatter of cups, the low chatter of customers—seemed to echo against that hidden tunnel beneath her feet.

She caught herself glancing at the floor more than once that morning, half expecting to hear the ghosts of jazz and laughter drifting up through the pipes. The chamber felt like a heartbeat now—steady, constant, pulsing just below the surface.

Jake hadn't texted since they'd sealed it back up the night before. That wasn't unusual for him—he respected space—but the quiet felt heavier than usual. There were things neither of them had said down there, things that couldn't be boxed up like the ledgers and bottles they'd found.

Ruby tried to focus on the steady rhythm of her morning routine—refilling syrups, wiping down counters, greeting the regulars who had no idea anything had changed. But everything had changed.

When the bell above the door chimed, she looked up automatically—and her heart stuttered.

Jake.

He stood just inside the doorway, snow still dusting his flannel sleeves, his expression unreadable but intent.

"Hey," he said, hands tucked into his pockets in that casual, careful way that was never really casual. "Got a minute?"

Ruby's hands fumbled the plate she was holding. She caught it before it fell, but not before Jake noticed her reaction. Something flickered across his face—awareness, maybe, or the same nervous energy that was making Ruby's pulse race.

"Yeah. Sure." Ruby set down the plate with exaggerated care. "What's up?"

Jake glanced around at the few customers scattered throughout Scattered Beans, then back at Ruby. "Maybe somewhere more private? About yesterday. The chamber."

Ruby's stomach flipped. She nodded toward her office—really just a converted storage closet with a desk—and Jake followed her back, closing the door behind them.

The space felt impossibly small with both of them in it. Ruby could smell that woodsy scent that always clung to Jake, could see the way he'd buttoned his flannel shirt wrong that morning like he'd been distracted getting dressed. The intimacy of noticing that detail made her chest tight.

"We need to talk about what happens next," Jake said, leaning against her desk. "With the discoveries. The speakeasy and the chamber."

"Right. Yes. Obviously." Ruby was rambling. She made herself stop. "What were you thinking?"

"Historical society. Mayor Greene. We'll probably get media attention—regional papers at least. It's the kind of story that travels." Jake ran a hand through his hair, making it stick up. "And we need to document everything properly—both the speakeasy room and the junction chamber. Create a proper catalog for the historical society."

"When?"

"This afternoon? After lunch rush? Mayor Greene is sending Carol Moore from the historical society—she specializes in historical documentation." Jake's eyes found hers. "It's both our buildings. Both our—"

"Both our discovery," Ruby finished.

The prospect of being in those confined spaces again with Jake—in the speakeasy where she'd kissed his cheek, in the chamber where they'd stood so close in the darkness—made Ruby's breath catch.

"Both of us," she managed. "Together."

"If that's okay."

Ruby met his gaze and saw the same awareness she felt, the same knowledge that this afternoon would be charged with everything they weren't saying. "It's your family's legacy. I wouldn't document it without you."

"It's both our legacy now," Jake said quietly. "That's what we found, Ruby. Evidence that these buildings were always meant to work together."

Ruby couldn't speak. The metaphor was too obvious, too perfect, too painful when she still didn't know if she was staying or leaving.

Jake must have seen something in her expression because he straightened up, putting professional distance between them. "Two o'clock? I'll meet you in my basement with Carol and Tommy."

"Okay."

Jake moved toward the door, then paused with his hand on the handle. "Ruby?"

"Yeah?"

"Whatever happens—whatever you decide about Derek—I'm glad we found it together."

He left before Ruby could find words to respond.

AT TWO O'CLOCK, Ruby descended into Jake's basement to find Jake and Tommy already there with Carol Moore from the Millbrook Falls Historical Society. The older woman had two camera bags slung over her shoulder and was setting up her equipment, while Tommy stood beside his brother with an expression of quiet pride.

"Ms. Ashworth," Carol said, extending her hand. "Mayor Greene speaks very highly of your preservation instincts. Two discoveries—the speakeasy room and the junction chamber. This is quite remarkable."

"Thank you for coming on such short notice."

"Are you kidding? This is the kind of find historians dream about." Carol adjusted one of her camera bags. "Let's start with the speakeasy room, shall we?"

Ruby followed Jake into the hidden room, acutely aware that this was where she'd kissed his cheek in her excitement, where everything between them had shifted.

The speakeasy looked different in Carol's professional LED lighting—less mysterious, more obviously historical. But still magical. The bottles on the shelves, the bar counter, the gramophone in the corner, all of it preserved by accident and waiting to tell its story.

"Extraordinary," Carol breathed, already photographing. "The preservation is remarkable. Now, I'll need some shots with you in them for scale and context."

For the next twenty minutes, Carol directed them around the speakeasy. Ruby held up recipe cards while Jake stood beside the bar. Tommy positioned himself near the shelves, his hand resting on the wooden crates with reverence.

"This is where it started," Tommy said quietly, looking at his brother. "Where great-grandfather built something that mattered."

"And where it connects to," Jake added, gesturing toward the basement wall. "The chamber under the street—that's where we see the full partnership."

"Then let's document that next," Carol said, packing up her equipment.

They made their way through Sullivan's basement to the

passage entrance. The narrow corridor felt even more confined with four people and camera equipment, but they moved single-file—Jake leading, Ruby behind him, then Carol, with Tommy bringing up the rear.

When they emerged into the junction chamber, Tommy went very still.

"Every time I'm down here," he said quietly, emotion thick in his voice, "I can't believe this is real. What they built together. The trust that took."

Jake's hand briefly touched Tommy's shoulder—understanding, connection, shared legacy.

Carol was already setting up lights, examining the carved inscription on the wall with professional fascination. "Partnership with J. Fairfield—Sullivan serves, Fairfield stores. Together we serve the town." She looked up at them. "This is the story, isn't it? Not just survival during Prohibition, but collaboration"

"That's exactly what it is," Ruby said softly.

Carol began photographing the chamber systematically—the walls, the crates, the carved dates, the map showing both buildings. "Now, I need you three by that inscription. This is about family and partnership—both historical and present."

Ruby shot Jake a look, but Tommy was already moving toward the wall, his fingers tracing the words their great-grandfather had carved ninety years ago.

Every posed shot felt loaded with meaning. Ruby stood between Jake and Tommy, three people connected by history they'd uncovered together. Jake's proximity made her hyperaware of every breath, every shift of his weight, the warmth radiating from him in the cool underground space.

Ruby was examining one of the crates when her foot slipped on the uneven brick floor. She gasped, arms windmilling, and suddenly Jake was there, hands catching her waist, steadying her against his chest.

"Careful," he said, voice rougher than the single word warranted.

Ruby's hands had landed on his shoulders, gripping his flannel shirt for balance. They were inches apart, close enough that she could see the flecks of gold in his amber eyes, could feel his breath against her face.

"There you go," Jake added softly, those three words that had become their private language, a promise wrapped in casualness.

But neither of them moved apart. The chamber felt smaller suddenly, the air thicker. Jake's thumb brushed across her hip—accidentally or deliberately, Ruby couldn't tell—and she felt the touch everywhere.

"Ruby," Jake said, and the way he said her name was almost a question.

Ruby's gaze dropped to his mouth, then back to his eyes. "Jake, I—"

Carol's camera shutter clicked, breaking the moment.

"Perfect," Carol said matter-of-factly, reviewing the shot. "That's exactly the kind of authentic moment that will resonate with people. The discovery, the partnership, the connection."

Ruby stepped back from Jake quickly, her cheeks burning. Tommy was watching them with barely concealed amusement.

Jake cleared his throat, his hand falling away from Ruby's waist. "Did you get everything you need?"

"Almost. Let me get a few shots in the passage itself—it's part of the story, how the two buildings literally connect." Carol moved toward the tunnel leading to Ruby's basement.

Tommy moved closer to his brother, his voice low. "Jake, man. Every time I'm down here, I think about what great-grandfather built. Not just the business—the trust. The partnership." His voice grew thick. "About believing that working together makes you stronger than working alone."

Jake's expression softened as he looked at his younger brother. "Yeah. It was about that."

"And you found it," Tommy continued, his gaze shifting to include Ruby. "You two. Just like they built it—together."

They followed Carol through the passage to Ruby's basement,

documenting the complete circuit. When they finally emerged back into Scattered Beans, dusty and exhausted, Carol was beaming.

"This is going to make an incredible presentation for the town council," she said, already organizing her equipment. "Two buildings, one story. Mayor Greene is going to be thrilled."

After Carol left, the three of them stood in Scattered Beans, the weight of documentation settling around them.

"Thanks for including me," Tommy said, looking between them. "This is... it means a lot. Being part of preserving this."

"It's your family too," Jake said simply.

Tommy grinned, squeezing Ruby's shoulder as he passed. "And Ruby made it possible to find it all. Both of you should be really proud."

After Tommy left, Ruby and Jake stood in Scattered Beans, not quite looking at each other.

"Thanks for doing this," Ruby said finally. "The documentation. All of it."

"We're partners." Jake's emphasis on the word made it feel like more than historical fact. "In this, at least."

Ruby wanted to ask what he meant by "in this, at least." Wanted to close the distance between them and finish what they'd started in the chamber. Wanted to tell him she was already choosing, that her decision was forming even if she couldn't say it out loud yet.

But Jake was already moving toward the door, putting physical space between them again.

"I should get back. Holiday rush."

"Yeah. Me too."

He paused at the door, turned back. "Ruby? About what almost—about earlier—"

"Don't." Ruby couldn't handle him apologizing for touching her, for that moment when everything had felt possible. "Please don't."

Jake nodded slowly. "Okay. But you should know—" He stopped, seemed to reconsider. "Never mind. I'll see you later."

After he left, Ruby stood alone in her shop, touching the place on her waist where Jake's hands had been, and tried not to think about Christmas, how it suddenly felt like both forever away and not nearly enough time.

THE NEXT FEW days blurred together in a haze of holiday customers, newly opened coordinated tours, and the aftermath of Friday's town council presentation where everyone had enthusiastically endorsed their partnership—both historical and otherwise.

Jake had been right about the partnership angle—people loved it. They loved hearing the story of two buildings designed to work together, loved seeing the underground chamber that connected them, loved the romance of illegal speakeasies and community cooperation during hard times.

What they loved most, Ruby realized, was seeing her and Jake work together.

They'd developed a rhythm without planning it. Jake would start tours in his basement, explaining Sullivan's role as the legitimate front business. Then he'd lead customers through the passage—narrow enough that they had to go single file, creating anticipation—into the junction chamber. Ruby would be waiting there with lanterns and stories about her building's role as the storage facility. Together they'd explain the logistics, the partnership, the trust required to make it work.

Then Ruby would lead everyone through to her basement, showing the receiving entrance, explaining how deliveries would arrive at the back alley. Jake would follow, answering questions, adding details about his great-grandfather's operations.

Every tour felt like an elaborate dance. Every meeting in the chamber felt charged with awareness. Every moment of their practiced coordination reminded Ruby how well they fit together.

It was Zara who finally said what Ruby had been thinking, pulling her aside after watching yet another tour group leave with stars in their eyes.

"You look like someone who's discovered a treasure and doesn't know if she gets to keep it."

Ruby laughed, but it came out shaky. "That's... actually pretty accurate."

"The Jake situation?"

"The Jake situation. The Derek situation. The entire future of my life situation."

Zara set down her cup and leaned forward. "Can I tell you something? As someone who's been watching this unfold from her laptop corner?"

"Please."

"That man watches you like you're the first sunny day after a long winter. And you look at him like he's home." Zara's voice was gentle but firm. "I'm working on a romance novel, Ruby. I know the real thing when I see it."

"It's not that simple."

"It never is. But sometimes the complicated choice is the right one." Zara squeezed Ruby's hand. "Just... don't let fear make your decision for you. Fear of failure, fear of commitment, fear of being happy. Whatever you're afraid of."

After Zara left, Ruby sat alone in Scattered Beans, the evening quiet settling around her. Through her window, she could see Jake in Sullivan's, closing up for the night. He moved with that methodical efficiency she'd come to recognize, straightening chairs and wiping counters like meditation.

Ruby's phone buzzed with a text from Vi:

VI

How'd the presentation go?

RUBY

Everyone thinks Jake and I are a perfect partnership

VI

Are they wrong?

Ruby stared at her phone, at the question she'd been avoiding for weeks.

RUBY

I don't know

VI

Liar

Ruby smiled despite herself.

RUBY

Fine. They're not wrong. But that doesn't mean I know what to do about it

VI

When does Derek want his answer?

RUBY

After Christmas

VI

Then stop torturing yourself until then. Enjoy Christmas. Meet Rose. Let yourself have this before you decide

It was good advice. Ruby just wasn't sure she could follow it when every day brought her closer to a decision she wasn't ready to make.

IN THE EVENING of December 13th, after the last tour of the day, Ruby was closing up when her phone rang. Jake's name on the screen made her heart skip.

"Hey," she answered.

"Hey. Are you still at the shop?"

"Just locking up. Why?"

"Can you come over? To my place?" Jake's voice held something Ruby couldn't quite identify. "Rose just called. She wants to talk to both of us about the discovery. She's... pretty emotional about it."

Ruby's stomach flipped. "Both of us?"

"She insisted. Said it wouldn't be right to hear about it without you there." A pause. "Is that okay?"

Ruby looked across the street at Sullivan's, at Jake's apartment windows glowing above the shop. "Yeah. Of course. Give me five minutes."

She hung up, locked Scattered Beans with shaking hands, and crossed Main Street wondering what Rose would say, how it would feel to be included in this family moment, whether it would make her decision harder or easier.

Jake was waiting at his apartment door when she arrived, his expression a mixture of excitement and nervousness that made him look younger somehow.

"Thanks for coming," he said, ushering her inside. "I know this is probably weird—"

"It's not weird." Ruby settled onto his couch, "She's important to you. The discovery is important. It makes sense she'd want to hear about it from both of us."

Jake sat beside her, close enough that their knees almost touched, and pulled out his phone. "Ready?"

Ruby nodded, and Jake called Rose on video chat.

The woman who appeared on screen had Jake's warm eyes and a smile that immediately made Ruby feel welcome despite her nerves. Rose looked to be in her late seventies, with silver hair pulled back in a neat bun and laugh lines that suggested a lifetime of finding joy in small things.

"Jacob!" Rose's voice was warm with affection. "And this must be Ruby. Oh my dear, let me look at you."

Ruby felt suddenly self-conscious under Rose's scrutiny, but the older woman's expression held only kindness and what looked like approval.

"She's lovely, Jacob. You didn't tell me she was this lovely."

"Rose," Jake said, a warning note in his voice that suggested this wasn't the first time his grandmother had embarrassed him.

"Oh hush. I'm old. I can say what I want." Rose turned her attention back to Ruby. "Ruby, dear, Jake's told me so much about you. The coffee shop owner who came to town and somehow convinced my stubborn grandson to actually make changes to the shop."

Ruby couldn't help but smile.

"The best things usually are accidents." Rose's expression grew more serious. "Now, Jacob said you've made a discovery. About the buildings. Tell me everything."

For the next twenty minutes, Ruby and Jake took turns explaining. The documents Rose had sent, the mysterious references to underground storage, the discovery of the sealed passage, the junction chamber beneath Main Street. Jake showed her Carol's photographs while Ruby described the artifacts, the ledgers, the wall inscription about partnership.

Rose listened with increasing emotion, her eyes shining with tears by the time they finished.

"Oh my dears," she said, her voice thick. "Oh, this is—I knew there was more to the story. I knew it."

"You knew about the partnership?" Jake asked. "About Fairfield's building being part of the operation?"

"Not the details. But my father—your great-grandfather, Jacob—he used to tell me stories when I was a girl. About how he always said the success of Sullivan's Coffee wasn't just about the shop itself. It was about the cooperation, the partnerships that made everything work." Rose dabbed at her eyes with a handkerchief. "He said there was a building across the street that was essential to the operation, but he never told me which one or why. Just that it was a partnership built on trust."

Ruby's throat tightened. "My building—what was Fairfield's import business—that was the partner."

"And you found it," Rose said, looking between them with obvious emotion. "You two found it together. Just like you were meant to."

The weight of that observation settled over Ruby like snow. *Just like you were meant to.*

"Rose," Jake said carefully. "It's Ruby's building now. She's the one who gets to decide what happens with it."

"Of course it is. And she'll make the right choice." Rose's gaze fixed on Ruby with surprising intensity. "My dear, do you know what the most important thing about that partnership was?"

Ruby shook her head, not trusting her voice.

"It wasn't just about logistics or business sense. It was about two people choosing to trust each other, to build something together that neither could build alone. It was about believing that partnership was stronger than doing it alone, even when doing it alone felt safer."

Ruby felt Jake go very still beside her.

"Your great-grandfather and John Fairfield took a risk on each other," Rose continued. "They could have run their operations separately, could have competed for customers, could have protected themselves by staying independent. But they chose partnership. They chose trust. And because of that choice, both businesses thrived for years. The town benefited. People were happy."

"When the partnership broke," Ruby said quietly. "When the buildings stopped working together."

"Yes. And it took ninety years to find someone brave enough to complete what was broken." Rose's smile was gentle but knowing. "Ruby, dear, I don't know what decisions you're facing. Jacob mentioned something about a corporate offer, but he won't tell me details because he says it's your business. But I want you to know something."

"What?"

"Partnerships—real partnerships, built on trust and respect and shared purpose—those are rare. Worth fighting for. Worth choosing, even when choosing them feels risky." Rose looked at Jake with obvious affection, then back at Ruby. "I've watched Jacob his whole life be careful. Cautious. Protecting the family legacy by refusing to change anything, by playing it safe. And then you came to town with your new ideas, and suddenly he's renovating and taking risks and discovering hidden history. You did that, dear. You helped him see that honoring the past doesn't mean being afraid of the future."

Ruby couldn't speak because of the the lump in her throat.

"So whatever you decide," Rose finished, "make sure you're not letting fear make the choice for you. Make sure you're choosing what you want, not what feels safest."

After they said goodbye and Jake ended the call, they sat in silence for a long moment.

"She's not subtle," Jake said finally.

"No." Ruby's voice came out rough. "But she's not wrong either."

Jake turned to face her fully. "Ruby, you don't have to—Rose doesn't understand the full situation. The statistics Derek mentioned, the risks—"

"She understands partnership." Ruby met his eyes. "She understands that sometimes the brave choice is the right one, even if it's scary."

"Is it?" Jake's voice was barely above a whisper. "Scary?"

"Terrifying," Ruby admitted. "Jake, I'm terrified. Of failing. Of letting you down. Of making the wrong choice and regretting it. Of—" She stopped, the words catching.

"Of what?"

"Of wanting this so much that I'm blind to reality. Of letting my feelings for you override practical concerns. Of choosing with my heart when I should be choosing with my mind."

Jake was quiet for a moment, then: "What if your heart knows something your mind doesn't?"

Ruby looked at him, at this steady, wonderful man who'd been patient while she figured herself out, who'd given her space while making it impossible not to see what she'd be losing, who'd been there for every crisis since she arrived.

"Rose arrives Christmas Eve," Jake said quietly. "Dinner at my place, six o'clock. You're still coming?"

"I promised."

"Good." Jake's hand found hers, his fingers lacing through hers with a naturalness that made Ruby's chest ache. "Because she's been waiting months to meet you. And because—" He stopped, started again. "Because I want you there. Whatever happens after Christmas, whatever you decide, I want you there for Christmas."

Ruby squeezed his hand, unable to find words for the tangle of emotions in her chest—fear and hope and longing and terror all mixed together.

"I'll be there," she whispered. "Jake, I'll be there."

He walked her to the door, and this time when they parted, he kissed her forehead—gentle and sweet and somehow more devastating than any passionate kiss could have been.

"Eleven days until Christmas," he said against her hair. "And then you'll meet Rose. And then—"

"And then I'll decide." Ruby finished.

Jake nodded, his arms coming around her in a hug that felt like goodbye and hello and everything in between. "Whatever you decide, Ruby, I'll understand."

Ruby held him tight, breathing in his scent, memorizing the feeling of being held by him, and let herself imagine—just for a moment—what it would be like to choose this. To choose him. To choose partnership over safety.

Then she stepped back, smiled through threatening tears, and crossed Main Street to her apartment where Derek's offer waited, and eleven days until Christmas felt like both forever and not nearly enough time.

But as Ruby stood at her window that night, looking across at Jake's building where the lights had gone dark, she realized something had shifted. Rose's words about partnership, about choosing trust over fear, had planted something in her chest that felt dangerously like certainty.

The buildings below stood silent in the December darkness, connected by tunnels and history and ninety years of waiting for someone to complete what had been broken.

Ruby pressed her forehead against the cold glass and whispered to her reflection: "What if Rose is right? What if the brave choice isn't the safe one?"

Outside, snow continued to fall on Main Street, covering both coffee shops in white. Making everything look possible. Making everything look new.

Ruby closed her eyes and felt the weight of the decision settling into her bones—not lighter, but clearer somehow. Rose had given her permission to want this. To choose with her heart instead of her fear.

She just had to be brave enough to actually do it.

CHAPTER
Fifteen

December 23rd dawned cold and clear, the kind of winter morning that made Millbrook Falls look like a Christmas card. Ruby watched from her apartment window as Jake opened Sullivan's, steady and reliable as always.

Tomorrow, Rose would be here. And Ruby still hadn't decided what she was going to say when Jake's grandmother inevitably asked about her plans.

The days since Rose's phone call had passed in a haze of peppermint mochas and coordinated tours and stolen glances that meant everything and nothing. She and Jake had fallen into a rhythm that felt both natural and impossible—morning coffee prep in their separate shops, tours through the day, brief conversations that stayed carefully professional, loaded looks that said everything they weren't saying out loud.

But today felt different. Charged. Like the air before a thunderstorm.

Ruby was reorganizing the sugar packets for the third time that morning—by color, then by brand, then back to color again—when the bells chimed and Zara breezed in, bringing cold air and the scent of winter.

"Emergency best friend check-in," Zara announced, unwinding her scarf. "You've been dodging my texts."

"I've been busy—" Ruby knocked over the newly organized sugar packets. "Okay, that's not helping my case. I mean, not dodging. Just. You know. Holiday rush and tours and the chamber thing, which is still—" She was gathering sugar packets frantically, avoiding eye contact. "I'm fine. Totally fine."

"You've reorganized those packets like four times since I walked in."

"Three times. And they needed it. People just grab them randomly, no system, complete chaos—" Ruby set down a pink packet, picked it up again. "Which is rich coming from me, I know, the chaos coffee lady lecturing about organization, but—"

"Ruby." Zara leaned against the counter, her dark eyes sharp with concern. "You're spiraling. Talk to me."

Ruby's hands stilled. "I meet Rose tomorrow."

"Jake's grandmother. I know. You've mentioned it."

"About fifty times, which is probably obsessive, but I can't stop thinking about it." Ruby looked up finally. "Zara, what do I even say to her?"

"Start with hello?"

"But after hello! She's going to ask about my plans, about the business, about why I'm even here, and what am I supposed to say? 'Hi, nice to meet you, I might be abandoning your grandson right after we discovered this amazing historical thing, but don't worry, I have statistics'?" Ruby was talking faster now. "That's not a good first impression. That's a terrible first impression. That's the kind of impression that makes grandmothers hate you forever."

"Breathe," Zara said gently.

Ruby sucked in air. "I'm breathing. See? Very oxygenated."

"You're terrified."

"I'm not—" Ruby started, then her shoulders sagged. "Okay. Yes. Terrified. But not just of Rose. Of all of it. The deciding part."

"The Jake part."

Ruby's throat went tight. She picked up a sugar packet, set it down, picked up another one. "That's not—I mean, it's not just about Jake. It's about the business and the partnership and whether independent coffee shops can even survive in this market, which Derek says they can't, statistically speaking, sixty-eight percent failure rate, and—"

"Ruby."

"And yes, fine, maybe it's partly about Jake." Ruby's voice dropped to almost a whisper. "Maybe it's mostly about Jake. Maybe that's the problem—I can't tell anymore where the business decision ends and the feelings start, and you're supposed to separate those things, right? Emotions and logic. Church and state. Coffee and—" She paused, lost. "I don't know where I was going with that."

"You're in love with him," Zara said quietly.

The words hung in the air between them. Ruby opened her mouth, closed it, opened it again like a fish. "If I say it out loud—if I admit it—then it's real. And if it's real, then leaving isn't about statistics anymore. It's about—" Her voice cracked. "It's about choosing to walk away from someone I—"

She couldn't finish. Didn't need to.

Zara came around the counter and pulled Ruby into a hug. "Oh honey. Why didn't you tell me?"

"Because saying it makes it bigger," Ruby mumbled against her friend's shoulder. "Makes it matter more. Makes everything more complicated."

"Or makes it simpler."

Ruby pulled back. "How is being in love with Jake simple?"

"Because now you know what you're actually deciding." Zara's voice was gentle but firm.

"What if I'm not brave enough?"

"What if you are?" Zara squeezed her hands. "Look, I'm not saying Derek's offer isn't tempting. Security is seductive. But you light up when you talk about this place. About the tours with Jake. About Mrs. Patterson's grandchildren. About historical speakeasies and partnerships." She smiled. "That's not someone who should leave. That's someone who's already home."

A customer entered before Ruby could respond, and Zara stepped back with a knowing look.

"I have to run—holiday shopping waits for no one. But think about what I said." She headed for the door, then turned back. "And Ruby? Whatever you decide, make sure it's what *you* want. Not what's logical or safe or expected. What you actually want."

After Zara left, Ruby stood at the counter thinking about her words. About what she wanted versus what made sense. About bravery and home and the way Jake's eyes crinkled when he smiled.

She was still thinking about it when Jake appeared in her doorway carrying two cups and a paper bag.

"You looked like you needed this," he said, setting a cup in front of Ruby. "And I know you forgot to eat lunch again."

Ruby stared at the cup—her usual afternoon pick-me-up, made exactly how she liked it. "How do you even know my order?"

"Ruby." Jake's voice was soft, almost amused. "I've been watching you make coffee for months. I know you take your afternoon latte with an extra shot, light foam, and that specific sprinkle of cinnamon you do that's somewhere between a pinch and a prayer."

The intimacy of being so thoroughly known made Ruby's throat tight. "You're watching me?"

"Kind of hard not to when your shop is directly across from mine." Jake pulled a sandwich from the bag. "Turkey and swiss. Also your favorite, before you ask how I know."

They ate standing up at the counter, falling into easy conversation about the morning's tours, a customer's funny question, Tommy's latest dating drama. It felt normal and precious and terrifying—this glimpse of what everyday life could be like if Ruby stayed.

"I'm going to miss this," Ruby said before thinking, then froze.

Jake went very still. "Miss what?"

"I didn't—I mean—" Ruby scrambled. "Miss having lunch like this. Easy. When everything gets crazy after Christmas."

"Right." Jake's voice was carefully neutral. "Yeah."

But they both knew that wasn't what she'd meant. And they both knew that she'd just admitted, accidentally, that she was already mourning something she hadn't decided to leave yet.

Jake finished his sandwich in silence, then gathered up the paper bag. "I should get back. More tours this afternoon."

"Jake, wait—"

"It's fine, Ruby. Really." But his eyes said it wasn't fine at all. "I'll see you in the chamber in twenty minutes. Mrs. Patterson's group."

He left before Ruby could explain what she'd meant. Or maybe before she had to admit that she'd meant exactly what it sounded like—that some part of her was already saying goodbye, even though she didn't want to leave.

Ruby looked down at the perfectly made latte, at the evidence that Jake had been paying attention to details she didn't think anyone noticed, and felt something crack in her chest.

THE AFTERNOON PASSED in a neck-breaking speed of holiday customers and coordinated tours. Ruby and Jake maintained their professional rhythm, but there was a new tension between them now. Every time their eyes met across the underground chamber, Ruby saw the hurt from lunchtime lingering. Saw him trying to hide it, trying to be patient, trying to give her space even though it was clearly killing him.

By the time the last tour ended and the shops closed for the evening, Ruby felt wrung out. She was locking up when she heard sounds from the passage—Jake was still in the chamber.

She found him adjusting new lighting equipment, the kind with adjustable arms and multiple brightness settings.

"Oh, those are nice," Ruby said, moving closer to examine them. "Much better than the lanterns for actually seeing details."

"Thought they might help with the tours. Create atmosphere without sacrificing visibility." Jake adjusted one of the arms, angling it toward the inscription on the wall.

Ruby picked up one of the artifacts—a recipe card—repositioning it slightly under the new light. "You're good at thinking of these things. The practical stuff that makes everything work better."

They fell into an easy rhythm, Jake setting up lights while Ruby adjusted displays to take advantage of the new illumination. But the silence felt heavier than usual, charged with everything from lunch.

"Did you know that speakeasies used very specific lighting strategies?" Ruby heard herself say, falling back on historian mode. "Low and atmospheric. Made people feel anonymous, safe. Like they could be anyone in the dark."

"And we're doing the opposite," Jake said quietly. "Everything visible. No secrets."

Ruby's hands stilled on the bottle she'd been adjusting. "Yeah. I guess we are."

She moved to the next display, but her fidgeting gave her away—picking things up, setting them down, unable to settle.

"Ruby," Jake said gently.

"I know. I'm nervous." She finally stopped moving, looked at him. "This is hard, being down here. After lunch. After I said—after I accidentally admitted I was already mourning although I haven't even decided to leave yet."

"Is that what you're doing? Mourning?"

Ruby's throat tightened. "I don't know. Maybe. I just—" She gestured at the chamber around them. "We're really good at this. Working together. It feels natural."

"Yeah, we are."

The words hung between them, weighted with everything

unsaid. Ruby could feel the pull of him, the awareness that had been building since the discovery.

"That's what makes this so hard," Jake said quietly, not looking at her now.

Ruby knew he meant her leaving. Every tour, every moment of perfect coordination, was evidence of what would be lost.

"Jake, I—" She stopped, twisted her hands together. "I'm not good at this. At feelings and big decisions. I'm much better at research and facts and things that have clear answers."

"I know." Jake stepped closer. "But Ruby—staying isn't the risky choice. Not really."

"It's a sixty-eight percent failure rate."

"For coffee shops that don't have what we have."

"Which is?"

"Partnership. History." His voice dropped. "Each other."

Ruby's heart hammered. "You're talking about the buildings."

"Am I?"

The question hung in the dim light of the underground chamber, and Ruby couldn't look away from Jake's steady gaze. This moment felt important, like the next words spoken would matter in ways she couldn't take back.

But before she could respond, Jakes phone buzzed.

"Tommy. He's locked himself out of his truck. Again."

"That's the third time this month," Ruby said, grateful for the interruption even as she hated it.

"I should go help him. He's got equipment in there he needs for tomorrow's job." Jake moved toward the passage, then paused. "Ruby? Think about what I said. About partnerships. About what we have."

After he left, Ruby stood alone in the chamber surrounded by evidence of a ninety-year-old partnership, touching the inscription on the wall that read "Together we serve the town," and knew with sudden certainty that she wasn't just deciding about a business anymore.

She was deciding about Jake. About partnership. About

whether she was brave enough to believe that together was better than safe.

RUBY WAS CLOSING up for the night when Jake appeared outside her front door, hands in his pockets, looking uncertain in a way that made him somehow more endearing.

"Hey," he said when she opened the door. "Got a minute?"

"Always." The word came out before Ruby could think about what it revealed.

Jake's expression softened. "I wanted to walk you home. If that's okay."

"I live upstairs."

"I know. But humor me?"

They walked slowly around the block despite the cold, their breath forming clouds that mingled in the winter air. Christmas lights twinkled on every building, and somewhere a caroling group practiced harmonies that floated through the quiet evening.

"Tomorrow's Christmas Eve," Jake said finally. "Rose gets in around four. Dinner at six, if you're still—" He stopped, started again. "I mean, you're still coming, right?"

Ruby heard the vulnerability in his question. "I promised I would."

"I know you're nervous. About meeting her. About—everything." Jake's hands were still in his pockets, but he was close enough that their shoulders almost brushed as they walked. "But Ruby, she's going to love you. She already does, kind of. From my stories."

"You tell her stories about me?"

"Every Sunday when I call. She thinks it's hilarious that the chaos coffee lady from across the street has completely upended my life." Jake's voice held warmth despite the cold. "Her words, not mine."

"Chaos coffee lady?"

"You did move here with seventeen kinds of coffee syrups."

"I was trying to make a good impression!"

"You made an impression, alright." Jake's tone was affectionate now. "Just not the one you were going for."

They'd circled back to Main Street, stopping between their two buildings—the spot that had become theirs without either of them planning it.

Ruby's hands were shaking. She shoved them in her pockets.

Jake turned to face her, and the Christmas lights reflected in his eyes, caught those amber flecks she'd memorized. "I know I said I'd give you space. I know I said whatever you decide, I'll understand."

"But?"

"But I need you to know something before you meet Rose tomorrow. Before Christmas. Before you make your final decision." He stepped closer, his hand coming up to cup her face with a gentleness that made Ruby's knees weak. "I want you to stay. I want you to stay so much it's killing me to watch you struggle with this."

Ruby's breath caught. "Jake—"

"Let me finish. Please." His thumb brushed her cheek. "But I also know that if you stay because I asked you to, and it doesn't work out—if the business fails or you get restless or you resent giving up Derek's offer—I couldn't live with that. With being the reason you gave up security."

"You're not the reason for anything," Ruby said, her voice stronger than she expected. "This is my choice, Jake. You're just—" She stopped, tried again. "When I made my plan to come here, it was supposed to be simple. Test the market, make a logical decision based on data. Very straightforward."

"But?"

"But then there was you." Ruby's hands came up to grip his jacket. "And the discovery. And everything we've built together. And I started to realize—" Her voice wavered. "Maybe the discovery isn't showing me what to do. Maybe it's just proving what I already knew."

Jake went very still. "Which is?"

"That I'm home." The words came out quieter now, but clear. "I've been home since the day I moved here. Since you made space for me. Since you saw possibility instead of competition."

"Ruby." Her name came out rough.

"Derek's offer doesn't matter because I don't want that life anymore. The statistics do scare me but I believe in what we're building." She looked up at him, tears starting. "I'm just terrified of trusting myself. Of believing I'm brave enough to choose this."

"What if you are?" Jake pulled her closer, his forehead resting against hers. "What if we can make this work?"

"What if we can't?" The fear was still there, honest and raw. "What if I stay and lose everything?"

"Or what if you stay and find everything?" His voice was barely a whisper. "What if this is exactly where you're supposed to be?"

They stood there breathing the same air, and Ruby felt something shift—not quite certainty, but close. So close.

"Tell me you're staying," Jake whispered. "Tell me Derek's offer doesn't matter."

Ruby wanted to. God, she wanted to say yes right now, make it simple. But—

"I can't. Not yet. Not until—"

"Not until you're sure." Jake pulled back slightly, devastated but understanding. "I know. I'm sorry. I shouldn't pressure—"

"Don't apologize." Ruby's voice was fierce. "Don't apologize for telling me what you want. That's not pressure, Jake. That's honesty."

"Then let me be completely honest." His hands framed her face, tilting it up until she had to meet his eyes. "I'm in love with you, Ruby. Not just attracted to you or interested in partnership. I'm in love with you. With your chaos and your rambling and the way you see possibility in old buildings. With how you convinced me to renovate a shop I was terrified to change. With the way you make seventeen kinds of lattes and believe in historical speakeasies and can't keep a plant alive to save your life."

Ruby's eyes filled with tears. "Jake—"

"You don't have to say anything. I'm not asking you to love me back right now. I just need you to know—when you make your decision, know that love is part of the equation. My love for you. What we could have if you stay."

And then he kissed her.

It wasn't careful or questioning. This was a claiming, a declaration; everything Jake had been holding back poured into the press of his mouth against hers.

Ruby kissed him back with equal desperation, her fingers tangling in his hair, her body pressed against his as if she could merge them into one being that didn't have to make impossible choices. Jake's hands slid down to her waist, spanning her back, pulling her closer as he deepened the kiss.

The world narrowed to this: Jake's mouth on hers, the taste of coffee and winter air, the solid warmth of his body against the December cold. Christmas lights twinkled around them, snow began to fall, and Ruby thought distantly that this was what every romance novel described but she'd never believed actually existed —the perfect kiss in the perfect moment with the perfect person.

When they finally broke apart, both breathing hard, Jake kept his forehead pressed to hers.

"Tell me that meant something," he said raggedly. "Tell me I'm not alone in this."

"You're not alone." Ruby's voice was barely above a whisper. "Jake, you're not alone."

"Then stay. Please, Ruby. Choose this. Choose us."

Ruby wanted to say yes. The word was right there, pushing against her lips, ready to spill out and make everything simple. But the responsible part of her brain—the part that had heard Derek's statistics and knew the risks—held her back.

"After Christmas," she managed. "Let me meet Rose. Let me have Christmas Day to be sure. Then I'll decide."

Jake nodded slowly, stepping back even though it clearly cost him. "Okay. After Christmas."

"But know—" Ruby caught his hand before he could move too far away. "Know that whatever I decide, tonight was real. This is real."

Jake brought her hand to his lips, kissed her knuckles with a tenderness that made her ache.

He walked away, leaving Ruby standing in the snow between their buildings, touching her lips where his had been, trembling with want and fear and something that felt dangerously close to certainty.

RUBY COULDN'T SLEEP that night.

She lay in bed watching snow fall past her window, replaying Jake's kiss, his confession, his plea for her to stay. The words ran through her mind on loop: *I'm in love with you. Choose us. What if we can?*

Her phone buzzed on the nightstand. Vi, because Vi always knew when Ruby needed her, even from an hour away.

VI

Merry Christmas Eve eve! Have you decided yet?

Ruby stared at the message, then typed:

RUBY

Ask me tomorrow night

VI

That good or that bad?

Ruby looked across at Sullivan's, dark and quiet, the Christmas lights in Jake's apartment window glowing softly. She thought about his hands on her face, his voice breaking when he said he loved her, the way the kiss had felt like coming home and jumping off a cliff simultaneously.

RUBY

That complicated

VI

Did something happen?

RUBY

He kissed me. He told me he loves me. He asked me to stay.

The three dots indicating Vi was typing appeared, disappeared, appeared again. Finally:

VI

And?

RUBY

And I don't know what to do

VI

Liar. You know exactly what you want to do. You're just scared

Ruby closed her eyes, letting the truth of that settle. Vi was right. She did know. Had known for a while, probably. The discovery had just made it impossible to ignore.

RUBY

What if I choose wrong?

VI

What if you choose right and it's terrifying and perfect and everything you never knew you needed?

RUBY

You're supposed to be the practical one

VI

I'm practical enough to know that love and partnership and finding your place in the world don't come around often. And I'm practical enough to know that you've been happier in the last five months than I've seen you in years

RUBY

Even when I'm terrified?

VI

Especially when you're terrified. That's how you know it matters

After Vi signed off with promises to call tomorrow, Ruby lay in the darkness thinking about what it meant to choose. Not just to want something, but to actively choose it. To say yes to risk and uncertainty because the alternative—safety without joy—was worse.

She thought about Derek's offer sitting on her kitchen table. About the statistics he'd quoted. About the secure, predictable future he represented.

Then she thought about Jake's eyes when he'd said he loved her. About the underground chamber that connected their buildings. About the way customers smiled when they saw her and Jake work together. About Daisy's mint plant thriving on her counter, about Frank Kowalski's first specialty drink order, about Mrs. Patterson and her grandchildren.

About home. About partnership.

Ruby got out of bed and went to her window one more time. Snow was still falling, covering Main Street in pristine white. Both buildings glowed with Christmas lights—hers chaotic and colorful, Jake's elegant and warm. Two halves of a whole, connected beneath the surface by brick and history and something that felt like destiny.

She pulled out her phone and typed a message before she could overthink it:

RUBY

I'm scared

She didn't expect Jake to be awake at almost midnight. But three dots appeared immediately.

JAKE

Me too

RUBY

What if we fail?

JAKE

What if we don't?

Ruby smiled despite her tears, despite her fear, despite everything.

RUBY

See you tomorrow for Christmas Eve dinner

JAKE

Can't wait for you to meet Rose

RUBY

Jake?

JAKE

Yeah?

Ruby stared at her phone, at the message thread that had become their lifeline through complicated weeks. She wanted to tell him she loved him too. Wanted to say she'd already decided, that the kiss had sealed it, that she knew what she was choosing even if she wasn't ready to say it out loud yet.

Instead, she typed:

RUBY

Thank you for being patient with me

JAKE

Thank you for being worth waiting for

Ruby clutched her phone to her chest and looked across at his building, wondering if he was standing at his window too, looking back.

JAKE

Ruby?

RUBY

Yeah?

JAKE

Whatever you decide tomorrow—after you meet Rose, after Christmas—know that tonight mattered. That kiss mattered. You matter.

RUBY

You matter too

JAKE

Get some sleep. Big day tomorrow

RUBY

You too

JAKE

Merry Christmas Eve, Ruby

RUBY

Merry Christmas Eve, Jake

She set down her phone and climbed back into bed, but sleep remained elusive. Tomorrow she'd meet Rose. Tomorrow she'd have Christmas Eve dinner with Jake's family. Tomorrow she'd get one more piece of the puzzle that was her decision.

And then, the day after Christmas, she'd have to choose.

Ruby closed her eyes and whispered to the darkness: "Please let me choose right."

But in her heart, underneath the fear and doubt and statistics, she already knew what right looked like. It looked like Jake's eyes when he said he loved her. It looked like their buildings connected by history and possibility. It looked like home.

She just had to be brave enough to choose it.

CHAPTER Sixteen

Christmas Eve dawned bright and impossibly busy.

Both shops were packed from opening until closing—last-minute gift shoppers, people picking up holiday treats, tourists wanting one more speakeasy tour before the holiday. Ruby barely had time to think between making drinks and running tours and trying not to stare across the street every time Jake appeared in Sullivan's window.

They coordinated three tours throughout the day, meeting in the chamber with practiced ease, telling their story of partnership to delighted audiences. Every time Ruby stood beside Jake explaining how the buildings worked together, she felt the weight of metaphor. Every time someone commented on what a great team they made, she felt her decision solidifying.

By four o'clock, Ruby was exhausted and wired and terrified because Rose would be arriving any minute, and tomorrow was Christmas, and the day after that she'd have to give Derek her answer.

She was wiping down her espresso machine, who had been running beautifully all day, when her phone buzzed with a text from Jake.

JAKE

Rose is here. See you at 6?

Ruby's hands shook as she typed back:

RUBY

I'll be there

JAKE

Ruby?

RUBY

Yeah?

JAKE

Breathe. She's going to love you

RUBY

How do you know?

JAKE

Because I do

Ruby stared at those three words—*Because I do*—and felt something settle in her chest. Not quite calm, but close. The certainty that whatever happened tonight, whatever happened tomorrow, Jake was on her side.

She closed up Scattered Beans in a daze, went upstairs to change into something that looked like she'd tried but not too hard, then stood at her mirror trying to give herself a pep talk that came out as: "Don't be weird. Don't ramble. Don't accidentally confess your entire emotional crisis to Jake's grandmother."

RUBY STOOD on the sidewalk between Scattered Beans and Sullivan's Coffee at 5:58 PM on Christmas Eve. Her breath formed clouds in the cold air. She was trying to remember how to act like a normal person who met their boyfriend's family.

Boyfriend. Was Jake her boyfriend? They'd kissed—memorably—and he'd told her he loved her, and she'd admitted feelings she was still terrified to name out loud, but they hadn't actually defined what they were to each other. Partners, certainly. In the discovery, in the tours, in the underground chamber that connected their buildings and their lives.

But "boyfriend" felt both too small and too significant for what Jake had become to her.

Ruby looked down at her outfit—the third thing she'd tried on, settled on because Vi had texted:

VI

STOP OVERTHINKING IT AND JUST GO

When Ruby sent her a panicked photo—and wondered if she looked like she was trying too hard or not hard enough or—

Her phone buzzed.

Jake's text glowed:

JAKE

Come now. Rose wants to meet you before dinner. Says she's been waiting months to meet the chaos coffee lady in person.

Ruby laughed despite her nerves, pocketed her phone, and crossed the street before she could talk herself into a fourth outfit change.

Jake opened his apartment door before she could knock, like he'd been watching for her. He looked nervous too—hair slightly messed like he'd been running his hands through it, flannel shirt buttoned carefully for once, the scent of something delicious wafting from his kitchen.

"Hey," he said, and the relief in his voice made Ruby's chest tight. "You came."

"Of course I came. I promised."

"I know, but—" Jake glanced behind him, then back at Ruby.

"Rose is very... enthusiastic. If she overwhelms you, just give me a signal and I'll—"

"Jacob Sullivan, are you keeping that girl in the hallway?" A woman's voice called from inside. "Let her in this instant!"

Jake grimaced apologetically, but there was warmth in his eyes. "Welcome to Christmas with Rose."

Ruby stepped inside to find Jake's apartment transformed. Christmas lights twinkled along every available surface, a small tree stood in the corner decorated with handmade ornaments, and the scent of roasting turkey mixed with cinnamon-sweet baking filled the air.

And in the middle of Jake's living room, rising from the comfortable armchair like a queen greeting a subject, was Rose Sullivan.

She looked exactly like Ruby remembered from the video call —silver hair pulled back in a neat bun, Jake's warm brown eyes, laugh lines carved deep from decades of smiling. But seeing her in person was different. Rose had a presence that filled the room, a gentle authority that explained Jake's quiet strength.

"Ruby!" Rose crossed the space between them with surprising speed, arms already opening. "Finally! Come here, dear, let me look at you."

Before Ruby could respond, she was enveloped in a hug that smelled like lavender and vanilla. Rose held her for a long moment, then pulled back to study Ruby's face with those knowing eyes.

"Oh, you're even lovelier in person." Rose's hands stayed on Ruby's shoulders. "I can see why he's completely smitten."

"Rose," Jake said, a warning note in his voice.

"Hush. I'm your grandmother. I get to say what I want." Rose squeezed Ruby's shoulders once more, then released her. "Ruby, dear, thank you for coming. Jacob's been nervous all day."

"I have not—" Jake started

"Reorganized his bookshelves twice and cleaned the bathroom

three times," Rose continued as if he hadn't spoken. "That's nervous for Jacob."

Ruby felt her own nerves settling as she watched Jake's ears turn red. "The bathroom is really clean. I noticed."

Rose laughed, delighted. "Oh, I like her. Jacob, I like her very much."

"I'm glad," Jake said dryly. "Since I wasn't asking for your approval."

"Of course you were. You're a Sullivan. We always ask for approval, we just pretend we don't." Rose linked her arm through Ruby's and guided her toward the couch. "Now, Ruby, I have to tell you—Jacob took me down to see it this afternoon, and oh my dear, seeing it in person." Rose's eyes shone with emotion. "To stand in that space, to touch those walls, to see the evidence of what they built together. It was overwhelming."

"It was pretty overwhelming for us too when we first found it," Ruby said, settling onto the couch beside Rose.

"Tell me what it was like for you," Rose said, turning to face Ruby fully. "That first moment when you realized what you'd found?"

Ruby glanced at Jake, who had moved to the kitchen doorway, listening. "Honestly? I thought Jake was going to have a heart attack when we broke through that wall."

"I didn't."

"You went completely silent," Ruby said. "Just stood there, staring. I thought maybe we'd broken something we shouldn't have."

"I was processing," Jake said with dignity.

"You were frozen," Ruby corrected, grinning. "Tommy had to physically push you through the opening."

Rose laughed, delighted. "That sounds like Jacob. He processes."

"I wanted to make sure it was safe," Jake protested, but he was smiling now.

"And then," Ruby continued, "when we got to the junction

chamber and saw the inscription—'Together we serve the town'—I think that's when it really hit us. What we'd found wasn't just about Prohibition or speakeasies. It was about partnership."

Rose nodded slowly. "That's what I felt today, standing down there. Not just the history, but the trust it represented. My father and John Fairfield choosing to build something together that neither could build alone."

"The logistics must have been complicated," Ruby said. "Coordinating deliveries, maintaining the legitimate front, keeping everything secure. It required so much communication and trust."

"Which is exactly what you two have now," Rose observed. "The coordinated tours, the way you've integrated both buildings into the story. You're honoring that partnership."

Ruby felt heat creep up her neck. Jake was watching from the kitchen with an expression she couldn't quite read.

"We're trying," Jake said quietly. "It feels important to do it right."

"You are doing it right," Rose said firmly. "I could see it today—not just in the physical space, but in how you talked about it, Jacob. How proud you were. Not just of the discovery, but of what you and Ruby have built together."

The weight of that observation hung in the air. Ruby twisted her hands together, unsure how to respond.

"Tell me more about the artifacts," Rose said, mercifully changing the subject. "I saw bottles, ledgers, a gramophone."

Ruby relaxed into safer territory, describing the cataloging process, the recipes they'd found, the evidence of the town cooperation during difficult times. Jake added details about the structural elements, how the passage was built, the engineering required to create the junction chamber beneath Main Street.

Rose listened with rapt attention, but Ruby noticed she was watching more than listening. Watching how Ruby gestured when she got excited about a particular artifact. Watching how Jake's voice softened when Ruby described discovering the recipe cards.

Watching the way they naturally deferred to each other's expertise, building on each other's observations.

"It sounds like you make quite a team," Rose said finally, and something in her tone made it clear she wasn't just talking about historical documentation.

Before Ruby could figure out how to respond, someone knocked on the door.

"That'll be Tommy and Zara," Jake said, wiping his hands on a dish towel. "Right on time, for once."

Tommy burst through the door carrying two bottles of wine and his usual infectious energy. "Merry Christmas! I brought red and white because I couldn't remember who likes what. Also, this is Zara, who you've all met but I'm introducing anyway because—ow!"

Zara had elbowed him gently. "Because Tommy gets nervous and talks too much." She held up a covered dish. "I brought dessert. Tiramisu. It's the only thing I can make that doesn't taste like cardboard."

"Zara!" Rose stood to greet them both. "Tommy's told me so much about you. And that you're a writer! How wonderful."

"Romance, mostly," Zara said, shaking Rose's hand. "I'm working on a novel. Contemporary romance."

"How perfect." Rose's eyes twinkled. "I'm sure you'll find plenty of inspiration in Millbrook Falls. All these young people falling in love and renovating historic buildings."

Tommy caught Ruby's eye and grinned. "She's not subtle, is she?"

"Not even a little bit," Jake agreed, but his tone was affectionate.

They settled around Jake's dining table—set with family china, Christmas napkins, and candles casting warm, golden light. Rose presided at the head, Tommy poured wine with running commentary about turkey pairings, and Zara observed everything with those sharp novelist's eyes that missed nothing.

"A toast," Rose said, raising her glass. "To partnerships—old and new. To family, chosen and born. And to the courage it takes to build something worth keeping."

They clinked glasses, and Ruby caught Jake's eye across the table. He was watching her with an expression that made her breath catch—tender and hopeful and full of something that looked a lot like love.

Dinner was traditional Sullivan family recipes—turkey with herb stuffing, cranberry sauce made from scratch, green beans with almonds, mashed potatoes impossibly fluffy and creamy. Ruby learned that Tommy told embarrassing childhood stories about Jake with devastating accuracy, that Zara's wit was dry as good wine, and that Rose asked questions that made you feel seen—really seen—in a way Ruby hadn't experienced since her grandmother died.

"Jake used to rearrange the shop furniture when he was ten," Tommy was saying, gesturing with his fork. "Like, systematically. Every few weeks, he'd come in before school and move chairs around. Drove Dad crazy."

"I was trying to optimize traffic flow," Jake protested.

"You were ten!"

"Traffic flow is important at any age."

Ruby laughed so hard she nearly choked on her wine. "You were a nerdy ten-year-old, weren't you?"

"The nerdiest," Tommy confirmed. "Had a clipboard and everything."

"I had a system," Jake said with dignity, but he was smiling.

"He still has a system," Ruby told the table. "For everything. The way he organizes his counter, the order he does morning prep, even how he hangs his dish towels."

"And yet," Rose observed, "he's learned to work with Ruby's more... spontaneous approach."

"Chaotic," Jake corrected, but his voice was warm. "Ruby's approach is chaotic."

"I prefer 'creatively flexible,'" Ruby said.

"You forgot where you parked your car last week."

"I found it eventually!"

"It was three blocks away from where you thought you'd left it."

"In my defense, all these streets look the same in the snow."

Tommy and Zara were grinning at their back-and-forth, and Rose watched with obvious delight. "This," Rose said, "is what partnership looks like. Complementary chaos and order. Spontaneity and system. Learning to work with each other's differences instead of against them."

The table went quiet for a moment, the weight of Rose's observation settling over them. Ruby felt Jake's foot brush against hers under the table—deliberate, gentle, a connection that said *we're in this together*.

"Speaking of partnership," Zara said, breaking the comfortable silence. "The discovery. The underground chamber. That's incredible."

"It really is," Tommy agreed. "When we broke through that wall and saw the passage—Ruby, you should have seen your face. Pure wonder."

"Jake's face was pretty good too," Ruby said. "Like he'd just found buried treasure."

"I had," Jake said quietly, and the way he was looking at her made it clear he wasn't just talking about the chamber.

Rose didn't miss it. Of course she didn't. "Jacob mentioned that the discovery has changed how you're thinking about the businesses. Integrating the tours more fully?"

Ruby nodded, grateful for the safer topic. "We're running coordinated tours now. Jake starts in his basement explaining Sullivan's role as the legitimate front, then leads people through the passage to the junction chamber. I meet them there and talk about the storage and receiving side—what my building did. Then we bring them through to my basement and show where deliveries would have arrived."

"And people love it," Jake added. "The partnership angle

resonates—two buildings working together, neither successful alone."

"Because that's how real success works," Rose said. "Not alone, but together. Not competing, but cooperating." Her gaze moved between Jake and Ruby with meaning. "Your great-grandfather understood that, Jacob. And John Fairfield understood it too. That's why their partnership thrived."

Ruby felt her throat tighten at the implication.

"I'm just saying, when I'm seventy-eight years old, I want to be as cool as Rose." Tommy declared.

"You'd have to live to seventy-eight first," Zara pointed out.

"With my luck?" Tommy grinned. "I'll probably lock myself out of my truck and freeze to death in a snowbank."

"Not if I find you first," Zara said, and there was something soft in her voice that made Ruby do a double-take.

Oh. Tommy and Zara weren't just friends who hung out. There was something there—tentative maybe, new certainly, but definitely there.

Jake caught Ruby's eye and raised an eyebrow slightly, clearly thinking the same thing. Rose just smiled into her wine glass like she'd known all along.

They finished dinner with more laughter, more stories, more of Rose's gentle observations. When dessert came out—Zara's tiramisu, decidedly better than cardboard—Tommy insisted on another toast.

"To historical discoveries," he said, raising his glass. "To family dinners that make you remember why family is worth it. And to finding people who make you want to be less of an idiot than you naturally are."

"Hear, hear," Zara said dryly, but she was smiling.

After dessert, they moved to the living room. Jake built up the fire while Rose settled into the comfortable armchair. Tommy and Zara took the loveseat, and Ruby found herself on the couch with Jake close enough that their shoulders touched.

They talked easily—Rose asking Zara about her novel, Tommy

entertaining them with stories from his contracting jobs, Jake occasionally adding dry commentary that made everyone laugh. Ruby felt herself relaxing into the warmth of it, the easy rhythm of people who genuinely enjoyed each other's company.

This was what family felt like. Not just blood relation, but chosen connection. The kind of belonging that came from showing up and being welcomed.

Around eight-thirty, Zara glanced at her phone and made a small sound of surprise. "I didn't realize how late it was. I have to be at my parents' house early tomorrow—my mom will kill me if I'm not there for Christmas breakfast."

"I should get going too," Tommy said, but the way he said it—reluctant, glancing at Zara—suggested he'd stay if she was staying.

Tommy stood and offered Zara his hand. She took it without hesitation.

Rose stood to hug them both goodbye. "Zara, dear, it was lovely to meet you properly. I hope we'll see more of you."

"I'd like that," Zara said, and meant it.

Tommy hugged his grandmother, then his brother. "Great dinner, Jake. Really great."

"Thanks for coming," Jake said, and there was real affection in his voice.

Tommy paused at the door, his arm settling around Zara's waist in a gesture that looked both new and natural. "Ruby, it was good seeing you. You should know—having you here tonight, it felt right. Like you're already part of this."

Ruby's throat went tight. "Thank you, Tommy. That means a lot."

After they left, Ruby caught a glimpse through the window of Tommy and Zara on the sidewalk below. Tommy was helping Zara with her coat, his hands lingering on her shoulders. She said something that made him laugh, then stood on her toes to kiss his cheek. Tommy's grin was visible even from three floors up.

"Well," Rose said, watching the same scene with obvious approval. "Those two are figuring something out."

"Finally," Jake murmured.

Rose stretched, stifling a yawn that looked only partially genuine. "I think I'm going to turn in, dears. Travel and wine have caught up with me." She kissed Jake's cheek, then surprised Ruby by doing the same. "Ruby, thank you for coming tonight. It meant the world to Jacob, and to me."

"Thank you for having me," Ruby managed.

"Oh, we'll be having you again," Rose said with a knowing smile. "I suspect we'll be having you quite a lot."

She retreated to Jake's guest room, closing the door with a soft click, and suddenly Ruby and Jake were alone for the first time all evening.

RUBY SETTLED DEEPER into the couch while Jake adjusted the fire, adding another log that sent sparks dancing up the chimney. Christmas lights twinkled around them, and through the window Ruby could see snow beginning to fall on Main Street.

"Rose likes you," Jake said, sitting beside her. Close enough that their knees touched, close enough that Ruby could smell that woodsy scent that had become synonymous with safety.

"She's wonderful. I can see where you get it from."

"Get what?"

"The ability to make people feel like they belong."

Jake turned to face her more fully, his expression serious despite the soft lighting. "Ruby, I need to tell you something."

Ruby's heart started hammering. "Okay."

"Whatever you decide—about Derek's offer, about staying, about us—tonight meant everything to me." Jake's hand found hers, lacing their fingers together. "Having you here, with Rose, with my family—it felt right. Like Christmas isn't complete without you."

Ruby felt tears prick at her eyes. "Jake—"

"And that terrifies me," he continued, "because I don't know if you'll be here next Christmas. I don't know if tonight is a preview of what could be, or a goodbye to what might have been."

"I'm not saying goodbye," Ruby whispered.

"But you haven't said you're staying either."

Ruby looked at their joined hands, at the way his fingers fit perfectly between hers, at the calluses from years of coffee work that matched her own.

"Tonight mattered to me too. Rose matters. You matter. All of this matters so much it scares me."

Jake pulled her closer, his forehead resting against hers. "I love you. I know I said it before, but I need you to know—I love you, Ruby. Not because of the discovery or the partnership or the buildings. I love you because you're you. And whatever you decide, that doesn't change."

Ruby closed her eyes, breathing in his scent, feeling the solid warmth of him against her. "Jake, I—"

But she couldn't say it yet. Couldn't make the leap from wanting to choosing, not when fear still had such a strong grip on her heart.

Jake seemed to understand. He always understood. "It's okay. You don't have to say anything tonight."

They sat like that for a long time, holding each other in the soft glow of Christmas lights, listening to snow fall against the windows. Eventually, Jake walked her to the door, and when he kissed her forehead, it felt like both a promise and a prayer.

RUBY CROSSED Main Street in the falling snow. When she reached her building, she turned to look back. Jake was still standing in his doorway, hands in his pockets, watching to make sure she got home safe.

She lifted a hand in a small wave. He did the same. Neither of them moved for a long, lingering moment.

Then Jake stepped back inside, the door closing softly. Warm light glowed in the apartment above his shop.

Ruby stood there, her hand on her own door handle. She could go inside. But instead, she turned and started walking.

The town was quiet, the kind of stillness that only came once a year—after the stores had closed, after the laughter had faded into homes and living rooms and Christmas lights. She passed the decorated shop windows, now dark for the holiday, the big tree in the town square standing silent and beautiful beneath its halo of snow. The only sounds were her boots on the pavement and the steady whisper of falling flakes.

Through a window, she caught a glimpse of a family laughing around a dinner table. Another window glowed with firelight, children in pajamas curled up against their parents. The historical society sat dark and watchful, its windows reflecting the shimmer of Christmas lights across the street.

Her breath came out in clouds that drifted upward and disappeared into the night. Snowflakes caught in her hair, melting against her cheeks. Somewhere far off, church bells began to ring, soft and distant.

Ruby kept walking until her coat was dusted white, until her fingers ached from the cold, until the lights of Main Street blurred into hazy color through the snow. When she finally stopped, she was standing in front of the old Fairfield building. Her building.

She looked up at the dark windows of her apartment, at Scattered Beans below, closed and waiting. At the brick and mortar that connected, beneath the surface, to everything she loved and everything she was still trying to be brave enough to choose.

The snow was falling harder now, softening every line and edge, turning the whole town quiet. Turning it possible.

Ruby stood there for a long time in the stillness, her heart full and her thoughts racing, circling back to the same truth she'd been avoiding all night.

CHAPTER Seventeen

Ruby woke on Christmas morning to sunlight streaming through her window and a decision settled in her chest like something solid.

She was staying.

Not because it was safe or practical or what anyone expected. She was staying because this—Millbrook Falls, Scattered Beans, the man across the street who made "There you go" sound like a love song—this was what she wanted.

Ruby got out of bed and went to the window. Fresh snow had fallen overnight, covering Main Street in pristine white. Across the street, she could see Jake already moving around in Sullivan's Coffee, probably making his traditional Christmas morning dark roast.

The sight made her smile. Of course Jake would open even on Christmas morning. That was who he was—steady, generous, always showing up.

And she loved him.

Ruby dressed quickly—jeans and the soft green sweater Jake had once said matched her eyes. She grabbed her coat and paused at the door, her hand on the knob, heart hammering.

This was it. No more waiting.

At 7.30 on Christmas morning, Ruby Ashworth walked across Main Street to tell Jake Sullivan she was staying.

Jake looked up from the coffee machine when the door chimed. His entire face transformed—surprise, hope, uncertainty flickering across his expression in rapid succession.

"Ruby." He set down the portafilter. "I thought you'd sleep in."

"Couldn't sleep. Kept thinking." Ruby closed the door behind her, suddenly aware of how empty Sullivan's felt with just the two of them, how the Christmas lights seemed to glow brighter in the silence. "About what I want."

Jake went very still. "Ruby—"

"Let me say this before I lose my nerve." She crossed to the counter, close enough to see the pulse jumping in his throat, the way his hands had stilled on the equipment. "I'm staying, Jake. I'm choosing to stay."

The words hung between them. Jake didn't move, didn't breathe.

"Say that again," he whispered.

"I'm staying because I want to." Ruby felt tears threatening but pushed through. "Because this is where I belong. Because I love you."

"Ruby—" Her name came out broken.

"I'm in love with you, Jake Sullivan. I've been falling in love with you since the day you got my mail and looked at me like I was the most interesting disaster you'd ever met." The words tumbled out faster now. "I'm staying because every time I make coffee, I look up and you're there. Because when we found that passage between our buildings, all I could think was that of course they're connected—because we're connected too."

Jake closed the distance between them, his hands framing her face. "Say the part about loving me again."

"Which part? The part where I'm in love with you, or the part where I've been falling since August?"

"Both. Say both."

"I love you. I'm in love with you. And I'm staying."

"There you go," Jake whispered, and then he was kissing her.

This kiss was different from the desperate one that came before. This one was certainty and promise and future. Jake's hands slid into her hair while Ruby's fisted in his shirt, trying to communicate without words what her decision meant: *I choose you. I choose this. I choose us.*

When they finally broke apart, both breathing hard, Jake rested his forehead against hers. "You're sure? Really sure?"

"I've never been more sure of anything."

"What about Derek's offer?"

"I don't want it." Ruby pulled back enough to meet his eyes. "I thought I needed that validation, the security, that proof I could make it in the 'real world.' But this is real. You're real. What I feel when I'm with you is the most real thing I've ever felt."

Jake caught her hand and brought it to his lips, kissing her palm. "I can't believe you're staying. Merry Christmas."

"I can't believe I almost left. Merry Christmas to you to."

They stood there for a long moment, holding each other while Christmas lights twinkled and Main Street slowly came to life outside. Ruby could hear the first sounds of the town waking—a car starting somewhere, someone scraping ice off a windshield, the distant church bells beginning their Christmas morning song.

"We should tell Rose," Jake said finally, his voice rough.

"We should." Ruby didn't move.

"She's probably awake. Making coffee and plotting."

Ruby laughed. "She knew before we did."

"Rose always knows." Jake kissed her forehead. "Ready?"

"Ready."

ROSE TOOK one look at their faces when they walked into the apartment hand in hand, and set down her coffee mug with a satisfied smile.

"Well, it's about time."

Jake groaned. "Rose—"

"What? You think I couldn't see it?" Rose's eyes sparkled. "I didn't drive all the way from Northfield just for your company, Jacob. I came to meet the girl who finally made my grandson smile like that."

"I'm staying," Ruby blurted out. "I wanted you to know. I'm staying in Millbrook Falls. I'm choosing—" She glanced at Jake. "I'm choosing this."

Rose stood up and pulled Ruby into a fierce hug "For being brave. For choosing what you want instead of what you think you should want." Rose pulled back, holding Ruby at arm's length. "For making my grandson this happy. For giving me the best Christmas present. Welcome to the family, dear. Officially."

They spent Christmas morning together—Ruby, Jake, and Rose—drinking coffee and eating Rose's traditional breakfast casserole that Jake had prepared according to her exacting instructions. Rose shared memories of her late husband Thomas, about the choices she'd made and the ones she wished she'd made differently.

"Partnership isn't always easy," Rose said, refilling her coffee. "Thomas and I fought about plenty—money, family, whose turn it was to deal with the broken hot water heater. But we faced those problems together instead of alone. That's what made the difference."

Ruby listened, absorbing Rose's words. This was the first time someone had talked to her about love as something that required work, not just feeling. Her parents had divorced when she was twelve, her grandmother had been widowed young—she'd never seen partnership modeled like this, honest and imperfect and still worthwhile.

Around one o'clock, Ruby excused herself to Jake's bedroom, her heart hammering as she pulled out her phone. Through the window, she could see Main Street below, both coffee shops quiet for the holiday, the town peaceful under its blanket of snow.

Derek answered on the second ring. "Ruby. Merry Christmas."

"Merry Christmas, Derek." Ruby took a breath. "I know you said I had until tomorrow, but I've made my decision. I'm staying in Millbrook Falls. I'm turning down the offer."

Silence. Then: "You're making a mistake."

"Maybe. But it's my mistake to make."

"Think about what you're giving up—the salary, the benefits, the career trajectory—"

"I'm not giving up anything, Derek. I'm choosing what I want."

"A coffee shop in a town no one's ever heard of?" Derek's frustration broke through. "Ruby, be realistic. You have real talent. You're wasting it."

Ruby felt a flicker of the old doubt—the voice that said Derek might be right, that she was throwing away security for a feeling. But then she looked at Scattered Beans across the street, at the building that had been standing for almost a century, weathering far worse than her uncertainty.

"Is that all?" she said quietly.

"I'm trying to help you."

"No, you're trying to make me doubt myself because you can't understand why anyone would choose something different than what you would choose." Ruby surprised herself with her conviction. "I appreciate the offer. I do. But I'm not that person anymore."

"So that's it? You're turning down a six-figure salary for some guy?"

"I'm choosing myself. The life I want to build, the work that makes me happy. Jake's part of that, but he's not the only reason."

"You're going to regret this."

"Maybe. But at least I'll regret choosing what I wanted instead of playing it safe." Ruby took a breath. "Good luck finding someone for the position, Derek."

"Yeah. You too." Derek's voice softened slightly. "For what it's worth, I hope I'm wrong. I hope it works out."

"Thank you."

"But Ruby? When it doesn't work out—and statistics say it won't—don't wait too long to call me."

Ruby smiled despite herself. "Goodbye, Derek."

She hung up and opened her group chat with Vi and Zara.

RUBY

I did it. I told Derek no. I'm staying.

Also told Jake I love him this morning. We're together. Really together.

The response was instantaneous.

VI

AHHHHHHHHHH!!!

I'M SO PROUD OF YOU

Also I told you so but I'm too excited to gloat properly

ZARA

RUBY!!! This is the most romantic thing I've ever witnessed

VI

Okay but DETAILS. How did he react? What did he say? What are you doing RIGHT NOW?

RUBY

He said he loves me too. And right now I'm at his place.

ZARA

"At his place" — ARE YOU STAYING OVER???

RUBY

Maybe? I don't know. It's been a really big day and I don't want to leave yet.

VI

STAY. Obviously stay. This is not the time for separate apartments.

ZARA

What Vi said. Also I'm bringing champagne tomorrow. The VERY good stuff.

RUBY

You guys are the best. Love you both.

VI

Love you! Now put down your phone and go be with your hot coffee boyfriend

ZARA

What Vi said but with better grammar :)

Ruby laughed, wiping at her eyes, and pocketed her phone. When she came back to the living room, Jake was watching her with barely contained anxiety.

"How'd he take it?"

"Like I expected. But it doesn't matter." Ruby sat beside him. "Vi and Zara are pretty excited though."

"Yeah?"

Ruby showed him her phone. Jake read the messages, a smile spreading across his face. "Hot coffee boyfriend?"

"Vi's words, not mine."

"I'll take it." Jake pulled her close, kissing the top of her head. "I'm so proud of you."

They sat in comfortable silence for a while, Jake's arm around her shoulders, Ruby tucked against his side. The apartment was warm, the Christmas tree lights twinkling, and for the first time in months, Ruby felt completely at peace.

AROUND FOUR O'CLOCK, Rose announced she needed to head back to Northfield. Ruby helped her pack while Jake loaded the car.

"Take care of him," Rose said as she zipped up her overnight bag. "And let him take care of you."

"I will. I promise."

Rose cupped Ruby's face. "And don't be a stranger. I expect to see you both for Easter."

"We'll be there," Ruby said, and realized she meant it. Easter felt suddenly real and possible, not some distant future she might not be part of.

They walked downstairs together. Rose hugged Jake tight, then Ruby, then climbed into her car with a final wave. They watched until her taillights disappeared around the corner onto Route 7.

The evening air was crisp and cold, Christmas lights glowing up and down Main Street. Ruby shivered, and Jake's arm came around her shoulders automatically.

"Come back up?" Jake asked quietly. "It's early still."

Ruby looked up at him, at the hope and uncertainty in his expression, and realized she didn't want to leave. Didn't want to cross back to her empty apartment, didn't want to spend their first night as a real couple separated by twenty feet of asphalt.

"Okay," she said. "Yeah. I'd like that."

Back in Jake's apartment, Ruby pulled out her phone while Jake moved to the kitchen.

Ruby laughed, looking up to find Jake watching her from the kitchen, a soft smile on his face.

"Vi and Zara?" he asked.

"Very excited for us." Ruby set her phone aside. "Vi keeps calling you my 'hot coffee boyfriend.'"

"I'm ok with that." Jake came over with two mugs. "Hot chocolate? Fair warning, Rose's recipe is ninety percent chocolate."

Ruby took the mug he offered, their fingers brushing. "This is perfect. You're perfect."

They settled on the couch together, and Ruby tucked herself against Jake's side, feeling the rightness of it settle into her bones.

"What are you thinking?" Jake asked after a comfortable silence.

Ruby set down her half-empty mug. "That I don't want to

leave. That going back to my apartment tonight feels wrong, like we're pretending there's still distance between us when there isn't anymore."

Jake went very still. "Ruby—"

"I know it's fast. I know we just decided this today. But—" Ruby turned to face him fully. "Can I stay? Tonight?"

The hope that flooded Jake's expression made Ruby's chest tight. "You want to stay?"

"I want to wake up here tomorrow. I want the first morning of our life together to actually be... together." Ruby felt suddenly nervous. "Unless that's too much too soon, or—"

Jake kissed her, stopping the words. When he pulled back, he was smiling. "Stay. Please stay."

"There you go," Ruby whispered.

LATER, much later, Ruby borrowed one of Jake's t-shirts and brushed her teeth with a spare toothbrush he found still in its package. The bathroom counter had his razor, his cologne, the kind of everyday intimacy that made this feel real in a way grand gestures never could.

When she came out, Jake was already in bed, reading glasses on, a book of poetry open in his lap. He looked up when she entered, and something in his expression made Ruby stop.

"What?"

"You're here. In my apartment. In my shirt." Jake set the book aside. "I keep thinking I'll wake up and you'll have changed your mind."

Ruby climbed into bed beside him, tucking herself against his side. "I'm not changing my mind. This is what I want. You're what I want."

Jake wrapped an arm around her, and Ruby felt him relax incrementally. "I love you," he said quietly. "I know I keep saying it, but—"

"Say it as much as you want. I'll never get tired of hearing it." Ruby tilted her head up to kiss his jaw. "I love you too."

They lay like that for a while, Jake's fingers tracing absent patterns on her shoulder, Ruby listening to the steady rhythm of his heartbeat. Through the window, she could see her coffee shop below—dark now, waiting for tomorrow.

"What are you thinking about?" Jake asked.

"Tomorrow. The tours we'll run, the customers we'll serve. How different it'll feel now that I know I'm staying." Ruby paused. "And how I want to tell people. Not hide it, I mean. That we're together."

"Millbrook Falls will know by noon whether we tell them or not," Jake said dryly. "This town has a very efficient information network."

"Good. I want them to know." Ruby yawned, suddenly exhausted. The adrenaline of the day—the decision, the confession, Derek's call, Rose's departure—was finally catching up with her.

"Sleep," Jake said softly, turning off the bedside lamp. "I've got you."

Ruby nestled closer, feeling safe and settled and home. "First day of the rest of our lives tomorrow."

"No pressure," Jake murmured, and Ruby could hear the smile in his voice.

She fell asleep in Jake Sullivan's arms, in Jake Sullivan's bed, in the apartment above Sullivan's Coffee that looked across at Scattered Beans. Fell asleep knowing she'd wake up here tomorrow, and the day after that, and that eventually—when they were both ready—this wouldn't be Jake's apartment or her apartment but theirs.

She was staying. She was home. And for the first time in her entire life, Ruby Ashworth was exactly where she wanted to be.

CHAPTER *Eighteen*

THE WEEK BETWEEN CHRISTMAS AND NEW YEAR'S PASSED IN A BLUR of planning, preparation, and the kind of giddy happiness Ruby had only read about in romance novels.

She and Jake worked together openly now. No pretending they were just neighbors, no carefully maintained distance. When Jake brought her coffee in the morning, he kissed her. When Ruby came over to discuss tour schedules, she stayed for dinner. They held hands walking down Main Street, and when Frank Kowalski made a gruff comment about "took you long enough," they grinned at each other.

The town had taken the news with predictable enthusiasm. Daisy had cheered when Ruby confirmed she was staying, and even Gladys Murphy had managed a stiff "I suppose that's reasonable"—which, from Gladys, was practically a blessing. Mayor Greene immediately started talking about tourism initiatives and historical preservation grants, while Tommy declared himself "personally responsible" for their happiness and demanded credit in the wedding toasts.

"We're not engaged," Ruby had protested.

"Yet," Tommy had corrected with a knowing grin.

Now, on New Year's Eve, both Scattered Beans and Sullivan's

Coffee were decorated for their first official joint celebration. They'd planned a progressive party—starting with appetizers and coffee in Scattered Beans, moving to Sullivan's for the main celebration, and culminating in a special midnight tour of the junction chamber where their buildings connected underground.

Ruby stood behind her counter, arranging the last of the appetizer plates. Vi appeared beside her.

"You look happy," Vi said, bumping Ruby's shoulder. "Like, genuinely, stupidly happy."

Ruby smiled. "I am."

"Good. You deserve it." Vi picked up a mini quiche, examined it, popped it in her mouth. "So—when's the wedding? Because I'm calling dibs on maid of honor."

"Vi!" Ruby's cheeks flamed. "We've been together for like a week."

"A week officially," Vi corrected. "You two have been circling each other since August. I'm just planning ahead."

Zara appeared at Ruby's other side, grinning. "I'm with Vi. The betting pool at the bookstore has you engaged by Valentine's Day."

"There's a betting pool?"

"Small town," Zara said with a shrug. "What else are we going to do? Also, Frank Kowalski put money on New Year's Day, so you're really letting him down by not having a ring yet."

Ruby laughed, shaking her head. "You're both ridiculous."

"We're both right," Vi said. "Look at you—you're glowing. When's the last time you stress-ate cereal for dinner?"

"Last Tuesday," Ruby admitted.

"Okay, but that was because Beatrice was acting up, not because of existential career dread," Zara pointed out. "Totally different category of stress-cereal."

"There are categories?"

"Definitely," Vi said. "There's job-crisis cereal, relationship-crisis cereal, general-life-falling-apart cereal, and acceptable-breakfast cereal. You've graduated to only the last two categories. Character growth."

The door chimed, and Ruby looked up to see Jake entering with Tommy. Jake's eyes found hers immediately, and that familiar warmth spread through her—that certainty she'd made exactly the right choice.

"Speaking of character growth," Vi murmured, "there's your leading man."

"Stop," Ruby hissed, but she was grinning.

"The speakeasy's ready," Jake announced. "Tommy finished setting up the lighting, and Zara will be stationed at the entrance to manage the tour groups."

"You put me in charge of crowd control," Zara corrected, but she was smiling. "Someone has to make sure Frank Kowalski doesn't monopolize the bootlegging stories."

"Frank's already down there, isn't he?" Ruby guessed.

"Has been for an hour," Tommy confirmed. "Pretty sure he's giving unauthorized tours to anyone who'll listen."

As evening fell, guests began arriving. The original plan had been small—just close friends and a few regular customers. But word had spread through Millbrook Falls, and by seven o'clock, both shops were packed with people eager to celebrate the partnership that had captivated the town.

Ruby moved through the crowd, greeting guests, refilling coffee cups, accepting congratulations. Mrs. Patterson hugged her and whispered, "I knew you'd choose right." Daisy brought homemade cookies shaped like coffee cups. Even Gladys Murphy showed up, claiming it was "just to see what all the fuss was about."

Mayor Greene made a short speech about historical preservation, working in several mentions of Millbrook Falls' bright future. Then the party moved locations, and the crowd flowed from Scattered Beans across the street to Sullivan's.

Jake caught Ruby's hand as they walked together, surrounded by their friends and neighbors. "You okay?"

"Better than okay." Ruby squeezed his fingers. "This is perfect."

Sullivan's Coffee looked magical. Jake had kept his traditional aesthetic but added touches that acknowledged the building's dual purpose—vintage photographs of the Prohibition era, subtle references to the speakeasy below, a menu honoring both his great-grandfather's recipes and the new partnership with Scattered Beans.

The crowd filled the space, talking and laughing, while Ruby and Jake worked behind the counter together. The ease of their partnership showed in every movement—Jake knowing when Ruby needed the milk pitcher, Ruby anticipating which beans he wanted. They'd developed a rhythm, a shorthand, a way of working together as natural as breathing.

At nine o'clock, they led the first group down to the junction chamber. Ruby watched their friends descend into the underground space, faces lighting up with wonder at the exposed brick, the art deco details, the physical proof that Sullivan's Coffee and the Fairfield family's building had been designed to work together.

"It's like a time capsule," Mrs. Patterson breathed.

"It's proof," Mayor Greene corrected. "Proof that partnership has always been at the heart of Main Street, even when we forgot it."

Ruby caught Jake's eye across the crowd, and he smiled—that private, intimate smile meant just for her.

They ran three more tours, each met with the same enthusiasm, the same sense of discovery. By eleven-thirty, everyone had returned to Sullivan's main floor, energized by history and champagne and the approaching midnight.

"Ten minutes to midnight!" someone called out.

The energy shifted—more focused, more anticipatory. Ruby felt nervous excitement flutter through her as she realized that in ten minutes, she'd be kissing Jake Sullivan at midnight on New Year's Eve. In front of the entire town. In the coffee shop where they'd first met during her chaotic moving day disaster.

"Nervous?" Jake asked quietly, his voice carrying that steady calm that had gotten her through every crisis since August.

"A little. Good nervous, though." Ruby looked around at the party—their party—in the space they'd rebuilt together. "I keep thinking about where I was last New Year's Eve. Stressed about corporate deadlines, drinking cheap champagne in my Hartford apartment, wondering what I was doing with my life."

"And now?"

"Now I know exactly what I'm doing. I'm building something real, with someone real, in a place that feels like home." Ruby turned to face him fully. "Jake, I need to tell you something."

Something shifted in his expression. "What?"

"I love you. Not just the way you fix things or help me through disasters or say 'there you go' like you're solving all my problems. I love that you read poetry and visit Rose every Sunday and that you trusted me with your family's legacy. I love that you supported my dreams even when they competed with yours."

The words hung between them, carried by warm air and laughter. Jake's hands came up to cup her face, his callused fingers gentle against her skin.

"Ruby. I've been in love with you since you kissed my cheek in the basement. Maybe since the day you moved in and apologized for chaos you didn't cause." His voice was low, meant only for her. "You changed everything. You helped me see that honoring the past doesn't mean being afraid of the future."

"Five minutes!" Mayor Greene announced, and the crowd began the familiar ritual—checking phones, finding loved ones, preparing for the midnight countdown.

Jake's thumb brushed across Ruby's cheek. She realized she was crying, not from sadness but because happiness had nowhere else to go.

"Ruby Ashworth, will you be my New Year's kiss?"

"I thought you'd never ask."

The countdown began, voices joining in the familiar chant

marking the end of one year and the beginning of another. "Ten! Nine! Eight!"

Ruby looked around at their friends and family—Vi beaming with satisfaction like she'd orchestrated this romance herself, Tommy raising his beer in a toast to his brother, Daisy clapping her hands with obvious delight.

"Seven! Six! Five!"

She thought about Derek's job offer, turned down without a second thought since.

"Four! Three! Two!"

Jake's eyes never left her face—steady, sure, completely present, his amber gaze holding promises about their future.

"One! Happy New Year!"

The crowd erupted in celebration. Jake leaned down and kissed Ruby with a thoroughness that made her forget the party, the noise, everything except the taste of coffee and winter air and forever on his lips. When they broke apart, both breathless and grinning, Jake pressed his forehead against hers.

"Happy New Year, Ruby Ashworth."

"Happy New Year, Jake Sullivan."

Around them, the party continued—friends embracing, couples kissing, neighbors toasting the year ahead with bootleg-inspired cocktails from Jake's great-grandfather's recipes. Ruby caught a glimpse of Tommy and Zara. They weren't stealing their first kiss—they'd already crossed that line—but as the celebration swirled around them, Tommy pulled Zara close and kissed her again, not tentative but certain. A public declaration that what had begun quietly was now real. A few friends nearby cheered, Vi lifted her phone with a grin, and the moment folded back into the celebration.

But Ruby only had eyes for Jake, for the way he looked at her like she was the best thing that had ever happened to his carefully ordered life.

"So, any New Year's resolutions?"

Ruby considered this, looking around at Sullivan's Coffee,

where their two separate dreams had become something bigger together.

"Just one. Keep doing exactly what we're doing."

Jake's smile was brighter than all the pendant lights in both their shops combined. "I like that resolution."

"Good. Because I plan to keep it for a very long time."

When Jake and Ruby finally stepped back, both still grinning, the crowd had dispersed into smaller conversations. That's when Ruby noticed Gladys Murphy making her way toward them. For once, the older woman's expression wasn't pinched with disapproval—something that might almost be called thoughtful instead.

"Miss Ashworth," Gladys said, her formal tone softening slightly. "Might I have a word?"

Ruby's stomach clenched, but Jake's hand found hers. "Of course, Mrs. Murphy."

Gladys glanced around at the packed coffee shop—Sullivan's transformed but still recognizable, honoring its past while embracing something new. "I want you to know that I was resistant to changes on Main Street. I've lived in Millbrook Falls my entire life, and I've seen businesses come and go. I didn't think Scattered Beans would last a month."

Ruby held her breath, waiting for the criticism she'd grown accustomed to.

But Gladys surprised her. "I was wrong." The words seemed to pain her, but her gaze was direct. "You've proven yourself a worthy addition to our town. More than that—" She gestured between the two shops. "Sullivan's Coffee and Scattered Beans together, what you've built—it works. You've honored the history while bringing something genuinely new. That takes character."

Ruby felt her eyes sting. "Thank you, Mrs. Murphy. That means more than you know."

Gladys nodded once, her usual briskness returning. "Well. Don't let it go to your head. You've still got a long way to go." But as she turned away, Ruby caught the unmistakable hint of a smile.

Jake squeezed Ruby's hand. "Did that just happen?"

"I think Gladys Murphy just gave me her blessing," Ruby whispered, feeling like she'd passed some final test.

"Told you she'd come around eventually."

People began mingling again, but the energy had shifted—less anticipation, more contentment. It was after midnight now, officially a new year, and gradually guests started saying their goodbyes.

Vi was one of the last to leave, pulling Ruby into a fierce hug. "You did good, Rubes. I'm so proud of you."

"Thank you for pushing me to take the risk. For believing I could do this when I didn't believe it myself."

"That's what best friends are for." Vi pulled back, holding Ruby at arm's length. "But you know what? You pushed yourself. I just reminded you that you could."

After Vi left, Ruby helped Jake clean up. They worked in comfortable silence, moving around each other with practiced ease, collecting empty cups and wiping down tables.

"Best year of my life," Ruby said as she loaded the dishwasher.

Jake came up behind her, wrapping his arms around her waist. "It's only going to get better."

"You're very confident about that."

"I am. Because we're going to make it better. Together."

When the cleaning was done, they stood at Sullivan's door, looking back at the space that had seen so much celebration. Then Jake locked up, and they climbed the stairs to his apartment.

The fire was still burning in the fireplace, casting warm shadows across the living room. Ruby kicked off her shoes and curled up on the couch, watching the flames dance. Jake went to the kitchen—she could hear him making tea, the familiar sounds of home.

She thought about her grandmother Doris, who'd always told her that happiness wasn't something you achieved—it was something you chose, every single day. Ruby finally understood. This life she was building wasn't perfect, wasn't guaranteed, but it was hers. She'd chosen it. She'd choose it again tomorrow, and the day after that.

"What are you thinking about?" Jake asked, settling beside her with two mugs.

Ruby took the tea, their fingers brushing. "My grandmother. She would have liked you."

"Yeah?"

"She always said the best things in life were the ones you chose bravely." Ruby leaned into him, feeling his warmth, the solid comfort of his presence. "I think she'd be proud that I finally listened."

Jake set down his mug and pulled her closer, his arm around her shoulders. "I'm glad you did."

They sat in comfortable silence, the fire low and steady.

"Stay," Jake said quietly.

Ruby smiled. "I wasn't planning on leaving."

"I mean always. Stay always."

She turned toward him, meeting the steady glow of his amber eyes. "Is that a question or a statement?"

"It's a hope."

"Then yes," she whispered. "Always."

He kissed her—slow, deliberate, full of promise. When they broke apart, he rose and offered his hand.

Ruby stood, fingers laced with his, the firelight catching in her hair.

He led her toward the bedroom, the last of the firelight following them across the floor.

The door closed softly behind them.

THERE YOU GO

Thank You

Thank you for reading! If you enjoyed this story, please consider leaving an honest review on your marketplace of choice. Your feedback helps other readers discover new books and supports independent authors like me.

Visit Clara at her website: www.claraashby.com

Printed in Dunstable, United Kingdom

76663511R00133